SPARROW
FALLING

First published 2016 by Solaris
an imprint of Rebellion Publishing Ltd,
Riverside House, Osney Mead,
Oxford, OX2 0ES, UK

www.solarisbooks.com

ISBN: 978 1 78108 381 9

Copyright © Gaie Sebold 2016

The right of the author to be identified as the author
of this work has been asserted in accordance with the Copyright,
Designs and Patents Act 1988.

10 9 8 7 6 5 4 3 2 1

A CIP catalogue record for this book is available
from the British Library.

Designed & typeset by Rebellion Publishing

Printed in the UK

GAIE SEBOLD

SPARROW FALLING

SOLARIS

*To the assorted rogues and rebels who
get their crowbars under the window, and make it
that little bit easier for the rest of us.*

The Sparrow School

THE WOMAN IN the purple hat picked up the Gladstone bag and scurried from the room. Eveline gave her time to leave, picked up her own Gladstone – the one that actually had the money in it – and walked, not too fast, not too slowly, towards the door. Too fast a walk attracted attention, made people wonder why you were so eager to leave. Too slow left you without enough time to make the door before someone raised the alarm.

Instead of exiting, she slapped the door with her hand, spun around and dropped the bag between her feet. "All right, ladies, who can tell me what that was?"

The handful of girls in the room, perched on hard wooden chairs, looked at the floor, the walls, and their neighbours. Finally one of them, a skinny creature with dark eyes and a forceful nose, put up her hand. "A pigeon drop, Miss Sparrow?"

"Good, Adelita. So where'd I almost come a cropper, then?"

Another girl, almost as skinny and with skin so pale it looked greenish compared to Adelita's warm gold, said, "Was it the bit where she started to open the bag, miss?"

"Yes. Good. Doris, in't it? Right. You got to make sure you're out of the way, or give 'em a good reason to get out of the way themselves, like I done then, saying I thought I seen a peeler. Now, she goes ahead and opens the bag, what do you do?"

"Run, miss?" Adelita said.

"No. Why'd that be bad? Anyone?"

"'Cos people'd be looking, miss," said another girl.

"S'right. Now, she's not gonna call the coppers if she thinks about it, because she's handling stolen goods – six months hard, you can get for that –" Eveline spun around, and raised a finger. "But. You got her on side to start with by *not* letting her think. All right? Anyone who gets took like this, they ain't the thinking type, generally – so relying on 'em to think ain't a good idea. So she might yell for a copper first and think later, and then *you've* got six helpful citizens holding you down and *she* realises she'd be better off somewheres else. So, she looks in the bag. What do I do? Anyone?"

There was silence.

"What I do," Eveline said, "is *plan*. Think it through. Think about everything that can happen. Use your brains, my birdlets, that's what you're here for, to learn to use your brains. There's plenty enough people in this world think we're only good enough to use our bodies, being as we're female – but if that was all there was to us, none of us'd be here. Right?" She aimed her finger at the class.

"Right, miss," the girls replied.

The purple hat poked back through the door, and fell off, to general giggles, revealing a mop of brown curls surrounding a worried expression. "Eveline?"

"All right, Beth?"

"There's someone to see you."

"Who is it?"

"You'd better come." Beth Hastings tended to look distracted whenever she was away from her precious mechanisms, but Eveline could see that she was more anxious than usual.

"All right. Ladies, before next class I want you to come up with what you could do *before* the drop that'll make it all right if she *does* open the bag, right? And three more things that could go wrong, and ways to deal with all of 'em. Now, before you go: what's the rules?"

"Keep it simple, miss."

"Good. And?"

"Make 'em think it's their idea, miss."

"Lovely. And?"

"Find out what they want to hear, and tell it to them,"

"Good. And what's the one we never, ever break?"

"We never rob the people we come from, miss."

"Not just the people you come from, Doris. 'Cos not all of us here came from poor, though none of us wants to go back there. *You don't rob the poor.* You don't take from them with less than you. I may be training you up to run a con, I may be giving you skills what lots of people don't think are right nor proper, but any one of you ever uses 'em against the wrong mark, knowing it, then you're going to answer to me. And I asks *really hard questions.* All right?"

"Yes, miss."

"And remember, no chattering to the other girls, I don't care how curious they gets. Class dismissed, then. You done well today, ladies. Keep it up."

The girls filed out, and Beth and Eveline walked down the corridor.

"You're a natural at this, aren't you?" Beth said.

"Me, a teacher. Who'd have thunk it? All right, Miss Hastings, give us the worst, you look like you swallowed a goose."

"It's the grocer's boy. *Again.* He's been told not to bring us any more unless we pay him. And this morning it was the butcher's boy. They won't give us any more credit, Evvie."

"Oh, they will," Eveline said, grinning, though inside, her stomach tightened.

She managed to charm the grocer's boy into one more delivery with a combination of a few quid on account, promises, wit and a little light flirtation – she was only a year or so older than he, and he wasn't used to smart teacher ladies who could turn a friendly insult like a barrow boy. She reassured Beth – who tried to look as though it had worked – and walked slowly out into the grounds, biting her lip.

She'd have to go talk to the butcher. She didn't want the girls going without meat. She'd spent enough time hungry that she knew, after a point, it did nothing to sharpen your wits.

None of us want to go back there.

The trouble was, there were only so many people who could afford to school their daughters who thought it worth the money.

Generally, those girls didn't end up in Eveline's 'special' classes, because of the risk they'd let something slip to their parents. The special girls were mainly runaways, street children, survivors by their wits as Eveline herself had been. And still was.

She was teaching these girls the skills she'd learned herself, but she didn't intend they should use them just to get money from marks – it was too risky, for one thing, in all sorts of ways.

Eveline scowled at the bright sunshine which showed up the cracked plaster and rotten window frames all too clearly. She'd had the money to buy the place, but keeping it up, that was another matter.

Still, she had schemes. Eveline Duchen – though it was Sparrow, not Duchen these days – always had schemes. She'd made connection with some old contacts of Ma Pether's, people who kept their ears open, for a price. After months of waiting, interspersed with occasional scraps of worthless information (for which they still expected to be paid – and she had to pay, you didn't risk losing sources like those by stiffing them) – they'd finally found her a business that would suit her purposes.

If everything worked out.

"YOU SEEM TROUBLED, Lady Sparrow."

"Hey, Liu."

"You are definitely troubled." Liu pulled a comically anxious face. "Where is my insult?"

"I don't insult you *that* much! Here, you're got up very fancy, what's going on?" Liu was always a natty dresser, whether in a frock coat and a homburg, or as, today, in deep blue silk with soft black shoes and a little round hat.

"Oh, I have some errands to run for which this is more appropriate dress. But first, I understand that the grocer is causing problems."

"Oh, you heard that, did you?"

"I can, if you wish, go and speak to him."

"No, Liu, s'all right."

"You think he will not speak to me for fear of some subtle Oriental evil? I do not *have* to look Chinese."

Liu, being half fox-spirit, had an enviable ability to change his appearance, though he could only keep it up for so long.

"It's not that, Liu." Evvie sighed. "You know we have to get some proper money, regular."

"Proper, regular money? That sounds most dreadfully respectable. I think maybe you are not Eveline at all, but some deceiver, wearing a glamour to fool me."

"I'm a schoolteacher now, Liu, it don't come more respectable."

"I too was, and still on occasion am, a schoolteacher. I should object to being called respectable, however."

Eveline scowled. "S'all very well, but I got responsibilities now. It's not just the girls, it's Mama. I got to look after her."

"This is true and most honourable. But must you do it by turning respectable? I shall not know you."

"I don't know as I shall know myself. But if I get arrested running some scam, what's going to happen to them all? Besides, people might start taking an interest. The wrong people. I can't risk it."

Liu sighed. "It is all gone, then? The money from the jewels?"

Eveline's sister Charlotte, who was something between a favourite and a pet at the Emerald Court of Prince Aiden of the Folk, had sent Eveline a gift of jewels – whether out of guilt for her abrupt and rather brutal refusal to return to her family, or meaning to let them know how much better off she was, Eveline wasn't sure. She tried not to think about Charlotte. It hurt. She knew her mother worried, that the Folk were always capricious and frequently lethal, but Charlotte had made her choice, and didn't seem to care, so Eveline tried not to care either.

Today the reminder flicked her on the raw, and she snapped, "Yes, it's gone! You think I forgot, or counted 'em wrong, or something?"

"I would never make such a foolish mistake. When it comes to money your senses are finely attuned."

"They've had to be. We can't all steal a chicken when we're hungry."

Liu stopped, and looked at her, his eyes unreadable. "I thought that stealing was your profession."

"So?"

"Have you become ashamed, Lady Sparrow? Is the company of a thief something you no longer wish for?"

"Don't be a goose, I didn't mean that."

"Ah, and there is the insult. Good, now the formalities are taken care of. I had come to wish you farewell, but perhaps it is not necessary, as it seems you find my company unpleasant."

"I do when you keep twisting my words."

"Then I shall leave, and no longer be here to do so." Liu bowed, and turned away.

"Where are you going?"

"As I told you, I have errands to run. I will return, however, if you feel you can bear it."

"Liu…" But he was gone, into the trees that bordered the school grounds, quick and silent as he always was.

Eveline swore. She didn't know what was wrong with Liu lately, he never used to be so touchy. And what was this errand of his? She hoped it wouldn't get him into trouble – but then, he was a slippery one, *and* he was Folk – or at least, half so. He could get himself out of most things easy as winking.

Still, she couldn't help glancing at the woods where he had disappeared.

THE FOLLOWING DAY the butcher came himself. He was a lean, pallid, liverish man, who put Eveline strongly in mind of one of the chickens that hung, head-down and beak-dripping, in his window.

"I wish to speak to the master of the establishment," he said.

"That'd be me. Or mistress, rather. How can I help you?" Eveline said.

"You can help me, young lady, by allowing me to speak to the proper person."

Eveline choked down a remark about not being proper but being the person he wanted anyway. He didn't seem in the mood for levity. Nor, to be honest, was she – it was just the way her mind worked. "I know it may seem unlikely, Mr Blaithwaite, but I am the proprietor. Our name, the Sparrow School, is on the gate, and I am the Sparrow in question. What was it you wished to speak to me about?"

He glared her up and down, looked beyond her as though hoping to see some reassuring male presence, but encountered only Beth, hovering, and looking at him as though he were a fox and she a rabbit.

Deciding that no more proper authority was about to appear, he waved a piece of paper under Eveline's nose. "I am a patient man, Miss… Sparrow. But my patience is limited, indeed it is, and my bill is now overdue by some weeks. I would appreciate payment at your earliest convenience. That is, I don't intend to leave without it."

"What is the total, Mr Blaithwaite?"

He named a sum. Eveline blinked. "Would you wait here a moment, Mr Blaithwaite?"

"No, Miss Sparrow, I will not. I want my money."

"As you will, Mr Blaithwaite. Miss Hastings?"

"Yes, E… Miss Sparrow?"

"Please bring my cash box from the study."

Beth swallowed. "Yes, Miss Sparrow." She darted off.

"A pleasant day, though unseasonably warm," Eveline said. "It must be hard to keep the meat fresh in this weather."

"My meat is always fresh. But I need to get back to the shop. I hope that young woman will not be long."

"The study is not far, Mr Braithwaite."

"Good."

Eveline thought furiously. She knew to a penny how much there was in the cashbox, and it wasn't nearly enough for the butcher's bill. She could ask Ma Pether for some of her counterfeit coin – Ma always kept some about – but even if she was willing to let on to Ma how bad things were, that was a half-minute solution at best. The butcher would be back, and with the Peelers at his tail like as not.

Besides, it wasn't as though he'd given short weight or rotten meat – the stuff was good quality.

She put her hand in her pocket and felt the comforting smooth weight of the little jade fox Liu had given her. The thought of selling it hurt, and Liu would be upset – as though he wasn't already – but for all his sense in some things he really didn't seem to understand how badly they needed money, or at least, why she wasn't going the old way about getting it.

There was nothing else left to sell. Even in her thieving days Eveline had never owned any jewellery for more than the length of time it took for Ma Pether to sell it or Evvie herself to want it less than she wanted a bite of bread and sausage.

Beth came scuttering down the corridor, somewhat flushed and with her madly curly hair escaping its bun, as it always did in moments of stress. "Here you are," she said.

"Thank you, Miss Hastings." *Ask him to wait a week, and sell the fox? What will I tell Liu? Go to Ma Pether? Which?*

She was still wrestling with it when she opened the cashbox.

There was far more in it than there should be. Eveline managed to control her expression, but it was a near thing. She shot a glance at Beth, who was trying to look innocent and only succeeded in looking pleading.

"I do apologise for the delay, Mr Braithwaite," she said as she counted out the coins.

"Well, I'm sure you do your best," he said. "But perhaps you should hire an accountant." He leaned down, and said, in a conspiratorial whisper, "I'm doing myself down, here, but perhaps you should order less. Girls don't need to eat meat every day, you know, not like boys." He gave an unused-looking smile, tipped his hat, and walked back to his carriage.

"Wish I'd stiffed him now," Eveline said. "Condescending..."

"I'm sure he meant it kindly."

"Because he thinks we can't cope, being *girls*. Trouble is," she said, closing the cashbox with a sigh, "he's right, isn't he? We ain't coping. And I'll thank you to tell me where that brass came from, Miss Magician."

Beth hunched her shoulders. "I had some."

"Beth…"

"I sold a couple of things. Tools. We needed the money."

"Beth, you can't sell your tools! You need 'em!"

"And we need to pay the butcher. So."

Eveline gave her a fierce hug with the arm that wasn't holding the cashbox. "Numbskull. What're you going to do, tighten bolts with your teeth?"

"I'll manage," Beth said, flushing. "We do need money, though, don't we? Eveline, this scheme of yours… I hope it works."

"So do I."

WHEN EVELINE RETURNED to the house, the post had been delivered. She winced at the sight of what she had already learned to recognise as yet another bill, and shoved it under the others to open when she had the strength.

The next envelope was addressed to Mrs Madeleine Sparrow. Someone was writing to Mama, and under her new name. That probably meant it was safe, but… Eveline thought about going to the kitchen and steaming open the envelope. No-one would question her if they caught her at it, but it would hurt Mama a great deal if she should find out. She ran her thumb over the lush cream stationery. The handwriting was neat and confident. It didn't have the look or feel of officialdom about it, but she hadn't a deal of experience with official letters.

On the other hand anyone who knew either Mama or herself under their old name, Duchen, would hardly bother writing first. They'd be bursting the door down with boot and truncheon – or bundling people into a carriage in the dead of night.

She thrust the other letters into her pocket, and went to look for Mama.

MADELEINE WAS IN her workshop. Eveline paused for a moment in the doorway to watch, and to listen.

Mama looked better these days. When she was first rescued from her unjust imprisonment in Bedlam at her brother's hands, she had been pallid, distracted, and slow in her movements, flinching at unexpected sounds and struggling to return to the world from which she had been so long barred. Then she had been seized by Eveline's former nemesis, the government agent Thaddeus Holmforth, and dragged half around the world, witnessing murder and various other unpleasant and disturbing things – though she had proved herself both tougher and a deal more adaptable than might have been expected.

Now, notebook in hand, she hummed along with her instruments, the gleaming, spinning, singing mechanisms of Etheric Science, that subtle and artistic discipline of sound and mood (which had, like the Folk, its lethal aspects).

Madeleine made an adjustment to one of the machines, a small, rosewood box with three dials set in its side and a small brass trumpet protruding from its top. It started to vibrate, and gave out a slow, rising tone, which at first made Eveline smile, and gradually rose to a penetrating whine which made her wince and clap her hands over her ears.

"Oh, dear," Madeleine said. "*That's* not right." She leaned close to peer at the dials, made a note, snapped off the machine with a flick of her wrist, and turned around. "Oh, hello, my love. Did you want me?"

"There's a letter for you, Mama."

"A letter? How delightful!" Mama's face lit as though the sun had shone through the window on her. Mama could be pleased by such small things now. Eveline handed over the envelope, hoping desperately that it was something nice.

Madeleine opened it neatly with the edge of one of her dozens of screwdrivers, and drew out the single sheet within. "Oh, dear, I really *do* need spectacles, how thoroughly lowering."

"Don't worry, Mama, we'll get you some nice ones." *Even if I do have to steal them,* Eveline thought. "Do you want me to read it for you?"

"No, no, I think I can manage." Madeleine walked over to the window and held the letter close to her face. "Dear Madame, etc. etc... oh!"

"What is it? Mama?"

"Octavius Thring! He saw my work at the scientific exhibition in Bristol, and wants to meet me, and look at the rest of the mechanisms! And talk about Etherics!" Mama's face positively glowed.

"Octavius *Thring?* Who's he when he's at home?"

"He says he's an enthusiastic amateur – a 'dabbler in the sciences' – and thinks my work is fascinating!"

"What's he want?"

"Why, to talk. I could perform a demonstration – though a subject would be useful – several subjects – would you object if I asked some of the girls? Oh, I must finish the Halciphon..."

"Mama!"

"Yes, my dear?"

"Are you sure this is a good idea?"

"Why would it not be? Just to have someone to discuss... your friend Beth is a dear girl, and an excellent engineer, but she really isn't at home with Etherics. From his letter it's plain Mr Thring has more than an amateur's understanding. It would be so good to talk to someone, to clarify some thoughts. I don't see the harm in that."

"It's just... Mama, I don't wish to upset you, but I was thinking of Uncle James. What if this *Thring* person should be the same? What if he tries to steal your ideas?"

"Oh, well, I have applied for patents, you know. It does take forever, of course, but one or two have come through already."

"And what if he finds out about... everything?" Even here, Eveline was reluctant to mention Holmforth, or Shanghai, out loud.

Madeleine frowned, sat on the bench, and held out her hands to her daughter. "Eveline. Come sit with me."

Eveline went.

"My love," Madeleine said, "I know you mean to look after me. But it is not a daughter's place to have to look after her mother, you know; not unless I should become helpless, and I'm not quite there yet."

"I didn't mean…"

"I know you didn't. But you must allow me to make my own decision in this. It was hard enough to send the instruments off to the exhibition without attending myself; there were a number of people there I should very much like to have spoken to. Besides, they are mine, and I am proud of them. And yes, I know it would have been a risk, but now I consider it, the likelihood of one of the staff from the asylum attending such a thing and recognising me is very small."

"You're right, Mama, I know. And it's not as though you ever did anything wrong, after all. You were put away under false pretences."

"Well, quite."

"But if someone found you, they'd find me. And my case is different. It's not the asylum authorities who'd be looking for me, it's the government. Not the proper public government, neither – though they're bad enough – but a bit of the government that hardly anyone knows about. They don't have to follow the same rules." She'd been about to say more – to mention bundlings away in the middle of the night – but Mama had had enough to trouble her, and Eveline had no wish to add to it.

"But my dear, both those vile men are gone, and there's been no sign that anyone else knew the slightest thing about it."

"One of 'em's gone," Eveline said, forgetting in her agitation to keep up the careful language she tried to use with her mother – drawing-room language, as she thought of it. "The other – who knows?" Sometimes she almost felt sorry for Holmforth, the government agent who had recruited her, and who had been turned into a hare when he tried to cross the borders of the Crepuscular, where the Folk lived. For all she knew, he was still running mindlessly about the swamps outside Shanghai. Then she remembered that he had threatened her mother, and any pity died a swift and merciless death. Besides, she didn't even know if the transformation was permanent. What if Holmforth came back to himself? He'd be naked, alone, and probably confused – but she'd bet pounds to pennies he'd still be vengeful. She'd seen his capacity for that first hand.

"If we are careful, and remain on the right side of the law," Madeleine said, "I see no reason why anyone should come looking for you."

"I am trying, Mama."

"I know you are, my dear."

"I still don't know about this Thring sort, though. I mean, what do you know about him?"

"I know that he is interested and enthusiastic and wrote me a most courteous letter. In that last particular alone, he is entirely unlike my unlamented brother. Also, he has inventions of his own, 'mere dabblings,' he calls them, that he should like me to take a look at. So he is capable of coming up with his own ideas, too. Now, you must have a class, do you not?" Madeleine stood up, still holding Eveline's hands in hers. She was the taller – in Bedlam at least the food had been adequate. Eveline was still making up her growth after years of deprivation. This slight difference allowed Madeleine to look down at Eveline with fond reproach. "My daughter the schoolteacher," she said. "This is far better than your... other life, Eveline. When I think of how you lived..."

"I know, Mama." She kissed her mother on the cheek and left her to her mechanisms.

It might be a better life, with less chance of getting transported or chucked in Newgate, but it didn't *pay*. Not enough, not when you couldn't resist bringing home a girl you spotted with a neat line in pickpocketing or patter, who would be an asset if you could only put her to use, but who hadn't a copper penny to put towards the fees.

She didn't dare risk bringing the law down on them, no. But there were reasons the girls learned how to pick a mark, run a con, break a window, and slide out with the swag without raising an eyebrow. There were reasons they learned what she could remember from her brief time at the Britannia School, being taught the elements of espionage.

She had schemes, she had plans, and she had ambitions. And she had an interview tomorrow, which, if she could be bold enough and lucky enough, might be the beginning of better times.

"Evvie!" A LARGE, leather-waistcoated figure strode towards her, a pipe clamped in one corner of her mouth, trailing blue smoke down the corridor behind her.

"Ma, *please* can you smoke that foul thing outside?" Eveline said,

"You got proper finical since you set up this place," Ma Pether grumbled, but she opened a window, knocked out the pipe on the frame, and pointed its chewed mouthpiece at Eveline. "Those girls are doing all right. You've got an eye for 'em, just like me."

"Told you so."

"Ah, you did. But, Evvie my birdlet, what're you planning to do with 'em? They'll get restless. They already are. And that can only lead to trouble."

"Who's getting restless? What've they done?"

"I caught that Doris – she may look like butter wouldn't melt, but she's a proper bobbish mort, that one," Ma Pether's admiration was unmistakeable. "I caught her trying to get into *my* room! Mine!"

Bobbish? Eveline thought. *Bloody daft, if she thought she could put one over on Ma P and get away with it. Brave, but daft.*

"What did you do?"

"Don't look like that. I didn't whack her, I know you don't hold with it – though I was tempted. I told her I'd be peaching on her to you." Ma gave her a look.

It was a challenge. Evvie knew it. Ma might have been talking about retiring from playing Fagin to a houseful of girls for as long as Evvie had known her, she might have shown every sign of gratitude for her new role, but she'd ruled her particular roost a long time, and thought she knew how it should be done.

"I'll deal with her."

"Hmm."

"I've said I will, and I will. And you're right, it's time they were put to work. I'm off about something for us tomorrow."

"What do you mean you're off about something?"

"Like I said. I'm sniffing something out, and that's all I'm saying. You're the one told me never spread a secret, Ma."

"True enough. But I hope you know what you're about."

"*Yes,* Ma. Honestly, you and Liu… you'll drive me distracted between you!"

"Yes, well, that boy's another thing. I don't hold with it."

"Don't hold with *what,* exactly?"

"Now don't you take me up so sharp, Evvie Duch… Evvie *Sparrow.* You know exactly what I mean. Boys is trouble."

"Liu is *not* trouble. He risked his neck for me, remember?"

"I got nothing against him personal. He seems a decent enough sort – but when all's said and done, you keep a fox in a henhouse you're going to get ruffled feathers."

"He hasn't been *ruffling any feathers*, if you mean what I think you mean, Ma."

"And you'd know that, would you?"

"Yes, I would."

"Well, you know your own business best, I'm sure," Ma said, "but don't say I didn't warn you. It's the cart you don't think's moving as runs you down."

"Evvie? Are you all right?"

"Oh, Beth." The bell rang, signalling the end of the day, and Evvie pulled Beth into an empty room as the corridor filled with chattering girls.

"Was Ma Pether bullying you again?" Beth said.

"She's all right, she's just got her way."

"I don't know how you stand up to her," Beth said. "She scares me."

"I won't let her do anything to you."

"It's you I'm worried about."

"She won't do anything to me, neither." Eveline leant against the wall and rubbed her eyes. "She's all right, is Ma, but she don't half go on. And Mama, too. Honest, Beth, I had no mother for the longest time and now it's like I got two, and it ain't that I'm not grateful, but sometimes…"

"You've taken on ever so much, Evvie. I wish I could help more."

"I couldn't do it without you, Beth. Who'd teach the girls mechanics and sums? You know how cack-handed I am with all that, and all them little numbers makes my head swim. And you're helping out with other lessons, too. You're doing plenty, don't you worry about that. And if we get this job, there'll be proper money coming in and we can get some more teachers. We can start up Bartitsu if we can find someone to teach it. I miss Bartitsu," she said. "I could properly do with hitting something today."

"Evvie? Are you going to tell your Mama?"

"Not yet. Not 'less it works. She'll only worry."

"And what about Ma Pether?"

"No. She'd interfere."

"Are you sure that's all she'd do?"

"That'd be enough. Why?"

"I don't know." Beth chewed her lip. "I just… I don't think she'll like it, that's all."

"Well of course she won't *like* it, it wasn't her idea. She likes to be the one doing the planning – doesn't think anyone else is up to snuff."

"Mmm. Evvie? What happens if we don't get this job?"

"I'll find another," Eveline said. "Come on, Miss Anxiety. I don't know about you, but I want a cuppa tea."

The *Times* was lying on the table in the kitchen, not yet having been used for the fire, and Beth disappeared behind it. Eveline made tea and dug some more bills out of her pockets. She'd taken to carrying a few about with her, hoping that somehow it would inspire her to find a way to pay them – but also because it made the pile of them on her desk slightly less intimidating.

"This is scary," Beth said.

"You're right there," Eveline said, glowering at a bill. "They start charging any more for coal I'm going off to dig me own."

"I mean Panjdeh. Have you heard about it?"

"The what? No, what is it?"

"Panjdeh. It's a place in Turkmenistan."

"Sounds a long way away."

"It is. Ev*eline*. Don't you remember any of our geography lessons?"

"Not a one. And I don't see a need to. I got no plans for any more travelling, thank you very much."

"I'd love to go to Russia," Beth said. "Such a huge country. So mysterious. But they don't like us – they want a lot of the same bits of country we want. There was almost a war over the Panjdeh Incident, you know – there still might be."

"What do they want some bit of land in the middle of nowhere for, anyway? Why do *we*? S'a lot of nonsense if you ask me."

"It might be nonsense, but if it comes to war people will still be killed," Beth said.

"Well they ain't going to be coming here recruiting us, are they?" Eveline said.

"I suppose not." But Beth still looked worried. Eveline couldn't help feeling a little irritated with her friend. It wasn't as though they didn't have problems of their own, without bothering about something that was happening on the other side of the world.

Eagle Estates

It took Eveline longer than she had intended to find the offices of Eagle Estates. They did not declare themselves loudly. A small brass plate screwed to the yellowish bricks, almost hidden in the shadow of the portico, was the only clue for the curious. She checked it twice, to be sure, and in the slight but unacknowledged hope that this might not be her destination.

It was a smart enough building and fairly new, but the squat pillars of the portico had a dropsical look, and together with the sulphurous bricks, black-leaded windows and spear-headed black iron railings they gave the place a sullen, hostile feel that sent unease capering up and down her spine.

You're just letting yourself get all unnecessary, she told herself sternly. *You're Eveline Duchen, the Shanghai Sparrow, and you've got through plenty worse than this.* The Britannia School had looked pretty forbidding, when she'd first arrived – and *that* door had had the headmistress, Miss Cairngrim, waiting on the other side of it. There couldn't be anything much scarier behind this one.

Eveline took a deep breath, and gave herself a last mental check. Smart, business-like skirt and jacket, in grey, trimmed with dark blue ribbon. Hat, straw, with a stiff, dark blue gauze bow adorning its crown. A bag that was something like a baby Gladstone, also in dark blue.

She was still getting used to these narrower skirts. For convenience they were definitely to be preferred to crinolines, but she did miss the sheer capacity of a crinoline. It was amazing what you could stash under there if you had to.

Not that she was planning on stashing anything today. Today she was respectable. And she was as sure as she could be that she *looked* respectable. Whether she looked like somebody a person might hire for a job, that was another matter.

"Well, if they don't, the more fool them," she said to herself, raised her chin and rang the bell.

JOSH STUG LOOKED out of the window of his office at the hat below. A woman? What could she want? It wasn't his wife, she never came to the offices and he would certainly have discouraged it had she shown any such inclination.

Not... not one of them, surely? He jolted back from the window, his hand unconsciously rising to his mouth. If anyone should see, should guess... But surely there was no reason? He was due, yes, with another payment – but not *over*due.

But why would they wait in the street? They had no need... the figure moved under the portico, and the next moment the bell sent its juddering clatter up the stairs.

That settled it. They would certainly never ring the bell. Unsettled, none the less, he snapped at Jacobs, "Well, answer it, man," even as his secretary was lifting the speaking tube to his lips.

"A representative from Sparrow's Nest Security, Mr Stug," Jacobs said, putting his hand over the mouthpiece. "I have the appointment in the book."

"From... Really?"

"It's written here, sir."

"Yes, yes, I'm sure it is, but I thought I saw... never mind. I'll see them in the main room. And Jacobs."

"Sir?"

"Don't correct me again."

Jacobs twitched and ducked his head. "Yes, sir. I mean no, sir."

*   *   *

STUG SEATED HIMSELF behind the immense leather-topped desk, propped his elbows on it and fixed his face in an intimidating glower. It came naturally – he was one of those men who look as though they were put together from drying clay by an angry child; thickset, bristle-browed and jowly. His looks did not trouble him, since they had never prevented him from getting what he wanted.

When Jacobs ushered the slight figure through the door he felt another, momentary jolt. It was indeed the woman he had seen from the window. His glower deepened. Barely even a woman – a mere girl, who was looking at him with far too direct an expression.

"Mr Stug?" she said.

"And who might you be?"

"I'm the representative from Sparrow's Nest Security, Mr Stug."

"Oh, now really. Why in the world would they send you? Is this their idea of a sensible approach?"

"It's the only approach we have, Mr Stug."

"Hmph." He leaned back and waved a hand at her. "Well, go on, since you're here, but be quick about it, I don't have the whole morning to waste."

"This is a very fine office you have, Mr Stug."

"I know that."

"I understand you are looking to increase your security."

"Well I assume that's why you're here. Do you intend to set yourself up as a guard, perhaps? Stand in the doorway and ward off all comers?" He smiled at the ridiculousness of the thought.

"Oh, no, Mr Stug," she said with irritating calm. "We would simply advise you on how to best improve your building to prevent intrusion, thievery, and disruption to your business."

"I suppose you have some new invention or miraculous device that will do the thing?"

"Not at all. I noticed that the windows on the lower floor are easily reached from the street, however."

"They are locked every night."

"Windows can be broken."

"A police officer patrols this street regularly, he'd soon notice the sound of glass breaking, I assure you."

"Windows can be broken silently, Mr Stug."

"Then the intruder would also have to deal silently with a pair of large, bad-tempered dogs."

"Dogs can also be dealt with. Silently."

"And how would you know all this?"

"We have advisers, Mr Stug, who have expertise in this area."

"Turned-off coppers thrown out for a fondness for the bottle, no doubt. No, I really don't think so, Miss... whoever. I would advise your employers to seek someone more appropriate to plead their cause. And as for you... I suggest you apply to be a governess, you have just that sort of niminy-piminy way about you. Good day to you. Jacobs will show you out."

The brown eyes under the smart straw hat regarded him steadily, and he felt a little jab of irritation. She should have been flustered, any decent female would have been. "Thank you for your time, Mr Stug," she said, rose, and left the room.

What a piece of nonsense! He picked up one of the papers on his desk. Those tenants in the house off Elsted Street were behind with their rent again. He leaned back in his chair. Elsted Street, Elsted Street – oh, yes. The Huntridge family. The husband a dockworker, no doubt out of work again, the wife took in sewing – and they had a gaggle of children.

Maybe something could be got out of this morning after all.

EVELINE LEANED AGAINST the closed door of the office with a cold dropping-away in her stomach, then realised she was being watched. "Excuse me, do you have a..." For a moment the polite word escaped her, but the tall young man in the stiff collar and the cheap suit was looking at her sympathetically. He was sandy-haired and long-nosed. Almost handsome, in a shivering-greyhound sort of a way, but had a stretched-out look, as though there hadn't been quite enough material for all of him.

"Yes, miss. Just through there, miss," he gestured, with an ink-stained hand.

You're used to people needing the jakes after seeing your boss, ain't you? She thought. *And you look like a rabbit in a snare yourself.* She didn't like Mr Stug, not one bit – but she already felt sorry for his secretary.

"Thank you," she said.

"Jacobs!" Stug shouted.

She saw how he jumped. "You'd better go," she said. "Don't worry, I'll see myself out."

"Yes, miss." He looked as though he wanted to say something else, but didn't – instead he scurried into the office.

Eveline straightened up. *Now what?* She looked around.

Next to the door of the water closet was the tiny room the secretary Jacobs was caged in, and the staircase leading down, away from humiliation and failure. But next to it was a staircase leading up: bare boards, stained black, a wooden handrail worn down so the knots in the wood stood out like islands.

She glanced back at the office door. Then she bent, unlaced her boots, shoved them in her bag, and darted up the stairs.

There were three doors at the top. One opened on a closet containing a balding broom and several grumpy spiders. The other two were locked.

Eveline never travelled without her picks. These were a rather splendid new set she'd bought from Tall Jimmy in Longacre with some of the money from Charlotte's jewels. She'd told herself they were an investment against everything going wrong, but as a matter of fact, she just liked having them.

She looked at the two doors. Both had round brass handles – one of which was tarnished to a dull brown. The other, though it wasn't polished up like the nameplate outside, had a faint sheen of use.

That was the one she chose.

The room beyond was dim, with heavy curtains drawn over the

windows, but there was enough light to make out the edges of furniture. Eveline stood still until her eyes adjusted a little. A heavy table, one leg propped with a book. Another book – an old, thick one by the look of it – on the table-top. Not a ledger, something else. Candlesticks and the sort of thick-glassed lantern sailors used. A shelf of buff files bound with red lawyers' ribbon. Bunches of herbs strung here and there. Ornaments and oddments. A curtained alcove.

She nodded, backed out, locked the door, slipped down the stairs past the sound of hectoring from the office, and out of the front door.

Ao Guang's Palace

THE PALACE OF the Dragon King Ao Guang of the East China Sea was, of course, magnificent. It was also under water, but in the way of magical structures, this caused no difficulty for visitors like Liu.

The palace was of white jade, tiled in pearl, and shimmered like a mirage in the shifting sea-light. It was surrounded by a forest of branching corals twenty feet high, shading from palest flush to deepest blood-red.

Great glossy seaweeds, jade green and purplish-red, curved elegantly about the tiered roofs like silk shawls. Vast jellyfish, bigger than a man, like huge pale mushrooms, dozens of webby tendrils trailing behind them, swooped overhead. Shoals of fish swirled, glinting, and scattered abruptly before the slow cruising shadow of a shark.

Liu looked down at his robes. Traditional, but not excessive. He had, after all, been summoned. Too much flamboyance might count against him. He wore his human shape but let his fox-tail hang outside his clothes. Had he been true Folk, he would have had, like his father, several tails to show. He would not attempt to hide what he was – which would be useless – and would not give anyone the excuse to think he was ashamed of it.

Shame was not an emotion he had much time for.

Perhaps he should have told Eveline where he was going.

No. She would undoubtedly quarrel with him. She seemed to have become quarrelsome lately. And besides... he looked up at the towering palace.

Eveline was sharp, and clever, and altogether quite his favourite human. But despite everything, despite what he had told her about the Folk, despite her own experience (which after all had been more a case of carelessness and lack of human feeling on the part of the Folk than actual threat), he wasn't convinced she understood how dangerous his father's people really were.

Safer that she was kept well away from any involvement at all.

By his very nature, of course, he linked her to this world, and these beings that given sufficient excuse and an attention span of more than a moment's duration could destroy her in a thousand imaginatively appalling ways.

He tried not to think about that. He did not see the point of dwelling on unpleasant things any more than he saw the point of shame, though these days, avoiding either seemed to be annoyingly difficult.

A summons to the Court was quite unpleasant enough, and potentially a very bad sign. He had not been able to get in touch with any of his usual contacts, and suspected they were avoiding him – also a bad sign.

But he had been in worse situations, and had talked, charmed, stolen and tricked his way out of them all. He fluffed his tail, set his face in an engaging expression of open, slightly stupid innocence, and started towards the gates and their guardians; great Shi lions, ten feet high at the shoulder, who had not yet decided whether to notice one small fox-spirit approaching their gates.

"SO, *YOU'RE BACK*," the Shi lioness said. She glanced across at her mate. "He's back."

"He carries the stink of the *biaozi* on him," said the lion, rolling the embroidered sphere below his foot back and forth.

"So he does. He should wash, or he will offend the court," the lioness said. The cub curled beside her opened his eyes, blinked at Liu, yawned, and closed them again.

"Perhaps he should *be* washed." The lion bared his teeth, and curled his tongue. "Come here and let me wash you, Little Fox. I will remove the stink of the creature who calls herself a Queen."

"I thank you for your generosity," Liu said. "But I fear I am not worthy of such a gift."

"No, indeed you are not. I suppose you wish to enter?"

"I must enter, or disobey." Liu held out the scroll on which his summons had been written, in letters of purple edged with gold. Matching silk ribbons trailed from it, each an inch wide and at least two feet longer than necessary. Really, his former master had no subtlety. That was one thing you could say for the Queen – she was as subtle as the edge of a razor.

The lion leaned down and sniffed at the scroll, shook his curly mane, and sat back. "It is as he says, our master has ordered it, we must let him enter."

"I do not trust him," said the lioness, "and it is *my* place to guard those within."

"Do you wish to disobey our great lord?" the lion growled. "*That*," he jerked his head at Liu, "might be in the habit of disobedience. *We* are not."

"I disobey no-one. I fulfil my duty. If he is to come in then *I* should be the one to say it."

"You are disputatious and wearisome."

"I ask only to be allowed to fulfil my function as duty requires of me!"

The lion snarled with exasperation, and waved his claw. "Go, go!"

The great gates of red lacquer, carved with peonies, peaches, and dragons, opened with ponderous gravity, revealing a long walk lined with huabaio pillars of green jade, carved with more dragons, twining sinuously and raising their translucent heads to stare at Liu as he walked, head high and tail up, along the path.

Behind him the Shi were still arguing.

Liu heard the jade dragons whispering to each other as he passed. Some were snickering.

Belgravia

STUG OPENED HIS front door and immediately Cora was there, all ringlets and perfume, her pale hands fluttering like trapped birds. "Oh, there you are, Joshua. Such a day I've had, you wouldn't believe!"

"Really, dear?"

"Yes, that maid that Eliza found for me, oh, quite the most dreadful creature you know, really, so *insolent,* I had to turn her out."

"I thought she seemed quite proficient."

"Well, yes, she was to start with, but then I realised how she was sneaking about, you know, the way these girls do, poking her nose into things and asking questions, and oh, *gossiping,* I caught her gossiping with cook just at the *most* inconvenient time, going on about her family and so forth, really not at all... in any case, I shan't ask Eliza for another recommendation."

"I'm sure you know best, Cora."

"Well, at least now I won't have to *worry.*" She took his coat from his shoulders and hung it on the stand in the hall. "Oh," she said, leading the way into the drawing room, "there's a tea, tomorrow, at the Sithwaites'. I know you won't mind if I go, though I know they're not *quite* the thing, but..."

"I didn't think they were your type of people," he said, sitting in one of the red plush chairs that stood in a rigidly maintained order about the blue-and-red Turkey rug. In a glass-fronted cabinet of wood as dark and shiny as treacle stood ranks of crystal glasses, soldiers ready to sally forth on the field of social battle. On the black marble mantle photographs in heavy, bedizened silver frames jostled Chinoiserie vases and cut-crystal candlesticks.

The curtains were open, but the setting sun just managed to miss this window; sun never quite found its way into this room. All the rich and precious things gleamed in corners like the eyes of animals hiding in burrows, and despite the constant ever-changing flow of maids and skivvies dust gathered in nooks and cast a patina over the crystal, the silver, the polished wood; the chandelier dulled with it, the curtains grew a bloom like mould.

Stug lifted his chin to stop the collar – heavily starched, and still only slightly wilted at the end of a long day – from digging into the flesh of his neck. "Cora?"

"Well, no," she said, shifting one of the picture-frames a little to the left, then pushing it back again. "They're rather tiresome. But she's heard of a mesmerist – a most remarkable man, apparently – she thinks he might be able to... well. You know, dear."

Stug felt a shudder clench his innards. "Cora. I hope you have not been mentioning our *personal affairs* to these people?"

"I hardly needed to," she said. "She's in an interesting condition. *Again*. This will be her fifth." Cora looked at him, briefly, her face ghostly in the gloom. Even her ringlets seemed drifted with dust; his pretty young wife for a moment a lost, dead thing, like some spirit-photograph set among the frozen pictures on the mantel. "So many children, the littlest is the dearest thing. I don't know if I can bear it."

"Then don't go," Stug said, suddenly unable to bear it himself. "If it upsets you so, stay away from them. I don't approve of this nonsense in any case. Mesmerism! Sheer flummery and fraud. I hear disturbing things about it, Cora, I forbid you to meddle with such stuff. Even if it is harmless, and I'm not convinced of any such thing, it carries the aroma of the sideshow. I don't want my wife running about with such people."

"But Josh..."

"No, absolutely not. No mesmerism, Cora."

She turned away, her shoulders drooping. Stug heaved himself out of the chair and made for the stairs. "I hope cook, at least, is still performing satisfactorily," he said. "And that she is not going to inflict mutton on us again."

"No," Cora said. "I believe it is a ham, tonight." Her voice was chilly. No doubt there would be a bill from some obscenely extravagant dressmaker soon. He would pay it, and Cora would not go to a mesmerist.

He stumped up the stairs to his dressing room, wrenched off the wretched collar and flung it on the floor. He hoped there would be enough maids left to keep the place in order, at least.

As he changed, he took his watch from his pocket and laid it next to his shaving things. It ticked softly, a sound that should have been reassuring – but it was only another reminder. Time clawed at him with every tick, with the way his hair crept from his scalp, with the loosening of his jowls and the deepening lines beside his mouth. When he shaved, it was harder now, because the skin had loosened and slackened, the stubble hiding in the soft flesh, escaping the razor's edge. He was not, he considered, a vain man – but he had no desire to look like a thug.

The watch glowed in the gloom. It was a fat, smooth, glossy thing; *Presented to J Stug Esq* curled in extravagant letters over the cover, entwined with grape-laden vines. It was a fine watch.

It should be his son's. It *would* be his son's. He would not permit anything to stand in the way of that.

Perhaps he should let Cora have her mesmerist – what harm could it do, so long as she took a chaperone? Not that ghastly Sithwaite woman, though, with her immense brood.

His hands curled into fists, crushing the collar. Sometimes life was simply, unbearably unjust. Look at the Huntridge family – living like rats, feckless, hopeless scum, yet popping out brats like peas from a pod. The red-headed girl, though – all the rest of them were pallid, listless little things, or grubby and caterwauling – she had a bloom on her, and a smile.

Cora would probably find her 'a dear little thing.' Stug had no particular liking for children, though he had no doubt he would develop a fondness for his own, if... but a man needed a son.

Who would inherit what he had worked so hard for, if not his own boy? Someone he could show the ways of the world to... though not everything. There would be no need for the boy to know *everything*.

Ao Guang's Palace

"CHEN LIU."

"Your Imperial Majesty."

Liu found it hard, as ever, not to stare at the imperial yellow silks which draped the walls near the throne. They were embroidered with scarlet phoenixes and peonies, and in among them, tiny human warriors.

The embroidery moved constantly. The warriors battled each other, spears thrusting, swords slashing. Tiny limbs fell to the ground. Embroidered scarlet blood spilled down the yellow silk. There were no screams, only a constant whisper as the silk threads shifted.

It was the liveliest part of the room.

Where the Queen's court gave the impression of a kind of chaotic carnival, the Court of Ao Guang was as ponderously smooth and regular in its workings as some giant, slow machine. The courtiers, each with their specific modes of dress, moved along their assigned lines at the assigned intervals. Here, the stratifications, the motions up and down the scale of precedence and influence, could be seen at a glance. Even now, not having been a member of the court for some years, Liu could tell who had risen, who had fallen, who had dug in.

Ao Guang was on his throne. It was, of necessity, huge; he did not confine himself to human form, generally considering it below him. The throne was of fine lacquer-work, as scarlet as the blood embroidered on the curtains, piled with cushions in yellow and crimson and purple. He curled among them like a great cat, his gold eyes with their slit pupils fixed on Liu.

Liu walked towards him, doing his best to look suppliant without losing all of his swagger. Too little would suggest he was already defeated – too much would be dangerous.

He was not aiming these subtleties at Ao Guang himself, but at whoever currently had his ear. This appeared to be an elderly man – or at least, someone who bore the shape of an elderly man. He raised his head. He had the long beard that denoted wisdom, and was carrying Ao Guang's own eating implements in a massive silver box.

Liu recognised him at once. Ao Min. He was not a man, but a sea-creature who in his other form was something like a kraken. Even as an elderly man he had a certain toothy, tentacly look about him, and his beard had a habit of moving and shifting about as though the hairs were looking for something to grasp onto. He looked at Liu as though Liu was something particularly unpleasant that had been spilled on the floor, and that he would take pleasure in ordering the servants to wipe up.

This was not promising. Between Ao Min and Liu's father, Chen Shun, there was an established hostility whose origins Liu had never discovered.

And Ao Min had obviously moved up in Ao Guang's favour. That was... unfortunate. But then, as soon as he had received the summons, Liu knew that this was likely to be a complex dance, where getting the steps wrong could result in the loss of worse than one's dignity.

Liu wondered where his father was. He was conscious of a faint sense of relief at his absence, which he tried to suppress, and considered his former lord as he approached the throne.

Ao Guang was in some ways easier to deal with than the Queen. She liked to do the manipulation, whereas he, often bored but lacking imagination, (possibly, Liu considered, he was bored *because* he lacked imagination) liked others to come up with new entertainments, new intrigues, and new insults for him to take offence at. But once fixed upon a course, he was stubborn as a mountain and harder to move.

One great claw, longer than Liu's entire body, tapped upon the arm of the throne. His latest concubine, a new one since Liu's last visit, played upon a *pipa* – quite well, as far as Liu could judge. Her eyes were courteously lowered. She was, or at least was currently, human, and very young; perhaps thirteen or fourteen years old. She was pale and delicate as a windflower, her gown jade green, her black hair elaborately dressed with white flowers and pearls.

Liu did not look at her after that first glance. Taking too great an interest in Ao Guang's concubines could be unhealthy.

He stopped at the prescribed point on the carpet, (deep blue, worked with peacocks in pink and gold), and made the kowtow. He had thought about this quite hard, as it would, almost inevitably, get back to the Queen. Either she would consider it a sign of too great respect shown to his former master, and would punish him for it, or she would consider it an amusing example of the barbaric ways of Ao Guang's court. He would do his best to ensure it was the latter.

"Chen Liu. It is strange to see you in this Court again."

Liu bowed again.

"You no longer belong here. I have no liking for having the barbarian woman's spies and toadies in my court. You carry her stink about you. You may speak."

"I abase myself in horror, my Lord, if I offend your nostrils."

Ao Guang looked at him with those vast, yellow eyes, then waved a claw, dismissing the matter. "It was necessary to summon you. You remember, I am sure, a certain mechanism of the humans. Made in my image. You may speak."

"Yes, Your Imperial Majesty." Liu felt a creeping cold. Surely, surely no-one had guessed the secret of the Etheric dragon? It represented, potentially, the only human weapon that might actually offer a threat to the Folk – though it had been altered so that this was no longer obvious. They had been so careful, and everyone connected with it was either aware of the danger the secret represented – or dead.

Evvie knew the dangers – could she have spoken carelessly? Or perhaps her mother, with her love of mechanisms, her desire that

Etherics be recognised as a science… but Madeleine was a woman of sense, who had a rather better idea of the threat the Folk posed than her daughter did. She, of course, remembered an earlier time, when the Folk of her country had much more to do with humans.

Evvie, if you've been so careless, I'll strangle you when I get back, he thought. The cold in his stomach deepened. *If you're still there when I get back. If I get back.*

"I was told that it was gaudy, ugly, inelegant: an attempt at my image that was not only poor but insultingly, even *amusingly,* so." His lip lifted, showing another inch of a tooth that was already, in Liu's view, quite sufficiently long. "I have since received a differing report. You may speak."

"Imperial Majesty." *Who? And different how?*

"Min," Ao Guang said.

"Imperial Majesty."

"Remind me, what was your opinion?" Ao Guang said, looking at neither Liu nor Min but over both their heads, as though at some higher plane of thought.

Min bowed. "Remembering always that my opinion is that of the most worthless and humble of your servants, Imperial Majesty, and that I would hesitate even to venture on such an opinion were I not concerned only for your Majesty's honour…" Ao Guang, who never seemed to tire of this sort of thing, gave the slightest of nods. Liu kept his face fixed in an expression of bemused innocence.

"I have gathered information from what the barbarian is laughably pleased to call her Court, Imperial Majesty," Min went on, "and it appears that the mechanical dragon pleases her greatly. Though it is not in the highest tradition of gifts, it was none the less obtained with sacrifice of time, and effort, and blood. And what is perhaps more troubling is that it appears it could have been of strategic worth to Your Imperial Majesty's human subjects. Its removal to the Queen's jurisdiction may prove disadvantageous to them."

"So." Ao Guang turned his gaze once more to Liu. "Among the humans, and indeed, here, were you still a subject of my Court, that might be considered an act of treason."

Relief that the Etheric dragon's true nature was still undiscovered drenched Liu like heavy liquid. However, this was still an unfortunate situation, obviously created by Min for reasons of his own.

How bad was it, though? Liu was *not* a subject of Ao Guang's Court, not any more. He had been banished, thus freeing him to become a citizen of the Queen's Court.

And there were rules, custom and practice.

Ao Guang would be unlikely to simply execute Liu, or restrain him from returning to the Queen. The rules of the Folk governed even their human subjects, though in terms of humans they were rather more complex, and dependent on which earthbound territory the human was in, and whether they had reached their majority, and other such things.

The fact that there were such customs did not mean Ao Guang could not make Liu's life unpleasant and difficult if he wished to do so – and if he so desired, terminate it entirely, and risk irritating the Queen. He was only one of the four dragons of the seas, but he was the most powerful – which was why he was able to demand and receive the Imperial form of address, and be considered sufficiently important to be noticed by the Queen.

However Ao Guang was, as a rule, insular; his interest in the battles his human subjects fought was maintained only as long as he found it entertaining and could be persuaded that sacrifices were being made in his honour.

Liu bowed again, thinking furiously.

"Well?" Ao Guang said. "You may speak."

"I am thrice desolated that such reports should have been allowed to bring Your Imperial Majesty a moment's distress. My situation is a delicate one, and only by persuading my mistress that she had something you would desire could I retain the position of trust in which she currently holds me."

He left it there. Ao Guang was sufficiently full of his own importance that he would easily accept the idea that Liu was establishing himself as a spy in the Queen's court in order to curry favour and a possible invitation to return to Ao Guang's court. Of course, if Liu was ever made such an offer, he would have to work out how to refuse without causing so much offence he would never be able to return either to Ao Guang's court or to China itself. That would be annoying.

Liu was fairly certain he could dance his way through that situation, but this one was not over yet. Ao Guang had summoned him here to do more than simply complain, and Min was looking far too smug.

"Summon Chen Shun," Ao Guang said.

Liu barely had time to control his face before his father appeared, in his mostly human form. His gown was dusty, his hat showing trailing threads where his button of office had been cut away. He trod lightly still, his tails glossy and full, his eyes bright, and he prostrated himself before his master with grace.

"You may stand."

Chen Shun bounced to his feet.

"Your son disgraced this court," Ao Guang said. Chen Shun waited, his expression one of injured innocence.

"You may speak," Ao Guang said.

"Yes, Imperial Majesty."

"His disgrace reflects badly on you. You may speak."

"I know, Imperial Majesty."

"You are only still at our court because of the entertainment you have provided us and because we wish to practise the virtues. Although I fail to recollect which one applies, except perhaps there is one regarding extraordinary generosity. You may speak."

"The generosity and virtue of your Imperial Majesty are beyond compare."

Min leaned over and whispered in Ao Guang's ear.

"Ah yes," Ao Guang said. "Now I recall. One of the eight virtues is filial piety."

Liu's father opened his mouth, remembered that he had not been permitted to speak, and closed it again. Ao Guang, having paused, fixed him with a stare, and said, "You have our permission to speak with your son. You may use the Room of Lesser Celestial Influence for your conversation."

"We humble ourselves in astonishment at Your Imperial Majesty's divine beneficence."

Ao Guang gave the smallest of nods in acknowledgement and clapped his great paws. "I am hungry. Bring me pork. And wine."

As servants scurried to his bidding, Liu's father came trotting over to him. Liu bowed. His father looked him over, and shrugged. "I see. Well, my boy, come along, come along."

Liu knew better than to ask questions while they were in the midst of the court. He followed his father along the corridors, hearing the murmured conversation and feeling glances on the back of his neck, where the hairs were already aquiver.

The Room of Lesser Celestial Influence was small, for the palace, being only large enough to hold about a hundred people in comfort. The walls were pale blue and painted with stars, planets, suns, and moons; these were all considered things of lesser celestial influence than Ao Guang himself – at least by Ao Guang.

Being beneath his notice, this was one of the few rooms that contained no image of him.

Liu closed the door after himself, gently, but still said nothing.

"Well, this is a fine thing," Shun said, flinging himself into one of the blue-silk-upholstered chairs, his tails draped over the arm. "I hope you brought some wine."

"No, Father, I'm sorry." Liu glanced back at the door.

"You might have thought of it. I have been wanting to try some new wine, and since your antics it's so hard to get any. Well you can get me some when you do what's asked of you."

"Father…" Liu glanced at the door again. The room appeared empty, but everyone who had been in the throne-room knew where they were, anyone who hadn't been would within minutes, and the chances that someone was listening to them were so high as to be a certainty.

"You think we're overheard?" Shun grinned. "Why should it matter? All they will hear is your father making a request of his son, which his son will not, of course, dishonour him by disobeying."

Liu's heart was already sinking. "You've been punished because of me?"

Shun shrugged. "Of course, but it won't last, if you do as you're told. Oh, do stop looking at the door, boy; if Min or one of his toadies is listening, much good may it do him. Our Emperor requires something and you are to get it. Any attempt to interfere with this can only harm the one doing the interfering."

"What does he want?

"A harp."

"A harp?" A chill spread from the backs of Liu's knees up towards his spine. He couldn't mean...

"Yes. A harp. One for which your new mistress has a fondness. He wants it. Go fetch it, bring me some wine while you're about it, and then everything will be as it should be."

"He wants the Queen's Harp."

"Have you been taking opium or some other drug that you are so slow and stupid? You used to be sharp, it's the only reason I ever knew you were my son."

Liu bit down hard on his lip. "My mother would never have dishonoured you in that fashion."

"What, by bedding another?" Shun waved a hand. "I suppose not, she didn't have the imagination."

Liu's hands clenched, out of sight in the sleeves of his gown. "Was it Ao Min who brought this to His Majesty's attention?"

"Oh, probably, what does it matter?"

"It is often useful to know who one's enemies are."

"Min is a grumpy old fool, clutching grudges to his breast as though they were finest jade."

"You never told me why he hates you so," Liu said.

"I bested him and he cannot forget it, that's all. So he told our Imperial Majesty, may he receive ten thousand blessings , that he had been cheated, and that the only way to overcome the humiliation was to receive something of equal value. Thus, the harp. And you, having been instrumental in robbing him of his gift, are to fetch it. It's all very simple." He grinned at Liu. "Don't tell me you can't do it, boy, after all, you *are* my son."

"What if I can't?"

Shun swung his legs back to the floor, and waved his hands. "Then your father will be, if he is very lucky, only disgraced, cast out, and humiliated. If not... the mountain of ice, or the platform above the lake of fire, if his Imperial Majesty is in a traditional mood. Or perhaps the bamboo, which he picked up from the humans, charming creatures. Have you encountered that particular delight?"

"No. Father..."

"One is bound above it, and it grows through the body. Of course, when the humans do it, the victim dies, whereas for us... well, I should say, for me, that will not be the case. An unpleasant fate, that – and extended as long as it should please his Imperial Majesty to do so."

"He would have you tortured."

"Really, boy, of course he would."

Torture. He will be tortured. Liu felt as though his skin had suddenly become far too thin – the soft folds of his own clothing scraped at him like rusty nails. *The lake of fire, the mountain of ice...* as a curious pup, he had visited the lake of fire. What he had seen there had destroyed any desire to see the mountain of ice.

He had never seen the bamboo torture. His guts writhed at the thought.

"Come, my boy, why such a miserable expression? You will not permit any of these things to happen to your father." Shun bounced to his feet. "Are you telling me you can't outwit the Queen? Must I come up with a scheme? Have you been distracted by your little human?"

"What little human?"

"Really, boy, I'm not completely ignorant of your doings."

"I am honoured by your interest."

"Don't look sulky, that's no way to answer a father's care. I happened to hear that you were spending a lot of time with the humans, I thought I should look into it."

In case you could find some advantage to yourself, Liu thought, before he could stop himself.

"Thank you, Father, but I think it best if I try to handle this."

"There, I knew you could if you only put your mind to it. Stop looking so gloomy, come with me and eat. Have you seen the newest concubine? Delicious little thing, isn't she? Now, put your eyes back in your head, I'm not a complete fool, you know."

"Of course not, Father. But if you will excuse me I won't stay to eat. "

"You're terribly dull today; don't tell me you're becoming like your mother, or I will certainly end up impaled on bamboo spikes."

Liu could not quite manage a smile – he knew it would show too many teeth – but he forced his expression to one of slight boredom. "Min glares so at the pair of us that it quite destroys my appetite."

"Oh, don't let that old curmudgeon get in the way of your food, come, eat, grow fat on the Emperor's bounty. Annoy Min by stuffing yourself with all his favourite dishes."

"If I am to come up with a scheme that is both effective and sufficiently pleasing, I should begin to consider it immediately." *Also, honoured Father, I am not sure I can bear your company for another minute.*

But torture… no. No. I cannot allow it.

The Sparrow School

EVELINE CHECKED HER equipment. Rope, picks, paper, treacle, drugged meat (Stug might have been lying about the dogs to throw her off, but there was no point taking chances).

She was just easing open the door when she caught the smell of smoke. "Hope you remembered your picks," Ma Pether said, from the shadows.

"Ma…"

"I ain't interfering. Just you be careful. You're out of practice."

"No, I'm not! I teach this every day!"

"You teach cons, my girl. That ain't the same as sticking a bust. Not one bit, it ain't. And you ain't been at any of my classes lately, I'da noticed."

"I haven't forgotten, Ma."

"You got your…"

"I have everything."

"Those fancy new picks you bought won't be no good if you've forgotten how to get in and out quiet. Remember what I always sez…"

"There's plenty of things you always sez, Ma. Which one'd you like me to remember?"

Ma pointed a stubby, tobacco-stained finger at her. "Don't you cheek me, my girl, you're not too big to be put over my knee."

"Oh really? You want to go back to running cons, do you?"

"You'd throw me out, would you?"

"I will if you try to get in my way. I'm doing this for all of us, Ma.

Now will you please go... do whatever you were doing, and let me get on."

"Just you mind yourself, Evvie Duchen."

"It's Sparrow, Ma. Sparrow. You should remember, you're the one called me it to start with."

"So I did. Little Sparrow's flown the nest, but there's still nets out there to catch little birds."

"Ma..."

"Go on then."

"Thank *you*," Eveline said, and went off with something that looked rather like a flounce.

Ma Pether took out her tobacco pouch and refilled her pipe, with a slight smile, as she watched Eveline go.

Eagle Estates

EVELINE FOUND THE office again easily enough, though the buildings in this square all looked a great deal alike. Once one knew where to look for the brass plate, it was simple.

Getting in was less so.

The back proved impossible. Great high walls around a small area, difficult to get in, even more difficult to get out of in a hurry. And he'd not been lying about the dogs, big ribby half-starved things. She could drug them, but she didn't have enough meat to drug the dogs belonging to the buildings on either side as well, all of them kept hungry, all of them excitable. Seemed everyone in these offices was more afraid of a prig than they were of keeping an angry dog hungry enough to bite anyone who happened to be passing.

Beth was working on a folding ladder which would be perfect for upper-storey work, but it wasn't quite finished. And though Beth was a finicky creature, if she said something she'd made wasn't safe yet, then Evvie believed her. Landing on her backside in the road with bits of ladder all around her and the Peelers coming to see what all the noise was about wasn't how she planned to end this evening's festivities.

So it would have to be the front door.

Mr Stug knew his locks, or at least could pay those who did, but so did Eveline.

Speed, and confidence. Those were the tricks of it. And a set of nifty new picks, of course. It took a little finicking. The sound of approaching boots sent Evvie flat against the side of the porch, barely breathing, until the Peeler had passed – but pass he did, and eventually the door clicked open.

The office was pitchy dark, smelling of ink and dust. It didn't do anything for Eveline's nerves – she *was* out of practice, whatever she'd told Ma. Practising on locks in the safety of the school was one thing, but actually sticking a bust was another. She straightened her back and headed for the stairs.

She paused by the office. Stug was probably just the sort to have all his important papers locked away, but it never hurt to pick up a little extra information.

No lock at all on this door. Foolish Mr Stug. If everything went as planned, she'd advise him to change that. Anything that provided a little extra trouble would deter the casual prig, as most of them were, and even a determined thief could be delayed long enough to decide the game wasn't worth the candle.

The room was bone-cold, with the faintest of light seeping through the shutters. But Evvie had a solution; a neat little lantern. Bless Beth Hastings and her inventive mind! The lantern lit at the turn of a small handle, silently, giving a gentle greenish glow that was almost invisible from more than a few feet away. Beth was so clever, if she ever turned that marvellous mind to making something dangerous she'd have the world asmoke.

The lantern's soft glow lit framed certificates on the walls and a presentation pen-set from one of the more nobby charities – the sort which gave balls, where people wore a mint of finery and where Eveline, dressed as a servant, had more than once helped herself to some charity of the rather more direct sort.

She shook her head at herself. She hadn't taken as much notice of these trappings as she should have – she, Evvie Duchen – (dammit, *Sparrow*, she reminded herself – couldn't afford to slip that way, not even in her own head) – Evvie Sparrow, always so careful to know her mark. Here was a man who wanted to present a respectable face to the world. She could have used that. She'd been all of a fither, and trying to think lawful. It wasn't just being handy with the picks she had to bring to this – a mark was a mark. What you wanted was for them to buy something, whether it were a pig in a poke or no, and the more you knew of them, the more you could convince them it was just what they wanted.

There was a pile of correspondence in a wooden tray. She flicked through it. Nothing of note, invitations to this and that... but one bore what must be Stug's home address, and a very toff ken too. She knew that street, couldn't throw a stone without hitting some swell. She made a note of it, and nosed around the rest of the room, picking up a pen-knife here and an inkwell there, finally, reluctantly, returning to the hall.

The stairs wound up into darkness, a thin draft tickled her neck.

Yes, she was out of practice, and yes, Ma had properly put the wind up her, but it wasn't like her to be so laggard. She breathed in, darkened the lantern so no stray light would sneak through the unshuttered window, and set her foot on the stair.

But the closer she got to the room, the slower her feet went. There was something – a scent, a sound – that was riling her nerves. She stood still, listening, and sniffed the air, but whatever it was wouldn't come forward and make itself known. There was a dog yipping a house or two away, and the rumble of wheels, raised voices – but all of it was outside, none of it had that quality that meant, *get out, now.*

Eveline shrugged it off. She had to do this and do it now, or they were all in the suds. She knew which pick worked on this lock and could already find it in the dark with ease – she'd spent hours with these picks, learning the exact shape of each so no troublesome and easily spotted lantern was necessary.

Snick. The door jumped a little on its hinges, and opened at a push. With her senses on edge, Eveline waited for a theatrically loud creak or groan, but there was none, only a faint, weary whine.

The room was even darker now, of course, with no daylight seeping around the edges of the curtains. Evvie stood for a moment, just breathing. There was not enough light for her eyes to find however long she stood there, so finally she pulled out the lantern.

The low, underwater light, which downstairs had been merely convenient, here seemed to elongate and twist what it fell on, so that the legs of the table took on a crouching look, the rods of the chair backs became prison bars, the curtains – both those at the window and the one over the alcove – shifted and stirred as though something waited behind them. *Stop it, Eveline.*

The book on the table was far too big. What she_wanted was something that would be easy to carry, but would be missed – not something shoved in a corner and forgotten. She trod careful as a cat around the dim space, blessing Ma Pether for getting her into the habit of trousers when she was out on a job like this. There was a lot of dust. *Whoever's cleaning up here en't doing much of a job,* she thought. But then, the office downstairs was somewhere visitors would see. Perhaps Stug didn't think it worth the trouble – or perhaps he didn't trust anyone enough to let them up here. Another little flicker of unease ran up Evvie's spine at the thought. *What doesn't he want them to see?* She could see nothing of such obvious value that Stug would fear thieving by his staff; no safe, no important-looking papers. Besides that poor secretary seemed far too cowed to be on the sneak.

She drew back the curtain over the alcove. There was a trunk there, its top covered with cushions. Out of habit she noted their position, so they could be put back in the same place – then mentally laughed at herself. She was planning, quite deliberately, to steal something that would be missed – and she worried about someone noticing disordered cushions!

The trunk, however, proved to be both unlocked, and empty of everything but an odd, penetrating smell that she associated with hospitals.

Yet another oddity, and she was getting twitchier by the minute. There were things here that didn't seem to belong in an office. Bottles and jars that looked more suited to a chemist's, bunches of herbs hanging from nails. Horseshoes, and other random things, that tugged at her with a sense of familiarity.

She could hear Ma Pether's voice in her head clear as day, *If it stinks of a trap, look for the cheese, birdlets – it's there as sure as eggs is eggs.*

But *trap* wasn't quite right. Something was off, yes – something was odd about this room and the strange mix of stuff here there and everywhere.

Following some not quite acknowledged instinct, Evvie ducked down, shining the light along the floor. A scatter of grains that looked like salt, tiny gleaming crystals. And poking out from under a heavy carved chest, a little girl's shoe, battered and holed and flattened, a shoe that had had a hard life, and if she was any judge had covered more than one little foot in its bruised history, a miserable barely-worth-it hand-me-down of a shoe. A foundling's shoe, the very sort of footwear she'd lived in for several years, when she had shoes at all.

She thought of her sister Charlotte – who had got wet feet one dreadful cold winter's night, from being taken out in her indoor shoes – and straightened up abruptly, almost hitting her head on the table.

Never mind what such a thing was doing there. Suddenly she loathed this room and wanted to get out.

And there, on the shelves behind the table, was a long slender wooden box about the length of her forearm, carved with leaves and little winged creatures that twined and danced in the green light. It seemed to leap out at her, though surely she'd passed that very shelf before. There was no dust on it, or about it. Recently used, then.

She flipped the catch and eased the lid up carefully – it didn't seem the right shape for a music box, but one never knew, and she didn't want it suddenly singing her presence through the building.

No, not a music box – the case for a wooden whistle, of some wood the colour of honey with darker streaks swirling through it. It was shiny about the mouthpiece with use, and something about it gave Eveline the sense that it was old. It didn't seem the kind of thing that should be in an office either, but perhaps Mr Stug liked to play a jolly tune when he needed a break from bullying his secretary. The image of the bulldog-jowled Mr Stug cross-legged on his desk, piping away, lifted her mouth in a grin and eased her nerves a trifle.

It was the work of a moment to slip the case into her bag. She paused a little longer, staring around, and then thought, *All right, Ma, I can hear you, I'm going.*

She forced herself not to hurry too much on the stairs. Hopping home with a sprained ankle – or being found by Stug, at the bottom of the stairs with a broken leg – that would put a right spoke in the wheels.

As she got out into the open air, she eased back her shoulders and breathed in the familiar smoke and sewage stench of London, with a sense of relief. Neat as ninepence, it seemed she hadn't lost her touch after all. She strolled off down the street, her appearance now projecting *respectable factory-girl on her way to work* with every stride.

All the same, she paused on the corner, feeling a little itch between her shoulder blades, the faint weight of eyes. Was that a man-shaped shadow, drawing back into the other shadows?

But a peeler would blow his whistle and raise the alarm. Nerves, that was all.

"WELL, WELL," THE man in the bowler hat said, though only to himself. "Evvie Duchen, as I live and breathe. Up to your old tricks, Evvie? There's me thinking you'd gone respectable. Now, here you are sticking a bust. And that says to me, Bartholomew, it says, maybe there's more to this than meets the eye, and maybe where Evvie Duchen is, Ma Pether is too." He wouldn't mind seeing Ma Pether banged up – she'd got in his way a few times too often, being as she didn't approve of various of his business interests. But Ma had been formidable, and maybe still was, and if there was one thing Bartholomew Simms didn't care to risk, it was his own skin.

But there might be other advantages to be gained. Yes, indeed there might. He tilted his bowler to a more impudent angle and walked off into the night, at home among its stinks and shadows, softly singing a music-hall song.

She was as beautiful as a butterfly and proud as a Queen
Was pretty little Polly Perkins of Paddington Green...

The Sparrow School

WHEN EVVIE ARRIVED home, Liu was waiting for her, seated on the step, his feet neatly together, his head cocked. She felt a little jump of relief and pleasure in her chest but determined not to show it. "You're back then."

"Either myself or my ghost, yes."

"You look solid enough to me."

"But ghosts can be deceptive. Why, I have seen ghosts that could quite be mistaken for a living person."

"Hah. Well, whether or not you're a ghost you got your business done, then."

"As did you. Are you going to tell me what it was, Lady Sparrow? Or is this a secret?"

"I'll tell you if you tell me where you've been, all dressed up and coming back looking like a week of wet Wednesdays."

Liu's mouth, which had been drooping in a way quite unlike him, turned up. "Oh, that is a most charming expression. But then, wet weather is very good for growing rice, you know."

"Not much good here, then. So, what's got you so mumped?"

"I am not mumped. I am concerned. You have been up to no good, and without me, which is the part that concerns me."

"You weren't here, were you? 'Sides, I can still do some things without your help, you know."

"I do, I was merely hoping for the chance to admire you at work."

"Well thank you, Lord Blarney."

"You don't believe me?"

"I shouldn't."

"But you do. What is in that bag, do I dare to ask you?"

"Well you already have dared, haven't you? Budge up, and I'll tell you."

Liu obligingly shuffled along the step, and Evvie sat next to him. The sun was rising through the smoke over London, and casting long tree-shadows across the lawn.

"S'nice," she said.

"It is the best time of day. Apart from the dusk. And the night. Afternoons, too, have their moments. And mid-morning is the best time for tea. But then, any time is a good time for tea."

"Not the way you drink it."

"Putting milk in tea is a barbaric and disgusting habit."

"D'you want to see what's in my bag or do you want to chatter about nonsense?"

"Show me."

"You gotta hear the story first. You know I been looking for something, well, all right, respectable to do?"

"This involved sneaking out in the middle of the night? It does not *sound* respectable."

"You want to hear this or not?"

He grinned and waved her to go on.

"Well, I found out this fella Stug's been asking around about making his offices more secure, see. Seems like he's everso worried about someone breaking in and making off with his rent. He's a landlord, right?"

"So far I am able to follow."

"So I went and told him we could do what he wanted, get the place all tightened up. Didn't tell him *how*, mind. But I gotta put the girls to use, haven't I? And this uses what they got and makes it all respectable, poachers turned gamekeepers, see? You know what a poacher is?"

"Someone who cooks eggs?"

"*Liu...*"

"A poacher is someone who takes without permission animals that someone else believes belong to them simply because they have taken title to the land. I am a poacher, by nature. Land is not owned, and nor are the wild beasts. They are simply claimed."

"Right. So a gamekeeper's the bloke what's supposed to make sure all the animals are nice and fat and ready when his Lordship wants to go hunting, and ain't no-one making off with a few rabbits stuck in their pocket. All right?"

"I see."

"So if a poacher turns gamekeeper..."

"I believe I follow the metaphor. You plan to be a thief turned policeman, in effect."

"They say it takes one to catch one. Only I don't plan to catch none, just show folk how to keep 'em *out*."

"I see."

"Liu? Something up?"

"Not at all. Please go on."

"Right. So I goes and tells this Stug fella, only he isn't having any due to me being a mere female and probably no more brains than a hen. So I decide I'll show him I know what's what, and go back and nick something from his offices, so tomorrow – today I mean – I'll turn up and say, 'Guess what, look what I got, now, d'you want me to make sure it don't happen again or what?'"

Liu stared at her for a few moments.

"You intend to go to this person and *confess* to stealing?"

"Not at all. I'll confess to having 'operatives' – good word, innit, 'operatives' – that can get in his offices. And it in't stealing if you give it back, is it? And then he'll know it's easy for someone to get in, and that if my 'operatives' know how to get in we'll know how to stop anyone *else* getting in."

"Are you feeling quite well? What is to stop him from summoning a policeman?"

"Oh, don't you worry about that, I can talk me way out of that."

"I should be intrigued to hear *how*."

"A girl gotta have some secrets," Evvie said, grinning, though it was more than a little bravado. Usually she was a good planner, but now, sitting here with Liu, she realised that maybe she should have thought a bit harder about what exactly she planned to say to Mr Stug when she presented him with evidence of her own breaking, entering, and theft. Would he believe in her 'operatives,' who were, as it stood, a bunch of eager, half-wild girls?

But no. Improvisation was her *other* strong point. One of them. And she was good. She hadn't lost her touch, she hadn't been caught, and she'd be right as rain.

"I hope this object you absconded with was worth the trouble," Liu said. "If you are to be arrested it should at least be for something of value."

"Don't be daft – I wasn't going to nick something *valuable,* was I? What if I'd been caught?"

"I see that you have indeed been most careful," Liu said.

"Are you being ironical?"

"Actually, I believe I was being sarcastical." She made to hit him, and he ducked away, grinning. "Show me?"

Evvie took the case out of her bag and opened it. "S'a whistle," she said, helpfully, when Liu only stared in silence.

"May I see it more closely?" Liu's voice was odd, distant, as though he were thinking of something else, but his eyes fixed on the whistle. "It is, in fact, a flute – or a whistle, if you wish."

"Yes, I said."

"It is made of elder wood."

"Is it? I wouldn't know."

"No, I do not suppose that you would. Eveline…"

"What? It's just a *whistle,* Liu. Why're you looking so green?"

He put the whistle back in its case and snapped the lid shut, not looking at her. "Eveline – my Lady Sparrow, I don't think you should do this."

"Do what?"

"Become involved with this man, this Stug. What an unpleasant name. Definitely a name of ill-fortune. I am convinced he will bring you bad luck, you know. I know about these things." He gave her his charming, foxy grin, but she sensed an effort in it; it did not quite reach his eyes.

"What are you on about? After all the trouble I went to, I'm not giving up because he's got a funny *name.*"

"Please, will you take my advice on this?"

"No! Liu, what's got into you? Is it because I'm going to turn respectable? It is, isn't it." Evvie felt a weight all over her, like a heavy gown. "Liu, you think I *like* it? I *like* being me, Evvie Sparrow, I was *good.* I was one of the best, and I was learning, and getting better. But I can't *risk* it any more."

"It isn't that."

"What is it then?"

"Tell me, when you found this flute, was it dusty? Tucked away in some hidden corner?"

"No, what would be the point of that? I wanted something he'd use – and miss. It was on a shelf."

"Eveline, a flute of elder wood is used to summon the Folk."

"What?"

"Yes. It is one thing they must obey, at least, the lesser Folk. They do not like it – in fact, it makes them angry. No-one wants to be summoned, and least of all the Folk. He is summoning them, he is using a discourteous method and he is getting on their bad side, and that is not a good idea."

"Oh." Eveline tucked her feet up under her skirts and wrapped her arms around her knees, and rested her chin on them. "Now why would someone like Mr Stug be summoning the Folk?"

"Do you understand me, Lady Sparrow?"

"Yes, yes, he's calling 'em up and he's hacking 'em off, that, I get. What's it to do with me?"

"What it is to do with you is that the anger of the Folk is something that may spread beyond its immediate object. People may become caught up. Even possessing the flute…"

"I'm not *keeping* it."

"Eveline, please allow me to guide you in this. You could give me that thing – I will dispose of it – no-one saw you, did they? No-one knows you were there. Stug did not wish to employ you – you can forget about him, and deal with something less troublesome. There is so much you don't *know,*" he said, turning to look at her. "I tell you and tell you how dangerous they are – and who should know better than I? But you do not listen."

"You're still alive, and you've tricked 'em more'n once. So's Charlotte – leastways she was…" Evvie's voice tailed off.

"I am alive because I know how to play their games. And I keep track. Do you know the dances of the court, Eveline? Do you know who is up and down? Even being polite to the wrong person can change one's status, dangerously. When the Queen is in one of her more fractious moods, all one needs to do is wear the wrong colour and the punishments could be more horrible than you can imagine."

"Liu, I spent years scrabbling a pauper's living since I was no more'n a kinchin mort. I had to eat things and do things and live through things that *you* never had to. So don't tell me I can't imagine horrible. I bin through horrible. 'Sides, I got no plans to cross the stream of blood, thanks very much."

"But you might not have a choice. If you only stay out of their way and out of their notice, you may be safe."

"May I indeed. How'd you know this Stug is doing anything at all to do with the Folk?"

"The flute."

"Who's to say he's using it? P'raps he just likes having it about. Maybe it belonged to his family. Anyway, s'nothing to do with me. I *need* this work, Liu."

"And is there no-one else who wants this kind of thing done?"

"Not so far. And how many more'll there be who won't even talk to me 'cos I'm female?"

"Then let *me* go. Let me negotiate with him. Then, if he is involved with the Folk, I can…"

"*No.*" Eveline stopped, and jammed her hands onto her hips. Her mouth was tight. "Liu, I'm not having you run this business for me. I can *do* this, and I will."

"I didn't mean…"

"Never mind what you meant. I'm not having it."

"Do you think I meant to take over from you, your *respectable* business? I am sorry you think so poorly of me."

Eveline heaved an exasperated sigh. "Don't take me up so sharp!"

"What else am I to think? Is that not what you meant?"

"You don't understand."

"Neither do you. I am attempting to protect you from your own foolishness, Eveline."

"Oh, so I'm foolish am I?"

"On this matter, yes. And stubborn. And innocent as a fox-kit on its first day out of the den. Your mother knows how dangerous my people are – she is wiser on this than you."

"Oh, she is, is she? Well, I'm not having nothing to do with any Folk."

"You already are," Liu said, gesturing to himself. "And that alone..."

"That alone what?"

"I am only trying to keep you safe."

"I can look after myself."

"Indeed? Do you know that you must never carry St John's Wort to a meeting with the Folk?"

"'Course I do. Ai... someone told me that."

"And do you know who is currently in her favour at Court, and who is not?"

"Why would *I* be going anywhere near her Court?"

"You would not need to, to be at risk. Only to have words with one of her people. Do you know who Baba Yaga is?"

"Baby who?"

"Baba Yaga is the Russian version of the Queen, in her way. And at the moment your Queen –"

"She en't mine."

"The Queen of the English Folk, then – she has some quarrel with Baba Yaga, over who knows what. But speaking to one of her people you might easily do something that could be seen as showing favour to Baba Yaga. All you would need to do is, perhaps, to mention that you had a Russian doll of which you were fond, or that you had enjoyed a performance by Cossack riders at the circus."

"What sort of riders?"

"Cossacks. Or people dressed as such, at least."

"I wouldn't know a Cossack if one should dance up and call me Nancy. Liu, you're not making any *sense*."

"I am trying to explain that should you have any dealings with the Folk, you could endanger yourself without even knowing it."

"I en't going to, I keep *telling* you."

"Then you will not stop this nor let me do this for you."

"No, I won't," Evvie said. "You're worse'n Ma Pether."

"Ma Pether did her best to keep you safe."

"Ma Pether sent me out on jobs and would have abandoned me in a blink if I'd been caught, Liu. People talk about honour among thieves but there ain't a lot where I come from."

"But you were very, very good..."

"Will you stop it!" She jumped to her feet and glared down at him. "You got a proper romantic idea of what being a thief is all about. Might be different for you, being as you can change what you look like and I don't know what-all other magic you might have going for you, but I could end up hanged. Or in prison. Or on me way who-knows-where in a sinking ship. And can I trust *you* to look after this lot? After Mama? You like Evvie the trickster, who didn't have anyone. Well I got people now and I got to look after them and I can't do that in prison. Or dead."

"The Folk can do worse to you, Eveline. They are dangerous, and tricksy, and..."

"Well you should know," Eveline said, "being as you *are* one. Leave me be. If you don't like what I'm doing, you can... you can look the other way, or you can just *go*." She glared at him.

Liu rose to his feet, shut his eyes and clenched his hands. His fox-tail puffed out straight behind him, his teeth grew sharp, and long claws pressed into the pads of his palms.

"Lady Sparrow, sometimes..." He took a deep breath, then he walked away, across the lawn among the shadows and sun, into the woods, where all the birds were singing as though their lives depended on it.

Evvie's chest was tight and her eyes brimming. She'd never argued properly with Liu before, insults, yes, and well, there was when she'd found out what he was, but not since they'd been proper friends.

But she was furious, too. How dare he! She felt as though she were trapped in brambles, with thorns snagging and tugging at her every which way. Well, she was going back to Stug and she'd get this job and more, too – and they'd all see that she knew what she was about.

She needed some sleep, first. Sleep and breakfast and then she'd be able to think, and deal with Stug.

She saw Beth on her way to her workroom, with a pencil behind her ear. Beth was such an early riser, unable to wait to get to her beloved mechanisms. Even Mama didn't get up so early, now she didn't have small children to care for.

"Oh, hello, Evvie. You're up early – or late," she said, looking at the bag still clutched in Eveline's hand.

"Things to do." Beth was about the only person she could stand to see right now. At least she wasn't forever going on about what she thought Evvie should do with her life.

"Are you all right, Evvie?" Beth peered anxiously at her face. "Would you like some tea?"

The kindness brought tears brimming. Eveline swiped at her eyes. "Go on, then."

Beth waited until they had tea in front of them, before she said, "What is it?"

"Oh, Liu was being stupid."

"Oh, dear. I'm sure he didn't mean it."

"He just thinks he knows better'n me, and it made me cross."

"That's men for you," Beth said.

Hearing one of Ma Pether's phrases come out of the mouth of Beth, who'd had almost nothing to do with men until Eveline had come into her life, bringing Liu with her, made Evvie smile, and feel a little better. "How would you know, you juggins?"

"I watch," Beth said. "I listen. I know you think I'm silly, Evvie, and never think about much that isn't made of metal, but I'm not completely foolish. I do know things. And I know that Liu is a good sort, only he's got a lot of pride. Like you."

"I ain't proud!"

"I don't mean it in a bad way. You're proud of what you're good at, and why shouldn't you be?"

"Right now my life'd be a lot easier if I had something else to be proud of, Beth. You can make machines, you can *invent*, and no-one thinks the worse of you for it – what you do, that's useful to anyone, and don't make trouble nor get you the wrong side of the law."

"Just being interested in machines got me into enough trouble, remember?" Beth said. "My mother threatened me with an asylum if I hadn't agreed to go to the Britannia School. And whether machines are legal rather depends on what they get used for. I just wish…"

"What?" Evvie said, a little snappishly, hoping Beth wasn't about to start on her.

"Oh, nothing." She looked forlorn.

"Go on, Beth, what is it?"

"I just wish there was someone I could talk to about it. I mean, your Mama's wonderful but Etherics is different from what I do, and there isn't really anyone else here. The girls try, but there's none of them… anyway. It's nothing you should worry about."

Eveline gave her a quick hug. "Poor Beth. I'll keep my eye out, see if I can find some lass with a mechanical eye, eh?" She snickered. "That sounded strange."

"Urgh, don't," Beth said. "Although…"

"You're wondering how to make one, now, aren't you?"

Beth grinned. "Maybe. You'd need lenses. And…" Her grin dropped away. "There's soldiers," she said quietly. "A lot of them lose eyes, and hands. Most of what's made for them isn't much good. And if there is a war… it would be good to have some designs ready."

"You still on about the war? What's it to do with us?"

Beth hunched her shoulders and drew a finger around the rim of her mug.

"Beth? You don't think they're going to come here, do you, just 'cos we've been teaching our girls stuff? They're hardly going to come swanning up going, 'Right, we hear you got females what can handle a machine, off to the front with you,' are they?"

"Women have been soldiers, you know. Artemisia of Caria was a famous one."

"Who?"

"She was a naval commander under Xerxes."

"What are they?"

"He was a very famous Greek person who won a lot of wars. And he said Artemisia was the finest officer in his fleet. And there was Boudicca."

"I thought Boudicca was made up, like Robin Hood and that."

"No, she's real. She was."

"Where d'you *find* all this stuff?"

"One thing we had at home was books. Not much else, but a lot of books. Explorations and politics and military history. They were left to Mama by one of her uncles, she used to say he must have thought she'd have a son one day. Then she'd cry, or break something." Beth looked down at the table, rubbing at a stain with her finger. "Anyway I read quite a lot of the military history. See, I had an uncle, too. My Uncle Bertie. He was a soldier. My Mama's brother. The only one of her family who still came to see her, once... once she had me, and was in disgrace."

Beth pulled out a rag from her pocket to blow her nose. The rag had probably been a perfectly good handkerchief before it got used to wipe down oily machinery and sop up various colourful fluids. It left a dark streak down one side of her nose.

When it seemed she wasn't going to go on by herself, Eveline said, "He came to see you."

Beth nodded. "That house was so quiet. Mama hated noise. The first thing I remember her saying to me is, 'Ladies do not shout.' She'd get headaches, and lie on the settee, and if one of the neighbours banged a door loudly or a carriage went past she'd moan. If I made too much noise she'd shut me away until she thought I would be quiet."

No wonder Beth hardly ever raised her voice much above a murmur. Now it was so low Eveline had to lean forward to hear her.

"Uncle Berry – it was Bertie, really, but when I was little I couldn't say it, so I called him Berry. I kept doing it, because it made him laugh. He used to come to visit and he had such a loud laugh, and sometimes he came in his uniform, all bright and brass buttons, he had a great big blonde moustache and when he smiled it bushed out, and it was like… he was like this big happy wind blowing through the house, waking things up. He'd bring me things, toys. Dolls, mostly. I'd rather have had a train set, but the only time I asked him for anything like that Mama…" Beth's hand wandered to her cheek. "She was so furious. I don't know if she was more angry that I'd asked for something that wasn't suitable, or that I'd asked at all. So I played with the dolls when he was there because it made him happy. I felt guilty that I didn't like them much. But I found the books, then when he came I'd tell him I'd been reading Vegetius or Polyaenus' *Stratagems*. He'd laugh and swing me up and call me his Little General. Mama hated it but she couldn't say anything, in case he stopped coming to see us. I think he gave her some money, sometimes. He'd take us out to the seaside. I remember him lifting me onto a donkey, and the sound of the gulls and the children shouting, and the beach, and the sea so long and wide and blue. There was a boat and I thought, I want to be on one of those." She sighed. "One day he told us he was going on campaign. He was very excited.

"Then we didn't see him for months. When he came back for a visit, I was so looking forward to seeing him. Mama had already threatened me with being sent to Bedlam, you see. I thought perhaps he would help me. But… oh, Evvie.

"When he came to the door I didn't know who he was until he said 'Hello, Elizabeth.' He was so thin. His hands seemed to have got bigger, but they hadn't – it was just his wrists had no meat on them, none of him did. And his face. His face was *grey*. His moustache had started to go grey, too, just a little, otherwise it was the same – but it was wrong, it was on the wrong face. Even Mama looked shocked. She asked him if he'd been wounded and he said,

'Oh, no. A little. Nothing.' He said he was glad to see us and Mama fussed about making tea and Evvie, it was all wrong. He was like his own ghost, all grey and drifting. I asked him if he was ill and he said yes, in a way, and that seeing me made him better, but it didn't. I knew it didn't, not really. He didn't call me Little General any more. And when Mama chattered at him about my going away to school, he just nodded, I think he barely heard her. He just stared through things until even Mama stopped talking. He put his arms around me, oh, so *thin*, and said, 'Thank God they'll never send you, Elizabeth,' and then he was gone.

"And he never came back. Mama wrote to his regiment, in the end. They told his parents, when he was killed, but his people didn't bother telling Mama, they..." She shook her head, and blew her nose again, smearing the other side. "They'd cut her off, when I was born, so I suppose they didn't think she deserved to know. I don't know if they even knew he'd been coming to see us. I stopped reading military history, because they talked about 'soldiers' and 'the men' but every one of them could be Uncle Berry, and maybe they all had people at home who wanted them to come home and they came home wrong or never came at all. So it matters, you see. It matters if there's a war, because there's people in it and they get broken."

Eveline tried to think of something comforting to say, but she couldn't. So she refilled the teacups and sat silently with Beth in the sunny kitchen, her eyes constantly drawn to the thick black headlines that marched, military and stern, across the pages. Her mind put people inside those headlines now. Old Jeff who pulled himself along Northey Street in a little cart, his uniform trousers wrapped over where his legs ended above the knee. Jenny Blake, whose five boys had all gone for soldiers, and not one of them had come home. Jenny who had gone quietly mad, wandering the streets asking strangers if they had seen her Davey, her Bobby, her William or Frank or little Joe with his red hair like his Da's. More, plenty more – men missing eyes and arms and smiles, women missing husbands and brothers and sons. And

Beth's big, laughing Uncle Berry, who turned into a ghost before he was even dead.

AFTER SLEEP AND sausages, Eveline felt better, more like herself. Liu would come around. And Mama would be happy.

Ma Pether... well, Ma Pether could either go on training the girls, or she'd have to find something else to do. Evvie felt a little chill around her heart at the thought of telling Ma to go, but in the end, if it came to it, she'd have to. And the war? The war was none of her business, even if it happened. The newspaper said it wasn't going to and that would have to be enough for her.

She went to visit Mama, and found her flushed and smiling over a letter. "You look wonderful, Mama, what is it?"

"It's Mr Thring, darling. He's coming over tomorrow. Isn't it wonderful?"

"I suppose..."

"Don't sulk, my pet."

"I'm not sulking, Mama. I'm just... worried. You won't let him..."

"Eveline, my dear girl. After what I went through with your uncle, and that horrid man Holmforth, do you really think I would let another man get the better of me?" She gave Eveline a stern look. "I am your mother, not a child. It is not your place to lecture me."

"I didn't mean..."

"I know you mean well, dear, but sometimes you do seem to forget which of us is the parent."

"I'm sorry, Mama."

"Yes, well. I don't mean to lecture, either. But I am concerned; that woman, Ma Pether. I know she was your mother when I couldn't be, but... I hope you don't allow her to be too much of an influence. She's not a respectable person."

"Well, no, she's not, Mama, but she's not had it easy. And she's trying to be respectable now," Eveline said, thinking of her earlier encounter with Ma Pether and mentally crossing her fingers behind her back.

"I do hope so," Mama said. "You still won't tell me what goes on in those lessons of hers."

"I will, Mama. But I have to go out now."

"Is it…"

"It's proper work, Mama, I promise."

"Well, be careful, dear. I worry about you."

"I know you do, Mama." *That makes two of us,* Eveline thought.

Eagle Estates

STUG'S BUILDING LOOKED no more pleasant by daylight than it had when she'd first come here; in fact, it made her more uncomfortable. It occurred to her that it was the first time she had ever returned to a building that she'd broken into. Not a good idea, as a rule, and Ma Pether would no doubt have told her as much.

She wasn't sure *why* she'd refused to tell Ma what she was about: it was as though, she thought, she had something precious, and fragile, like an egg made of china, and was worried that rough handling would break it. Maybe because it was the first properly complicated idea she'd had that wasn't just a con, or was – but an *honest* one. A legal one, that would harm no-one.

Or maybe it was because Ma was always going to be on the other side from the law, and never mind finding holes in Evvie's scheme, she'd disapprove. Maybe to the point of leaving the school, maybe taking the more talented of the girls with her – and now having knowledge of what Evvie was up to.

For the first time Evvie wondered if she could properly *trust* Ma Pether. Taking her on had seemed so natural, so right – and by means of being thanks, too. After all, though Evvie knew she was clever and a good prig, she also knew that without Ma, she'd not have survived on the streets, and never have learned everything she had.

But Ma's loyalties lay first and foremost with Ma, and after that with the girls under her wing. And Eveline wasn't exactly under her wing any more…

But if there was one thing Ma Pether had taught her – among the many – it was that when you were on a job, you thought about the *job,* nothing else. *If you're thinking about the door when you're climbing in the window, you won't get out of neither with nothing.* And here she was, mithering on about things she couldn't do a thing about, especially not right now, when what she needed was all her mind on persuading Mr Stug that he wanted to take them on, without him calling in the Peelers, and maybe having her locked in that creepy upper room for good measure while he waited for them to appear.

Of course, now she knew why that room was so bothersome. And knowing that – knowing *anything* about a mark – that was always a useful thing.

She took a breath, straightened her skirts, marched up to the door and rang the bell with a determined jab.

The secretary – Jacobs – it was always useful to remember names, too – opened it with a look of anxiety that changed to sympathy in a moment. "Oh. Miss, I'm sorry, but he won't see you. He don't change his mind, Mr Stug. Not for nothing he don't. There's no good you wasting your time."

"Tell him…" She'd meant to use a different approach but something – the thought of Liu, trying to push her around, maybe – pushed the words out. "Tell him I've come about a musical instrument, that he might be interested in. A very special one."

"A musical *instrument?* I don't think…"

"He'll want to know," Eveline said. "He really will. It's a very *old* musical instrument, you might say *elderly.* If you'd be so kind as to tell him that, exactly in them words, I'd be everso grateful. And so will he."

"An elderly musical instrument."

"That's it. You're a very good secretary. Hope he appreciates it."

The young man looked as though he'd like to say something, but shook his head. "I'm not promising," he said. "He's not generally amenable to… but I'll tell him."

"Thank you," Eveline said, with her brightest smile.

"You'd best come in," he said, but didn't take her upstairs, instead he left her in the small chilly hallway with its black and white tiles and an umbrella-stand of Indian brass that Eveline automatically valued, though it was a big clumsy thing and ugly to her mind. There was only one umbrella in it, which was worth a bit itself. It had a silver bird's-head for a handle, and looked sneery but lonesome, all by itself in a stand big enough for a dozen umbrellas. She heard the office door shut and a murmur of voices, then a thunder of feet on the stairs and Jacobs was with her again, looking startled.

"You're to come up, miss."

She followed him, smiling to herself.

STUG CLENCHED HIS hands under the table as the young woman walked into his office. Brassy, for all her respectable dress, looking him in the eye that way. That was like them, too... bold. Full of their own importance.

He waved Jacobs out. "Well," he said. "What is it exactly that you wanted to see me about?"

"You remember what we talked about yesterday."

"Of course."

"I thought you might be willing to think again."

"And why would I do that?" Stug said. He hated this, hated that this wisp of a girl should have power over him – but power she had.

Because he couldn't be sure. She'd thrown him off balance by turning up – just when he had started looking to improve his security – by being young and female and apparently respectable.

But it could be that she was none of those things. It could be that she was one of the Folk, and without asking straight out – which would almost certainly be unwise and in any case unlikely to result in an honest answer – he had no way of knowing.

Treat her as though she was what she claimed, or as though she was one of them? He had wrestled with the question from the moment Jacobs had told him who was here and what she had said.

"Because I have something of yours," she said. "Here."

She opened her bag, took out the case and put it on the table.

He looked at the flute-case, then studied her face, which was open and bright and interested and perhaps a little pleased with itself.

"And what am I supposed to conclude from this," he said, "apart from that you are a thief?"

"Why, that I can tell you how to prevent such unfortunate things from happening in the future, Mr Stug. After all, someone got in, and took something of yours. You don't want that happening again, do you?"

No, he most certainly did not.

"Next time it could be something far more valuable," she said, with an apparently casual air. "Our rates are extremely reasonable, Mr Stug."

He put out his hand and closed it over the case, drew it towards him, opened it. The flute was still there – and it appeared to be the exact same flute, though until he tried to use it, he would have no way to tell.

"You have an interesting way of proving your point," he said.

"I was simply trying to be convincing."

"And is there a good reason why I should not send Jacobs to summon the police?"

"And what would you say to them, Mr Stug? There's nothing missing from your offices now, is there? If something was taken, it's come back. And it wasn't even something very valuable, unless perhaps it's worth more than it seems." She had her head slightly cocked, and a faint smile on her lips.

"What do you want?" he asked.

"Twenty-five pounds to go over the place in detail. We will tell you what you need and what it will cost, including fitting. We will then hire any necessary services, such as locksmiths. We have a list of excellent, reliable people who are reasonably priced."

"You weren't able to work all this out when you stole that flute from me last night?"

"Now Mr Stug, would a respectable businesswoman do such a thing?"

"How do I know it isn't just an excuse to go over the place and find out all its vulnerabilities, so you can strip it bare?"

"As you yourself said, Mr Stug, if someone did take that flute from you, they already know what needs to be known."

"I could get someone else."

"You could. But..." She glanced significantly at the flute. "Perhaps you might consider that Sparrow's Nest Security is the best option."

He still couldn't be sure. There was something about her, a swagger and confidence beyond her years, a kind of polish... and the very fact that she'd chosen the flute, that most of all.

But what she – or they – *actually* wanted if this was just an elaborate charade, that was another matter. He was not sure why they had not just taken the flute from him themselves – he was sure it was not beyond their powers – but it might involve some of those strange, tricksy rules of theirs, that a man could forever be tripping over. Damn them and all their works.

Still. If there was any chance, any chance at all, that by refusing he would offend them... He could not take the risk.

"Very well then," he said. "The contract?"

She drew a sheaf of paper from her bag and laid it neatly on the desk. He read it, carefully, watching her for signs of impatience, for any sign at all, but she waited calmly, her hands neatly folded in her lap.

He could find nothing wrong with the contract; the language was all correct, if simple. There were no oddities, no hidden clauses. He looked with particular care at the space for his signature, but if there was anything else there, he could not see it.

Nonetheless, he hesitated over the document, peering for any clue. It wasn't as though he were required to sign in blood, and contracts, at least ones on paper, contracts that certainly *read* as though they were drawn up by lawyers, were not the Folk's usual method.

But in the end, what choice did he have?

He signed, the pen sputtering with the force of his hand.

He opened his desk drawer with a snap, jerking at it when it jammed, tugging so hard there was an audible crack. He snatched out a wad of notes, and counted them off, slapping them onto the green leather surface.

"Here."

"Thank you." She took the money, but didn't count it – careless, or did she actually not care?

"When can I expect you?" he snapped.

"Well, I could have a look about now, if you like."

"No! No. Today's not convenient."

"Whenever would suit you, Mr Stug. We're here to serve you, you know."

"Are you indeed. In that case, in three days. At three. Will it be just you? I don't want to deal with all your people tramping about the place until I must." He put an emphasis on 'all your people' and peered at her, seeking a reaction, but her face was calm, pleasant, unreadable.

"Just as you wish, Mr Stug. It's a pleasure to do business with you."

And that, that could be true, or a lie, depending on who – or what – she was.

It was the flute. Had it been anything else he would have dismissed his fears. But it was the flute she had taken.

Whatever she was, he disliked her with an intensity that soured his throat and tightened his muscles as he went to the window to watch her leave. Pert, improper young woman. Had he been sure, he wouldn't have given her a moment of his time. The very idea!

And of course, if it proved she was only what she claimed, he would take great pleasure in throwing her off, and giving a piece of his mind to any business associates he could think of about the perils of allowing women – young, impertinent women – to become involved in one's business.

In the meantime… he turned away from the window.

He would have to provide his next payment soon.

He felt the familiar shudder of distaste, the brim of fear along his nerves. Was it just to show him that even with the flute, he had no power over them, that they had the upper hand? Perhaps they were simply trying to get him to give up.

But that would not happen. He would not be defeated. One way or another, Josh Stug *always* ended up in charge.

EVELINE BOUNCED ALONG the pavement, brimful of pleasure. There. She had done what she set out to do, she had proved herself smart, and she had got them a respectable job.

She had done it by stealing and conning, admittedly – but only because Stug was so unreasonable. And that part of it would please Ma Pether and Liu, at least.

She slowed, her walk losing some of its energy. Liu had been… she knew Liu cared for her. He'd risked his life for her, in fact – though she also knew that risk was his lifeblood, the way it was hers… or had been. But was he right? Was she doing something stupid?

And could she make up to him for what she'd said? The memory of it chilled her and leadened her feet. *You should know,* she'd said. *You are one.*

Stupid, and cruel, and unfair – but he'd got under her *skin* so. He could do it like almost no-one else; because she cared for him, too, whether she liked it – and whether Ma Pether liked it – or not.

Maybe she should check Stug out. A bit more. Because he was obviously up to *something.* Many people might dismiss the Folk as a spent force, something between history and myth, now they stayed away from the cities; she knew better. They were still there, and if Liu was right – and it was true, he really *should* know – still dangerous.

What she knew about them was that they – at least real Folk, not half-Folk like Liu – didn't think like people, and that made them tricksy.

So someone who got involved with them either didn't know what they were doing, or did, and thought it was worth it.

Like you, something whispered in her head, and she made a face. She'd never got involved with the Folk on purpose, it had just happened. And she hadn't seen Aiden of the Emerald Court in years. When she was little, she'd thought of him as a friend. Later, she'd realised that he thought of her as more of a half-trained puppy. Her sister was his lapdog now.

Charlotte had been offered the chance to come home, and had refused. It hurt Mama more than she tried to show and it had hurt – it *still* hurt – Eveline fiercely.

But Charlotte was irrelevant. She wasn't coming back. Mr Stug was what mattered right this minute.

He was a landlord, that much she knew. She couldn't risk going back to his offices, not now. But though she hadn't taken anything but the flute… she'd looked at every paper that was in her eyeline the two times she was in the offices, and had an address in Limehouse fixed in her mind. *Knowledge, and the means to use it.* The school's motto, taken from one of Ma Pether's sayings. It never hurt to have as much information about a mark as you could gather.

Of course, respectable people didn't think of the people they did business with as marks. Well, you couldn't change everything at once.

Limehouse

SHE DIDN'T BOTHER with a cab, besides, they cost money. She liked to walk, to keep her eye on things. Within an hour the familiar stench and babble of the slums surrounded her. Limehouse, where she'd spent much of her life.

She felt wrong, out of place. It wasn't the clothes – she'd moved around these streets respectably enough dressed when she lived with Ma, because Ma kept sets of decent clothes for the very purpose of making her girls look respectable enough to get into places they'd otherwise be kept out of.

She was still Evvie Duchen, Evvie the Sparrow, underneath – but now she was something else, too.

These people crowding around her, these pressing, smelly, desperate, exhausted, yelling, drunk, diseased, skinny people – it was these people she'd survived amongst, all that time; these people who'd given her a scrape of their own tiny portion or chased her off their own sleeping-hole behind a draper's or under a bridge or a broken cart. The children were still everywhere – pallid and grimy, trying to dip a pocket – not much to be gained, not around here – playing hopscotch and begging and yelling and fighting. She'd been one of them, and then she'd been one of Ma Pether's girls – under the shabby but protective umbrella of Ma's influence and the fearful respect she was held in.

Did Ma feel like she did now, out of place? *Softened?*

Stop it, Evvie. Keep your mind on the job.

It isn't a job. It's snooping for Respectability, like that feller who came around asking after Fallen Women and accused Ma Pether of being a... what did he call her? A Procuress. I thought it sounded grand until I knew what it meant. Oh, did she ever give him an earful.

You've turned, Evvie Duchen. You've gone over to the side of starched linen and lecturing, the ones with money who tell the poor how to live.

I have not! And anyway, I was respectable to start with, before Papa died and we had to go live with Uncle James – I was respectable until I ran away...

Her head suddenly seemed so full of yammering voices she wanted to sit down on the filthy pavers and clap her hands over her ears, as though that would help.

"You crossing, miss?"

The words came from not much above her knee. Looking down she saw a small, dirty boy; he could have been any age between six and ten for size, given how scrawny and undergrown most of the street children were, but the curves still remaining to his face suggested he was no more than seven. His eyes were brown, his hair a thick mat of unidentifiable colour, and he wore the remains of a pair of trousers and a jacket that would have been comically oversized to anyone who hadn't had to wear similar clothes as often as Evvie had, just to keep warm. Sleeves cavernous as tunnels had been folded back over their full length to allow small hands to emerge, which grasped a broom almost twice as tall as the boy himself.

On his feet were boots. Terrible boots, that had not ever been a pair; one was of faded dung-brown, the other, once black, had withered to an indeterminate grey. The brown one was too big, wrapped about the ankle with string to keep it on. Both gaped at the front, showing small bare black-nailed toes.

"No, I..." She looked again. "All right," she said. The boy moved ahead of her, manipulating the broom with determined energy and little grunts of effort, sweeping away horse-droppings and leaf-litter and the paper a pie had been wrapped in and the corpse of a rat.

"What's your name?"

"Bat, miss."

"Bat?"

"On account of I lives in a belfry, miss."

"You never do!" The old Evvie emerged, jaunty and rough. "No-one lives in a *belfry*. You'd go deaf. 'Sides they'd never let you."

He looked up at her, considering, and gave a wide, gappy grin. "Well, that's what I tells 'em, miss. People like a story."

"So they do," she said. "What's the real reason, then?"

"I dunno, miss, it's just what my brother called me."

"And where's he?"

"Gone off to sea, miss." Bat looked wistful. "I wish I could go to sea. I might meet pirates."

"Why'd you want to do that?"

"It'd be an adventure, miss. And there'd be treasure. Maybe one day my brother'll come and fetch me to go with him. And we can go fight pirates."

"Maybe he will," Evvie said. They'd reached the other side by now. "This crossing much good? I wouldn'a thought anyone around here's got the blunt to pay a sweeper."

"You'd be surprised, miss. We get all sorts through here, church and everything."

"Coming round doing the charity?"

"Oh, yes. And when the duns or the landlords come oftentimes they want a sweeper."

"I see. Here." She paid him – generously. "You know what's what around here, then?"

"Maybe, miss," he said, suddenly wary, clutching his broom across his chest.

"Don't fret yer gizzard. I en't looking to make trouble, I just wanta know who lives in there." She pointed to the address she'd memorised.

"'Bout six, seven families, miss – none of 'em uses my crossing," he said, resigned.

"I don't suppose they do," she said, looking at the building, which seemed to be held together as much with soot and general grime as with actual bricks and mortar. "Here, Bat."

"I gotta work my crossing, miss."

"Look, there's another brown in it for you if you'll tell me anything you can about the people in that house – and I'll buy you a pie and coffee while you're telling me. I'm not with the church and I'm not with the Peelers – I just need to find out some things, that's all."

He looked her over, and, finally, nodded. "We'll have to eat it here, though, miss. We don't, someone'll have my crossing."

"All right, then. Where's the best pie shop?"

"Albey's Eel and Mash on the corner, miss."

She nodded, and started off – he was wary, but skinny enough that she'd have to trust the chance of a pie in the hand, and the need to mind his crossing, would be enough to keep him there until she got back.

"Miss?"

"Yes?"

"I don't like coffee, miss. C'n I have milk?"

"'Course," she said, swallowing against a sudden stupid lump in her throat and the memory of her sister Charlotte's baby mouth, silky with milk and blowing a fat, happy bubble of satisfaction.

The pie shop smelled good enough she decided to get a pie of her own. She'd not eaten since breakfast, and her hunger, though more easily satisfied these days, never deserted her for long. It was as though her body, used to deprivation, could never quite believe the days of plenty would last. She still had the habit, too, of shoving the occasional piece of cheese or apple or chunk of nearly-solid stale crust in her bag, just in case.

When she came back the boy was standing leaning on his broom, looking world-weary as only a tired, hungry, seven-year-old trying to look older, bigger and tougher can look.

"Here."

"Thanks, miss."

"Someone taught you manners, anyroad."

"My brother'd thump me 'less I said my thankyous, miss," came the somewhat muffled reply in a shower of crumbs.

"Didn't teach you not to talk with your mouth full, though. S'not polite, and you might spill the food, that'd be a waste."

He swallowed hastily. "Sorry, miss."

"Never mind," she said, wondering why she was trying to teach this scrap of humanity manners, it wasn't as though he'd have much chance to use them; most of the people who used his crossing, he'd be lucky to get a bent ha'penny off them, never mind another pie. "So, what about that house, then? Who lives there?"

"I dunno much, miss," he said, but between bites he proved willing enough to talk – and he even tried to remember to swallow first. "There's Juicy Peg, and Blind Will. And Loaf, he's simple, he goes aaaah but he can't say words. He lives with his Ma, she takes in sewing. There's the Farleys on the top, and all their bantlings, I dunno what he does but she makes lace, she comes out sometimes to sit on the step. There's the Glucks – they talk funny – and the Pritchards, they talk funny too but you can understand 'em, he coughs all the time. The Pritchards are church, they always go out Sundays. The Pritchards got seven, or maybe eight, the Glucks had a boy and a girl, and now they just got a girl, she don't talk much, and the Farleys, half theirs are off to work 'cept Bert cos Bert's back went bad on him and he can't walk no more, he waves at me through the window sometimes. There's the Stones, they've five, no, four, he's scammered all the time. Gin," Bat said solemnly. "She don't half yell when he lays on. And there's the Huntridges, they en't been here so long as the others, they got maybe six, I can't keep 'em all straight. There's more go in and out, but I dunno the names."

"Any visitors?"

"Juicy Peg gets lots," he said. "And Loaf's Ma gets a few, men, mainly. She turns Loaf out when they come, unless it's the draper man come to pick up the shirts. Sometimes Loaf comes to the crossing. He tried to take my broom, I had to yell and his Ma come for him."

"You do all right holding on to it like you do, how'd you manage?"

"Oh most of the time s'all right, cos they know me round here, but sometimes a bigger boy's tried to have it off me and I kicks 'em. I kick good, and I bite." He wrapped his hands protectively around the broom. "But Loaf's real strong, his Ma says what didn't go into his head God put in his body. He's all right, mostly, he's sort of like a dog. Anyways... That's mostly it."

"What about toffs? Landlords and that?"

"Oh, *them.*" There was a wealth of scorn and distrust in the word. "There's Bowler, and the Viper. The Viper don't come often himself, mostly he sends Bowler. I don't like 'em. Time they came together they used my crossing, Bowler looked at me like I was a pie, only he wasn't sure what was in it, and he said to the Viper did he think I'd do, and the Viper told him he was a flat. Bowler only guv me a fadge *and* it was clipped."

"So the Viper, he's the landlord?"

"'S'right." Bat was looking at the remains of Evvie's pie with a ravenous eye.

"Here," she said. "I'm full." She wasn't, but she reckoned he was earning it. "Why'd you call him the Viper?"

"S'what everyone calls him, Viper Stug. I asked Juicy Peg once and she said it was cos he's the devil himself in disguise, not that this was the Garden of Eden she said, I din't understand that bit, only anyway she called him a... she said I wasn't to say it. I dunno what it means anyways."

"Why'd she say he was the devil?"

"She says he's bad luck and carries evil with him."

"Why's that then?"

Bat shrugged, picking the last crumbs of pie off his filthy trousers with a wetted finger. "I dunno, miss."

"But often he doesn't come himself, you said, he sends Bowler? Who's Bowler?"

"He's the Viper's nobbler, miss. You don't pay up, he gives you a basting. We calls him Bowler on account of his hat – never seen him without it, miss. I don't like him. He's..." The boy seemed to choose, and reject, several words, possibly ones Juicy Peg had told him not to use, before settling on, "bad, miss. *Proper* bad. I reckon *he's* the devil, not Viper. There was horns under that hat of his I wouldn't be a bit surprised."

"Well, well. You're a noticing one, you are. You all done? I gotta take these mugs back to the shop."

He handed her his mug.

"You been a proper help to me," she told him. "You keep this hidden and don't go flashing it about, you hear?"

Bat gave a wide stare at the handful of coins she slid into his small palm and nodded vigorously. "Right you are, miss."

"Good boy. Here, you know when the Viper was here last?"

"Not for ages, miss. But Bowler was here two days back."

"Everyone paid up?"

"S'far as I know, miss. He was right nettled."

"Why'd he be nettled?"

"He likes it when they can't pay up, miss. Makes him happy, that does. Like I said, he's a bad 'un."

"You're a good boy, Bat."

"Thank you, miss."

"You stay away from them fellas."

"Oh, I will, miss. Less they wants the crossing, cos that's me job, that is."

"Yeah, I know. All right, Bat." She felt an odd impulse to say, "Be good," but being good had never done her any favours, not when she was out on the streets. There was one other thing she could do for him, though. "Here, Bat. One of them boys comes after your broom again, I can show you something to put 'em off, you want to see?"

"What?" He was wary again, clutching his broom close to his chest.

She put her hands over his. They looked very clean by comparison, and she felt that sense of dislocation again. "You hold it like this, so they can't grab it so easy. Then, one of 'em comes at you, you jab it like this – see? That'll wind 'em proper, and you can get away. Or give 'em a bit more to remember you by, if you've a mind – but getting away's usually better."

"That's smart, that is. Show me again?"

She showed him twice more. She remembered that much from

her Bartitsu lessons, and a broom was as good a weapon as any. "You could see if you can find someone to shave a coupla feet off the end, and you'll get by easier, and you can still jab with it – better, even."

"I dunno about that, miss. It makes the ladies go a bit soft, seeing me with this broom."

He gave her that gappy grin again and she grinned back, feeling a little better and glad to give him something more than a few coins – the move would last him longer than they would, especially if he had a chance to grow a bit.

She made her way to the miserable collapsing heap of a house.

JUICY PEG PROVED to be at home, if you could call her room 'home.' She flung open the door of a tiny little cupboard of a place, which Juicy Peg filled like a bunch of big, blowsy flowers jammed into a small, ugly vase. She was a full-figured woman, wearing a pink sateen wrap thrown over scarlet corsets. With her bright ginger hair, the combination was startling, but cheerful.

Peg looked Evvie up and down. "You ain't my usual sort of customer," she said, "but I'm accomodatin'. Come in."

"I ain't here for wapping, love," Evvie said. She felt perfectly at home, instantly; the room was crammed with cheap colourful junk – brightly painted fairground china, luridly dyed shawls and artificial flowers. A scrapbook and a pot of glue lay on the small rickety table. Red-cheeked cherubs frolicked over its pages among finely-dressed children. More cherubs were paused in flight across the table top, ready to be pasted in. A boy doll in a sailor suit perched on a chair, the crisp whiteness of his jacket startling against the grimy cushions. Crammed among the gimcrackery were dozens of brightly-tinted picture postcards of elaborately dressed children. There were damp stockings and undergarments hanging off the furniture. It smelled of sausages and Dr Mackenzie's Arsenical Soap and cheap Mille Fleurs perfume and sex, and, of course, of sewage. Everywhere around here smelled of sewage.

"What you want then?" said Juicy Peg. "I'm about to have me breakfast."

"Don't mind me."

"If Viper sent you…"

"He didn't. I wanta ask you about him."

The sausages were steaming in a greasy wrapper. Peg unfolded it and picked a sausage out, delicately, with the tips of her fingers. "What about him?"

"He's the landlord, right?"

"So?"

"So… I heard maybe he isn't on the up and up."

Peg opened her mouth, closed it on a big bite of sausage, and chewed, eyeing Evvie thoughtfully. Eventually she swallowed. "This room," she said, gesturing with the remaining sausage, "it en't much, but it's what I got, and it's no worse than some. Better'n others, 'cos I got it to meself, and my customers likes a bit of privacy. I can charge more. So I can't afford to be on outs with the V… Mr Stug, right?"

There was a porcelain dog with an expression of sneering idiocy and a dusty ruff around its neck staring down at Evvie from the grimy mantel. She looked at it while she considered. "All right," she said. "I know. I ain't planning to make trouble and I ain't naming no names. Anything I hear, I didn't hear off of you."

"S'all very well," said Peg, "but how do I know?"

Evvie let out a small sigh. It was partly genuine, too – after talking to Bat and seeing the room, it was almost too easy to guess where Peg's lever was.

"I think," she said, "he's up to no good – and it's something to do with children."

Peg wrapped her arms around herself, as though she was cold. "Here," she said, "you fancy a drop of porter? I always has a drop of porter with me breakfast."

"All right." Evvie hated porter.

Peg poured the dark stuff into two mugs, both chipped. She leaned forward confidentially, enveloping Evvie in the smells of sweat and cheap perfume.

"Every time he comes here, him or Bowler, there's something bad happens. Every time."

"Some people are like that," Evvie said.

"But it's children. Always the children. Now me, I ain't got none, I caught pregnant once and it ended bad, I near died of it, but I likes the little 'uns." For a moment her jolly face drooped mournfully and she looked old, something old and lonely left out in the sun too long and drying up. "But anyways, the Viper comes round – normally he doesn't want his fancy self carrying our stink, so he sends Bowler, who's as bad, or worse. But every now and then round he comes, and I swear, day later or two, something happens to one of the children. Mrs Pritchard's boy died of a fever, the *very next day*, and he hadn't even been that sick. And the Viper promised work for the Glucks' boy but the lad never wrote nor come home, and it just about broke Gluck's heart. He was a good, likely boy – handsome as the day, and the hope of that family, he was. There was a girl found at the foot of the stairs, with her neck broke, and another boy just faded away, like he had the consumption but he never even coughed, just faded.

"And last time, it was the Stones' girl. Just disappeared. Lovely little thing, she was, like a little daisy, all white and gold, used to make me think of when I was a girl in the country, just looking at her. But the day after Stug's visit, she disappeared. And Bat... he's the sweeper boy, he told me he sworn he saw the Viper's carriage, that night. Stone's never been the same. I mean, he wasn't never what you'd call a good man, but he got his head out the bottle now and again and got work, and he never used to baste that poor woman so bad. I thought maybe I should go and look, you know, around one of the bawdy-houses, but..." She looked down at her hands, shiny with sausage-grease. "I couldn't bear it, I can't see the little 'uns like that. 'Sides, there's so many of 'em. I din't know where to start. But there's one not a mile from here."

"Why would he take her there? S'not like he needs the money."

"Because he's evil, that's why," Peg said. "He's the devil, and that Bowler, he's the devil's red right hand, he is." She shuddered, and pulled her pink wrap tighter. "I shoulda gone," she said, turning away. "I shoulda gone looking but I'm just a scared old whore. I'm scared of Viper and Bowler and the Peelers and I'm scared of what I'da seen, in those places."

"You wasn't the one took 'em," Evvie said. *If anyone did.* "'Sides, if they were in one of those places, he'd take 'em further away, not close by where they could run home. You wouldn't'a seen 'em anyway."

"Poor little things," Peg said, and snuffled, and picked up her porter. "Poor little things."

Children died of fever all the time, there was nothing new in that. When Eveline was at Ma Pether's, in the surrounding rookery a week without a death or two was a rare one, and sometimes, they went two and three in a day, from the typhoid or the whooping cough or some new thing that came in with the ships.

Children fell downstairs. Sometimes children fell downstairs because a parent had had enough, because there was too much misery and not enough money and too much gin and not enough hope.

These were the rookeries. Children died in their hundreds; or just disappeared into the chaffering crowds of mites who swarmed the rooftops and the parks and the alleys.

But there was something. Something in what Peg had said that niggled her.

She thought of Bat and his dreadful boots. She'd worn boots like that herself. Now her feet were cased in neat, laced boots – that *fit,* and kept her feet dry. She wondered how many people, like Stug, knew what it was like to be so grateful for a decent pair of boots... and why was she thinking of boots, and feet, and shoes... Charlotte's little wet feet in the snow....

A child's shoe. A slum-child's shoe in a place where no such thing had any right to be.

Under a carved chest, in an office, miles away from here.

She felt a chill go through her despite the warm coat and thick stockings she would once have had to steal for.

Oh, Eveline, what have you stumbled into?

Maybe it was nothing, maybe it was just coincidence. Shoes got everywhere, you saw them on railway embankments and the tops of walls and who knows where – though if there were a slum-child about, they didn't stay there long. Shoes were precious.

So such a child wouldn't voluntarily leave a shoe behind.

She'd come meaning to check Stug out, and maybe had got more than she bargained for.

What was he up to? And did she want to know?

She'd meant – she'd thought – that perhaps she could do something, once she was safe, and established, and had money and a respectable name. That maybe she could do something for the people who had no-one else fighting their corner.

But she wasn't safe yet. And there was Mama, and Beth – who was bright, but out here would be completely helpless. And the others she had taken on and promised to protect.

She could feel the weight of the slum all around her, a great lump of heavy, seeping, stinking darkness.

"So," Peg's voice broke into her reverie. "If that's all…"

"No. Do us a favour?"

"Maybe."

"All I want is you should tell me when either of 'em turns up next, that's all. Get us a message. Send… I dunno, send Bat."

Juicy Peg looked at Eveline over the rim of her mug. "Why'd I do that, then?"

"'Cos if you're right, he's a bad man, and if I can find out what he's up to, maybe I can do something."

"You? What are you, the Peelers? Even if you was, you couldn't get Bowler. He's snake-slippy, he is."

"Maybe he is. And maybe I'm the snake-charmer."

"That's all very well but if he finds out I peached, I'll be in an alley with a red smile round me neck soon's winking, like them poor girls over Whitechapel."

"I'm not going to let on, what d'you think I am?"

Peg scowled. "And what about Bat? I'm not getting that innocent in trouble with Bowler, not for any money, I'm not."

"What makes you think Bowler'd know anything about Bat being in it? All he's gonna be doing is running an errand for a sixpence, like as he might do any time."

"He won't leave his crossing, anyroad."

"Find another, then – there's enough little 'uns round here'd do it for a penny or two. Or someone else, not little. But it's *about* the little 'uns, Peg. All of 'em. He's up to something with 'em, I know it. But if you're too scared to do anything, even without a ha'porth of risk to yourself, I suppose I'd better find someone as actually *cares* about the poor innocents, instead of just rambling on all pious, and doing nothing."

Peg slammed her mug down and started yanking still-damp stockings from the bedrail, shaking them like a terrier with a rat, and moving them to the back of the chair, for no good reason Eveline could see.

Eveline waited her out. She'd set her crowbar, now to see whether she'd applied enough pressure to wheedle the window up.

"All right!" Peg burst out. "All right. And if Bowler strangles the pair of us and throws us in the Thames I hope you'll be properly remorseful."

BAT WAS NOWHERE in sight when Evvie left, scurrying away from the slum as though it might reach out long filthy fingers and grab her back.

It wasn't until she was nearer the school, with fields in sight, that her shoulders unhunched and her pace slowed.

Now what? She'd given Peg the address to send a message, but it might lead to nothing.

She would have to talk to Liu… but what if he wasn't there, what if she'd annoyed him so much he'd taken off?

She bit at her nails, made herself stop. *Think, Evvie.*

Stug had promised her the job. She'd take it, and find out more, and when she had enough information, she'd do something. What, she had no idea.

The Sparrow School

"MRS SPARROW?"

It took Madeleine a moment before she turned around, with a screwdriver in her hand. "Oh, Beth dear." She gave a sad smile. "I do *forget,* you know."

"I know." Beth smiled back. "I don't know what I'd do if I had to change my name. I forget things enough as it is."

"Aren't *you* worried someone will come looking for you?"

Beth shrugged. "Once I was at the school my mother never cared to come looking, and my father hadn't any interest except to keep me out of the way. I don't know what the school will tell her, and I don't care much – *they* don't know *where* I am and no-one else cares *who* I am."

"That sounds dreadfully lonely."

"Oh, no, ma'am. I was. At the school, and before. But not since I met Evvie."

"I'm very pleased to hear it. Beth, did you want me for something?"

"Oh! Oh, yes, I'm sorry. There's a gentleman. A Mr Thring? He said you had an appointment?"

Madeleine's hands flew to her mouth. "I forgot! Oh, dear... and he's come all this way... Beth, please, would you arrange some tea, have them bring it here, show him through. Oh, I meant to have this ready... and this..." She started to adjust the device in front of her, a beautiful creation of brass and cherry wood, with a spiral metal groove set into its upper surface. A bronze ball-bearing sat in the centre of the spiral, quivering slightly.

Beth grinned and hurried away.

OCTAVIUS THRING WAS a small, slightly rotund gentleman with a battered hat sitting at an angle on exuberant grey curls, a waistcoat brightly adorned with embroidered peacocks, a large case, a set of extremely complicated-looking goggles hanging around his neck, and a beaming smile.

"Mrs Sparrow?" He thrust out a somewhat oil-stained hand. "What a charming name. Octavius Thring. I know, I know, a ridiculous moniker but I'm used to it. Oh, there they are! I say, isn't that one of the ones that was on display in Bristol? May I look?" He was bouncing on his toes, his curls dancing in rhythm. He seemed to have more enthusiasm than could be contained in such a comparatively small frame – he barely reached Madeleine's shoulder and was peering around it with intense eagerness.

Madeleine had been standing, somewhat protectively, in front of her devices, and now moved aside, smiling. "Of course, that is why you're here, Mr Thring."

"Do call me Octavius, if you don't feel it too forward of me. Now, am I right in believing this is the Ruminator? A wonderful idea, quite wonderful. And just the sort of thing I would find most useful myself. I have a butterfly brain, you know, forever flitting from one idea to the other. I am convinced that such a means of focussing the attention on one thing for more than a moment would be most beneficial. And not just to myself. Can you conceive of how much art, how much literature, might be produced under its influence? What wonderful things might burst into existence if the notorious digressifications – I know, I know, it is a word of my own invention, but I feel it has a place in rational discourse – of the creative mind were to be suppressed?"

"Indeed," Madeleine said, once she was certain the torrent of enthusiasm had ceased for the moment. "But I fear I have not yet perfected it. I am attempting to induce a state of calm, focussed attention. Unfortunately it acts on some subjects as a most effective soporific, not at all the effect I intended."

"Ah, but there is certainly also a place for a soporific device! Perhaps it may need to be adjusted to the individual subject? It might, indeed, be capable of performing both functions – focussing the mind when needed, and inducing restful slumber when that is required?"

"My dear sir! I have been wrestling with this wretched device for months, trying to force it to be just one thing, and I believe you may have presented me with the very solution I should have been attempting!"

"Oh, no, well, that is most kind, but it's only a thought, you know. Tell me, when I saw it on display, of course it was open, but not running. I could see the workings, and I wondered – how do you counteract the noise created by the pump? Did you not find it interfered with the vibrations?"

"Oh, I had to dampen it. It required some thought, but I was quite pleased with the result. Let me open the lid for you…"

By the time Beth returned with the tea – she was far too interested to give the errand to someone else – they were deep in a discussion about regulating steam-pressure and the possibilities of Etheric science to improve the working conditions in the manufactories.

"Oh, Beth dear – Octavius, this is Beth Hastings. She is an exceptional engineer. Beth, would you care to show Octavius the *Sacagawea*?"

"Oh, I…"

"Another intriguing name! May I ask what the *Sacagawea* might be?" Octavius beamed at her.

"Well," Beth said, "she's sort of a steam car, only I've boosted the engine with… fluid. A fluid. That I made."

"Now I am most certainly intrigued. But you seem a little reluctant, my dear. Don't worry. I know what it's like, one's creations are so very much like one's children – I haven't been blessed with children of the flesh, alas, but my children of the mind, as it were, well, one does so hope strangers will be kind. Don't feel you must show it to me unless you are quite ready."

"Well, you're not here to see *me*, after all," Beth said, torn between eagerness and nerves. The case had been unpacked and a scatter of intriguing instruments lay over the bench and floor. She longed for a closer look, but Mr Thring's kindness only made her feel more awkward. "I... um... I'd better go."

"Another time, then? If you feel able."

Beth made a gesture somewhere between a nod and a curtsey, and hurried off, casting longing glances over her shoulder and colliding with Ma Pether in the corridor.

"Keep your eyes in front of you, child, or you'll run right into trouble."

"Sorry, ma'am."

"No matter," Ma Pether said, looking at the door Beth had just come out of. "Beth."

"Yes ma'am?"

"Don't call me ma'am, child, how many times've I told you? I'm Ma Pether, to you and everyone else. Who was that talking to Eveline's mama?"

"Mr Thring. He's an inventor."

"Is he. Hmm. Pretty nicely turned out for an inventor, considering most of 'em I've come across ain't got two farthings to bet on a lame dog."

"Maybe he makes money from his inventions?"

"Like Mrs Sparrow done so noticeable?" Ma Pether said, rolling one of the smelly cheroots she alternated with her even smellier pipe between yellow-stained fingers, and fixing Beth with a cynical eye.

"She will," Beth said.

"I'd bet more money on you, meself," Ma said. "You got a knack for fixing, and people always want stuff fixed. Sometimes they'd rather that than something new. People hold onto the old, and try and make it fit, you ever noticed that? They'll bodge something up to keep it working, sometimes because they en't got money for new, but sometimes just acause they like the old thing, it's comfortable

94

and they understand it. And they'll keep it going long past time. Even me. Stuff I kept in Bermondsey... rats'll have got most of it by now if the river en't... still..." Ma in pensive mood was new to Beth and more than a little disconcerting.

She seemed to come back to herself with a shake of the head, and glared at Beth. "Well?"

"I have to get on, ma'am... Pether." Beth scurried away, hearing what sounded like a snort of laughter behind her. Ma Pether always made her feel stupid and more than a little uneasy, though she hadn't ever done anything bad to Beth.

She was a criminal, of course. But then so was Eveline, and Eveline was her best friend. Pretty much her only one, in fact. Mama Duchen (*Sparrow*, she scolded herself) was unfailingly kind but could hardly be said to count as a friend.

It wasn't so much the criminality, that made Ma Pether uncomfortable to be around; it was that she thought most other people were fools, and didn't hesitate to say so.

Beth sighed. Compared to Ma Pether she *was* a fool, she knew, about most things other than engines. People were too complicated, and couldn't be solved with a bit of reengineering or a drop of oil in the right place. But she couldn't see anything wrong with Mr Thring, he seemed nice, and interested, and one day Mama Sparrow's Etheric studies would make money, she was convinced of it.

"MYSELF, I FIND children of the mind to be somewhat less troublesome than those of the flesh," Madeleine Sparrow confessed, as she tightened the seating of a radial arm.

"Indeed?" Octavius Thring was up to his shoulders in one of her larger devices, but popped his head out to look at her. His shirtsleeves were rolled up and his curls in even more disarray, his hat having been discarded on a side-table.

"I have a daughter. She is... we were separated for a long time, and her upbringing was... unorthodox. She has managed so well, but I fear... Oh, I don't know why I'm chattering about such things! Tell me, you said you were working on something of your own, which also used vibratory principles?"

Thring regarded her for a moment, then withdrew fully from the machine, and straightened. "Yes. I have a theory, regarding cats."

"Cats?"

"Do you keep a cat?"

"I am rather fond of them, but in recent years my situation has not permitted a pet," Madeleine said.

"I am very fond of cats. I have three. I broke a leg, a few years back."

"Oh?"

"Yes, and the break healed with remarkable speed. I believe there may be a connection."

"A connection?"

"With the cats. One of them, Blanc de Neige, had a habit of sitting on my leg as I lay immobilised in a cast – oh, I had so many ideas, I considered having myself immobilised for a month every year, to see if the same effect could be obtained – where was I? Oh, yes, Blanc de Neige, she purred a great deal. I suspect she was rather pleased to have me at rest and able to pay her the attention she believed she deserved. The doctor commented on the speed at which I healed, and I believe the vibrations produced by her purring may have had an effect on the knitting of the bone. I have been attempting other experiments, but finding it rather difficult. I know that the great scientists are happy to experiment on themselves but alas I could not bring myself to break another bone on purpose. I dislike the idea of breaking an animal's bone simply to see how it heals, even alongside the application of ether, which is in any case dreadfully tricky to use, especially on the smaller beasts. Also, alas, the cats do have a tendency to *eat* the other experimental elements, given the chance. So… but I still think the theory has merit."

"How very interesting," Madeleine said, struggling not to laugh.

"I have been wondering if it is possible to reproduce the effect by other means, but since it is so difficult to find out how a cat produces a purr in the first place, and I have no desire to dissect my poor darlings, nor to do so to any of their fellows, even if one could do so while maintaining the cat in a sufficiently calm and happy state for it to continue to purr, which seems almost certainly impossible and the mere attempt distressing for all parties…"

"I doubt such extreme measures would be necessary," Madeleine said. "What one needs is to measure the vibration with as much accuracy as possible, and then find means to reproduce it. If one could record the purring, say, upon something like a phonogram disc…"

Limehouse

"MR STUG, IF you could just see your way…"

"Huntridge, don't waste my time. Can you or can't you make your rent? I've been patient, Huntridge. Very patient. My patience has limits. I'm a businessman."

"Yes, Mr Stug. I understand, Mr Stug. I'm just waiting to hear about a job…"

The man was pale and skinny, dark sideburns standing out stark against his pallid skin, his hands long-fingered with large, scarred knuckles. His wife stood behind the room's one piece of furniture, a battered, age-worn table, as though it were the only thing protecting her from Stug, and clutched her youngest child to her chest. She did not look at Stug, nor at her husband, but stared dully at the bit of ragged cloth that served as a curtain, rocking the baby mindlessly, a motion without care or comfort, only something that she had done so many times, that once a child was in her arms she could no longer stop herself.

The rest of the children huddled on a pile of… something. An unidentifiable heap of what might be clean clothes, or dirty ones, or bedding, or all of them promiscuously piled together. They ranged from a couple of years to about eight and were all as pale and thin as their father and as dull-eyed as their mother, apart from one.

The girl was probably seven or so. She had copper curls that, despite probably never having been washed in her life, were still the brightest colour in the dim, miserable room. She was watching her father and Stug anxiously; her quick, clear eyes going from one to the other, her arms spread protectively in front of the children on either side of her.

"Girl, come here," Stug said.

She looked at her father.

"Come on, Pearl, it's all right," the man said.

The girl got up off the pile, and went to her father's side and slipped a hand into his. She looked up at Stug, her face still and unreadable. In this light it was hard to tell, but he thought her eyes were green. Would that do? It might. In any case she had something – something he was learning to look for but could not yet, quite, identify.

He felt a deep shudder move through his gut. If he got it wrong too many times... he had seen the Queen's Harp.

One of the brats mewled and he straightened his spine. Look at them, look at them all, it was unfair, it was wrong. It *had* to work. And soon, soon, he had been promised – no more of this, he could leave all this behind him.

"Can you speak, girl?"

"Yes."

"You should say, 'Yes, Mr Stug,'" her father said.

"Yes, Mr Stug." Her voice was hoarse, legacy of damp winters in rooms like this. That would mend.

"Can you recite?"

"I know a passage from the Bible, Mr Stug."

He shuddered. That wouldn't do at all. "Anything else?"

"I know a story," she said. "I heard it from a man in the street who told tales. It's called Death the Sweetheart. But it's quite sad, perhaps you shouldn't like to hear it?"

"Death the *Sweetheart?*" It sounded like the worst kind of nonsense, but perhaps the Queen might like it. "Go on," he said.

Pearl set her feet and put her hands behind her back. "There was once a pretty young girl," she said, "who had no father nor mother nor brothers or sisters. She lived all alone and saw no-one. And one day a man came to her door and said he had been travelling far and was very tired. She was a kind person, and let him in..."

The story was, indeed, nonsensical, with the foolish female falling in love with the pale stranger who came to her door, when anyone of sense would have turned him away and no nonsense about it, and she died, of course, as could only have been expected. But the child did the thing without self-consciousness, and with a kind of innocent gravity that perhaps might appeal – dammit, it was so hard to *tell*.

Stug was overwhelmed with a sense of being hard-done-by. All this. This stinking room, these worthless people, this dance he must go through, never knowing, never being sure – all for something that the merest dog could do, the most wretched flea-bitten cur.

He should never have married Cora. She had had such a delicate, porcelain look, with her tiny waist and fragile hands, like a little figurine, but so it had proved – too delicate, too fragile.

But a divorce was out of the question. Respectable persons did not divorce. And Cora's family had influence and few scruples.

"I may be able to come to some arrangement," Stug said. "I know of a couple. They have no children…" He felt his face twist, and fought to still it. "They would take her, perhaps. If she were cleaned up. And behaved herself. I owe them a favour."

"A couple…" the father said. "I don't…"

"Let me take the girl and pass her on to them, and I'll let you off the month's rent. If they take to her, there'll be some money in it for you."

"But…"

"How much?" the woman said. She was not looking at Stug, but still staring at the filthy window-rag as though something terrible would happen should she turn her eyes away. "How much money?"

"Fifty pounds. Perhaps more."

"No," the father said, pulling the girl closer to his side. "No, Mr Stug, it's a generous offer, sir, it is, but…"

"Fifty pounds," the mother said, still in that flat, dull voice. "When did you last see fifty pounds? Have you ever seen all that money, at once? They none of them have shoes. If I can put Mabel into shoes and an apron, she could get a post in service, we could get a doctor to Joe..." She still did not look at her husband, or her daughter, or Stug, but clutched the sill and addressed the grimy pane. "Pearl's a good child, they'd like her. You'd be a good girl, wouldn't you, Pearl, and please these nice people, and send money home to your parents to help them? Wouldn't you?"

Only then did she turn her gaze to her daughter. Pearl returned her look gravely, then looked up at her father.

"It's the only offer you'll get," Stug said. "Otherwise you're to leave by tonight. I have plenty of people who want this place. Plenty. The streets are full of feckless sorts like you with nowhere to sleep, and what do you think would happen to her there? That, or a respectable household. It's up to you."

"Sir... Mr Stug..."

"Well, man? I haven't got all day."

"I can learn some more stories," Pearl said suddenly, fixing her eyes – yes, they were definitely green, startlingly green – on Stug.

"There, you see, it's not as though she's unwilling," Stug said. "A bright girl like her could go far, given the right opportunities. Can *you* give them to her?"

The man bit his lip, and frowned. "But what if they... I don't mean, sir, that they're not... but we look after them, sir, best we can, it's not easy, no, but..."

"Let her go!" The wife turned, suddenly animated. It was shocking, like seeing a doll brought to life, or someone you'd thought dead gasp in a breath and sit up. She held the baby, now, like something she might throw – at Stug, at her husband, her other children, at the whole roiling world. "Let her go, what is there for her here, what life, let her go for the love of God, Samuel, or she'll end where we are. She's your favourite, I know it, we all know it, is this what you want for her?"

"Martha..."

"Don't talk to me," she said. "Leave me be. But let the girl out of here. Whatever she goes to, it can't be worse than this."

As though something in the air had snapped, the decision was made.

It was easier this way, Stug thought, satisfied. This way, he didn't have to involve Simms.

Pearl didn't cry. Huntridge clenched his jaw and gave a trembling smile as he told her to mind her manners and do as she was told and send to let them know how she was doing. The other children, understanding nothing, but feeling their father's misery and their mother's fury, set up a whining and wailing.

The mother tied a ribbon – a pathetic, frayed strip of still almost green ribbon – into the bright curls with jerky movements. "There. You'll be a good girl," she said.

"Yes."

There were no kisses, which was a relief to Stug. He took the small dirty hand in his, grateful for his gloves, and left.

The child was not the babbling sort, which was also a relief. She stared at the steam-car that stood puffing and hissing in the roadway, got in, and sat when directed on the cloth he kept there for the purpose. She asked no questions, only observing everything with those striking green eyes. Unlike some, she did not attempt to smear grubby finger-marks on the fittings or pull at the curtains that covered the window.

Stug sat back. He did not look at the girl again.

The Crepuscular

"NOW REMEMBER, SPEAK only when you are spoken to. Don't gawp like a simpleton, smile and be pleasant. And for God's sake don't scratch or pick your nose or any other urchin tricks, you understand?"

"Yes, Mr Stug." The girl's voice came in a hoarse whisper. She was gripping the cloth of her new cloak with both hands, her knuckles white. Her eyes were huge, the green irises all eaten up with black. Her dress too was new – a plain green gown, soft shoes. Her hair was washed and teased into ringlets and glowed like life in the cool, shifting light. He had taken some trouble; though this sort of frivol was beneath him, it would be worth it if this worked. Everything would be worth it.

He understood the girl's astonishment. He had felt something like it, though of course, unlike this creature, he had had some education and knew a little more of the world than a few stinking square yards of Limehouse.

But then, this wasn't, quite, the world.

"I bring a gift for the Emerald Queen," he said.

"Do you?" said the Gate. "Bring it close and let me see."

Stug pushed the girl forward with a hand on her shoulder and she stumbled a little, staring around with wide, dazed eyes.

"Here she is."

The Gate was made of wood and metal, bone and flesh, all woven into patterns that changed constantly. Faces – or fragments of faces – appeared and disappeared, mouths opened and gasped, or laughed, or whispered, or sang. Eyes flickered open, moved, winked, wept, shut, disappeared. They slid and climbed around each other, in an obscene dance, a writhing minuet of root and branch and muscle. If he tried to follow the movement it gave him a fierce headache that lasted for hours, so he had learned instead to stare at something else: the pale silvery sky, or the field of grass, dotted with tiny, brilliant flowers, that stretched towards the horizon and the hint of spires in the distance. Behind him the Stream of Blood gurgled quietly through the grass.

A number of eyes opened at once, in pairs, and focussed on the girl. Grey, blue, brown eyes; yellow and bronze eyes, slit-pupilled like cats' or with oblong pupils like a goat's. Faceted like the eye of a bee, or round and pupilless as a cabochon jewel. The girl gasped, but did not whimper or sniffle. The eyes blinked, span into a circle, blinked again, and disappeared.

The Gate swung open.

The path to the Queen's residence wound across the green, lined with ferns. He wondered how long it would be today, and hoped not too long. Though the temperature here seldom varied from the pleasant cool of a summer evening, he was always, inevitably, sweating by the time he arrived.

Not that it mattered. The Queen could smell his fear whether he sweated or not. He hoped the Harp was out of the way, along with all her other little jokes and pleasantries; the girl throwing a fit of screaming hysterics would do nothing for his cause. Or probably not, at least. It was so hard to tell – that was part of what made this business so endlessly frustrating.

He had hopes for this girl, but then, he always had hopes. So far, they had proved without foundation.

Today it seemed the Queen was impatient: they were walking only a few minutes before the Palace was in front of them, the spires having slid up over the horizon, dragging the buildings behind them, in the dreamlike way things moved here.

"How did we get here so quick?" the girl asked.

"Because we were allowed to," Stug said. "You'll see some strange people in here. Don't scream or make a fuss."

"I won't."

She hadn't fussed over the Gate, he allowed that. He gritted his teeth. So far, so promising, but so much could still go wrong.

The courtiers were already gathering. *Some in rags, some in bags, and some in velvet gowns,* a strange, high, childish voice sang in his head – but these were no beggars. He felt the girl tremble under his hand.

A tall, attenuated creature in clothing – or skin – that looked like ancient bark bowed and shuddered as though it were a tree in a high wind, waving skinny arms and walking past on backwards-bending legs, turning to watch the girl with eyes like flickering candle-flames. A shimmering-satin exquisite, dressed in the style of a long-gone century, whose wig, at a foot tall, was almost as tall as he, tittered behind a fan made of animal-skins, joined with gold wire. A woman of pure-carved, painful beauty in a night-blue velvet robe looked them over with chilly indifference, and turned around so that the face on the back of her head, which was male, but no less beautiful, could see as well. The face made a *mou* and the shoulders shrugged as the creature moved away.

A unicorn trotted out of the woods, saw the girl, and tossed its head; she laughed and clapped her hands. The unicorn caracoled, then lowered its horn and came towards them. Close to, it was no larger than a pony; it walked warily around them, looking them up and down, avoiding the girl's outstretched hand, then stepped away, flirting its purple-smoke tail.

"Is this a fairy-tale?" the girl whispered.

"Something like." Stug said. He kept moving forward, bowing, bowing, not too deep, one must leave something for the Queen.

The crowd parted to let him climb the steps of silver and glass. Between columns of milky-blue agate lay the doors to the inner palace – at least, so he hoped. Judging by the ease of his walk today she was feeling amenable, but one never knew.

The doors were of brass set with hundreds of jewels, some no bigger than a fingernail, others big enough to buy entire kingdoms; some of astonishing beauty never seen in the other world, some that looked like killing growths taken from dead stomachs. Jewels were currently out of fashion at court, but it had pleased the Queen to allow these to remain.

Stug fixed a smile to his face and said, "Remember what I told you. We are about to see a lady who is a Queen, and if you please her, she will give you many pretty things."

The doors opened at their approach. Another good sign.

Beyond them was a carpet of flowers, and beyond that, the Queen upon her throne.

The girl stared open-mouthed at the Queen, then remembering who-knew-what half-heard story, lifted the sides of the skirt and attempted a curtsey. For what was probably a first attempt it wasn't entirely graceless, but a low snickering ran through the Court like a poisoned stream.

"What pretty hair you have," the Queen said. Stug's heart pulsed in his chest.

The Queen rose from her throne, and drifted towards the girl with her undersea walk that never quite touched the ground. The first time he had seen her even Stug, who had little appreciation for beauty and none at all for mystery, had been struck. Now, he just stood with a dry mouth, trying to hide his impatience.

The Queen was all pearl-pale skin and yards of flossy hair that drifted about her like the seeds that float on a summer breeze. Her eyes changed colour with her mood; now storm-grey, now sky-blue, now opalescent and opaque.

The girl reached out a hand – thoroughly scrubbed as Stug had instructed – towards the Queen's gown, and hesitated. The little hand hovered in mid-air like something trapped in amber. The Queen laughed, and said, "Do you like my gown? Maybe you will have one like it, if it pleases me."

The gown was of living flowers, each a different shade of yellow. Buttercup and celandine and daffodil and primrose (the Queen might not command the seasons, but she could make flowers bloom out of their time), hawkbit and trefoil and cowslip – though no St John's Wort. St John's Wort was not welcome here. Whether it was actually effective against the Folk, Stug did not know, but carrying it was considered an insult.

He had made the mistake of having it with him the first time he had been invited across the Stream of Blood. That visit had not gone well, and he knew, now, how lucky he had been to get away with his skin, and his mind, intact. The Queen had been in a beneficent mood, and it seemed she might be so today.

She ran her fingers through the girl's hair. "Look up, child."

The girl did so. "Hmm. Your eyes... your eyes match the shade of my favourite slippers. If I have you sitting at my feet, that will be pleasing. Tell me, can you sing?" The girl cast Stug a pleading glance.

"Not well enough to please you, my lady," he said. "But she can recite. I thought you might enjoy that."

"Recite? Recite what?"

"Poems, ballads... she has a most retentive memory." He had tested the girl, and given her more poems to learn. Of course, she could not read, but she was extraordinarily quick to memorise.

"Recite something for me," the Queen said.

"What would you like, ma'am?" The girl said.

"Something..." The Queen tapped her chin with one finger. Her hands were very long, and narrow, and white; she had touched Stug, once, and it had taken all his control not to whimper. The girl had seemed unaffected by her touch, but then she was a slum child, and probably had no more sensibility than a snail.

"Something sad," the Queen said.

"Yes, ma'am. Would you like to hear about Sweeney Todd the barber, ma'am?"

"And what is a barber?"

"Someone who cuts people's hair. Only this one's wicked, ma'am, and murders people..."

"Stop." The Queen cut the air with her hand and Stug shuddered. *No, no, it was going so well...*

"You should never give away the ending of a tale in its beginning," the Queen said. "If you are to recite for me, you must learn these things. Will you remember?"

"Yes, ma'am."

"The Stug says you are retentive. If this proves true, and you please me, then you may stay." She turned back to Stug.

There was a whisper and rustle at the door, a genteel commotion of silks and shimmer. Stug felt the nape of his neck shiver. *Not now, not now!*

"Lady, we have news!"

The creature was something like a horse, and something like a ferret. It had a long sly face, hooves, teeth. Clinging to its forearm was a naiad, trailing water, her long green luminous eyes inhuman and lovely as the moon. Gills pulsed in her neck, her shining red-kelp hair brushed the floor.

"News?"

"The ugly old woman, of the most grand and high Court of Chicken-foot." The horse-creature sniggered as though at some fine joke. "Oh, wonderful gossip, my Queen – you will be most amused!"

"Indeed, indeed," the naiad half spoke, half-sang, her voice flying with gulls and gales.

The Queen turned away from Stug and the girl, swept back to her throne of pearl and bones, and arrayed herself on it, chin propped on her hand. "Bring me essence of moonlight. And a sugar-cake. And poppy wine, with... let me see... with ant's eggs. I have a fancy for them."

The lower members of the court scattered frantically to do her bidding. Stug thought about clearing his throat, but did not, quite, dare. If she forgot them they could be here for hours, and back home that could mean days – or more. Time slipped and slid, here, and could not be relied on.

"Child, come to me," the Queen said, and gestured to the girl. Stug gave her a little push, though she was already going, willingly enough, still agape and perhaps not sure she wasn't dreaming.

The Queen turned to Stug. "We will speak in a quarter-moon, little man. If the girl still pleases me..."

Stug opened his mouth to plead, and shut it. This was the closest he had come to success. None of the other children had pleased her.

He had had to give them to Simms. What happened after that was none of his concern.

"Yes, ma'am."

"Go away now, little man." She flicked her fingers at him, as though he was something stuck to her nail. "Go. *You* do not please me."

The girl did not plead, or beg to be taken home. She did not even watch Stug leave, but instead stroked a flower on the Queen's gown, as though, with all the wonders surrounding her, a simple buttercup was the most amazing of them.

The Sparrow School

EVELINE WAS SCOWLING at the kitchen cupboards – they were almost out of everything – when there was a quiet knock at the back door. She jumped as though jabbed with a pin. Back in the days when a slow hand on a plump pocket would have been enough to send her to Newgate she'd never been so nervy – but then, she'd only had herself to worry about. Now, she felt like that fella Cinquevalli that she'd seen at the music hall, who balanced a man on one arm and juggled three balls with the other.

Whoever it was had simply tapped, not rung the bell – she waited. Maybe it was just a branch.

But then the knock came again. "Whyn't you ring, if you're so all-fired eager?" she muttered to herself, then straightened her spine, put on her most formidably schoolmarmish expression, and flung open the door.

And there, looking like a bit of dirty paper blown all the way to her doorstep, clinging to his broom as though it were his anchor to the world and peering wide-eyed at the nearby woods, was Bat.

"'Ullo, miss," he said, glancing at her briefly before scanning the woods some more.

"Bat! What are you… never mind. Come in, then."

He bolted past her and watched as she shut the door.

"You all right?" she said. "Was there someone after you?" Her stomach chilled. What if someone were out there right now, watching the school? If they knew where she was…

"No, miss." Bat shook his head vigorously, his dreadful hat sliding back and forth.

"What were you all in a pucker for then?"

"It's awful... big, out there, miss. And quiet. And it don't half smell funny."

"That's cos it ain't full of smoke and other people's shit," she said. "Come sit down. How the devil did you get all the way out here?"

"I come on the horse bus, miss. Juicy Peg made me, she paid. They made me put my broom on the roof, miss. Nearly drove off with it, they did."

"Well it's safe now. Lean it by the wall before someone falls over it. You want some milk?"

"Yes please, miss."

While he drank his milk she bolted the kitchen door, in case someone should come wandering in. She fetched him a bowl of the stew left from the girls' lunch and put it in front of him. "Now, what's going on?"

"A couple days back, Viper turns up. And his coach is outside and Peg comes down and I seen her watching so I goes over, and she told me to stay out of sight, but she's watching and so I watch too. Then we seen him come out with one of the Huntridge girls, the copper-top, and get in his coach, and Peg she gets all of a flither, and says she knew it, and calls him a filthy beast. And I ask what she means but she says all she knows is he's up to no good, and maybe she should call a peeler, only if she does what would she say, and..."

"So what happened?"

"I got in, miss."

"You got..."

"I got in the steam car, miss."

"*What?* Don't tell me Peg told you to do any such thing!"

"No, miss. Only the car wouldn't start, miss, and he was pulling levers and swearing, and I give Peg me broom and run over and nip into the basket on the back for the luggage and pull the lid down, and off we go."

"But what..." She looked at him, and shook her head. "*Why?*"

"I don't rightly know," Bat said. "Except I thought, maybe, p'raps he was selling her to pirates?"

"*Pirates?*"

"Well, he could'a been, couldn't he?"

"And what were you going to do if he was?"

Bat shrugged, and spooned up more stew. "Chase 'em," he said, muffled.

"So what happened?"

"We bounced along for ever such a long time. I maybe fell asleep for a bit. It was all right in that basket, there was a blanket and everything, but it did throw me about, 'specially the last bit." He held out a sticklike arm and displayed a massive bruise. "I nearly yelled when I got that, but I didn't."

"Good boy."

Bat grinned and shrugged. "I don't suppose he'd have heard me anyways, the noise it made. Anyways we stopped, and I heard 'em get out. I snuck a look and we was by a building, maybe in the City, I dunno. I was going to get out but I thought I'd better wait, on account of I wasn't sure where I was, also he'd left it running so I reckoned he was coming back. When they came out she was all done up fancy and her hair different. I shut the lid again and he drove and drove; and I thought maybe we really was going to sea, only then it stopped, and it was everso quiet. And I heard the doors open and shut and he says, 'Mind what I told you,' and there's sounds like them moving off and so after a bit I opens the top and looks out. It's getting on dark, and I can't see no lights or nothing, just a bit of road and grass and a hill, like a park, but bigger. They're going up the hill so I gets out and goes after 'em, but they just – the air went funny and then they wasn't there no more. I tried to follow them but then..." He took another spoonful and chewed as he considered. "There was sort of a stream, only it looked wrong. I thought maybe it was the sun, at first, 'cos it was going down and everything, and the stream was all red, but I got close and it wasn't water, miss, it was blood. I was going to try and go over, see if they'd gone that way, but it disappeared. And I didn't know where they'd gone, and there was a big yellow thing with eyes, miss, sorta like a horse only fat, that made a noise – *Muuuh* – and blew at me, so I ran, and got back in the basket, then he come back without her and then we goes off again. And I wakes up in the basket back in town and gets home and tells Peg, and she put me on the bus and makes me come here."

"That'd have been a cow, that fat horse," Eveline said, absently, her mind working. "And the other was the Stream of Blood. Just as well you didn't try to cross it. You'da been in trouble for sure."

"Did I do right, miss?"

"You done bloody spectacular. You'd better stay here the night, and I'll send you home tomorrow." She'd have to come up with the fare, somehow.

Stug was stealing children, and taking them over the border, into the Crepuscular. To the Emerald Court? To the Queen? Why?

And what was Stug getting in return?

Eagle Estates

Simms was waiting when Stug got back to his offices.

"I told you not to come here during the day," Stug growled.

"I had some news I thought you'd want."

"News? If it's about the tenants, it can wait." Stug glowered at the man. It was a risk, being involved with someone like this – he was a thug, a nasty brute of a man, but he was useful. "I've nothing for you, not this time."

Stug didn't mind having him along when he went to see the tenants, but respectable people came to these offices, and having this fellow around – he stank. Not physically – he kept himself neat and clean, but nonetheless, he stank, of back alleys and unpleasant dealings and knives in the dark. The reek of bad deeds rose from his flaunting sideburns and the tilt of his midnight-black bowler.

"Well now," Simms said. "I could go away, and not tell you, and by the time you saw me this evening, and I told you, you might be saying, well, I'm right in it now, you shoulda' told me. And then you'd blame me, and I'd be doleful about that, I'd be very doleful. Acause we've got a good business relationship, you and me, and I'd hate for that to be done over because you could have got some information from me, at the right time, and didn't. See?"

The man's theatrical flair made Stug's skin itch and tighten. "Well don't hang about the step, then, come in."

"Don't worry, I ain't been here long enough for any of your respectable clientele to notice my humble presence, Mr Stug. I made sure I waited until I saw you coming before I *hung about your step*. After all, I know we're not of a type, eh? I'm not a man of reputation like you." He paused, one foot in, one out, the shadow of the door cutting across his face. "Well, I am," he said, thoughtfully, "only not the same kind of reputation."

Stug led the man up the stairs, aware of a crawling sensation between his shoulder-blades the whole time. He poked his head through the door of Jacobs' cubbyhole. "Go take those papers over to the bank," he said.

"Yes, Mr Stug."

"And take your time, make sure they're checked properly. I don't want any mistakes. And don't disturb me when you go out, or come back, crashing about, I want some quiet. I've things to do."

"Yes, Mr Stug."

He shut the door behind him, and waved the man into his office. "Well, Simms? What is it?"

"So, you've been looking to tighten things up around here, I see."

"What? Oh, yes. Security. I have to be careful. The world's full of rogues."

"So it is, Mr Stug, oh, yes indeed. Only that's the thing, you see. That's the very thing I wanted to drop in your shell-like, that was."

"What are you going on about, man?"

"A young woman, Mr Stug. A certain young woman who came a'visiting. Now at first I thought, maybe she was here to see that rasher of wind you've got doing your under-stair work. But then I thought, Mr Stug, he's a respectable sort of person, he wouldn't want those kind of goings on... going on, not he. He wouldn't be having with it. And I didn't think she was the kind of person who he would be having personal doings with, perhaps an indigent relative or such, because she didn't *look* indigent, oh, no, got up very smart, she was. Respectable smart. Because the idea of any other sort of smart lady a-visiting of Mr Stug, well, that would never cross my mind. Wouldn't even begin to consider the thought of crossing my mind, that wouldn't."

"Do get on."

"As you wish, Mr Stug, as you wish. Rogues, you said. Well, not to put too fine a point on it."

"Oh, so there *is* a point?"

The man paused, one eyebrow afloat, then when it was clear Stug had nothing more to add, he went on, "She's a rogue, Mr Stug. Oh yes. I got a clearer look at her on her way out, and that young woman is someone I know of old, and a rogue she is indeed." He held up a hand. "You might not wish to think it, I know, her seeming all respectable, which is something I admit she's exceptional good at, but she broke into your place, for a start of it, which is, you'll admit, roguish behaviour."

"Oh, I knew that."

Simms' chair, which had been tilted back, slammed down level, and Simms' bowler slid low over his eyes. He glared at Stug from beneath it, putting Stug firmly in mind of something hiding under a rock.

"You knew." His voice was flat.

"She told me as much. Simms, are you telling me you *know* this young woman?"

"Indeed I do, though I never persuaded her to work for me. But obviously you know all about it, and it doesn't bother you that she's a prig by profession, that is, a noted and accomplished filching mort, that is to say, a thief, and a gulling, sham-cutting trull that's got the eye of Westminster on her. I'll be on my way then, Mr Stug, and sorry to have wasted your time this fine morning." Simms was out of the chair and on his way to the door before Stug got the words out.

"What? Wait!"

"Oh, so that she *didn't* tell you?" Simms paused, one hand on the door handle, and looked over his shoulder.

"Didn't tell me what? Sit down man, tell me what you mean. Westminster?"

Simms span around, whipped the chair under him and planted himself in it.

"Thereby hangs a tale, Mr Stug. Oh, yes indeed. Our little Evvie, Mr Stug, Evvie Duchen, she was a common thief and trickster of the most adept, only she was took up by a government man. He come looking for her. By way of being very generous, he was, when he was on the hunt for her. Now he didn't know I knew he was government, but I'm a cautious man, Mr Stug, I like my buttons buttoned and my braces braced, I do, so I made enquiries of my own, and I found out. And then Evvie Duchen disappeared. And it seems like not long after that this government man disappeared, along of another fella of some importance, off overseas somewhere. Most mysterious and maybe a bit embarrassing, you might say, being as government men aren't supposed to just disappear off of the face of the earth, without a by-your-leave or a fare-thee-well. Now they've never come home, those fellas, but it seems like Evvie Duchen did, only not going under that name no more, is she?"

"No," Stug said, staring at the wall beyond Simms and tapping his fingernail on the desktop. "No, she isn't."

"And there's them as might be interested in knowing that while their ever-so-clever government fellas, with all of their schooling and such, managed to get themselves lost in foreign parts, one little street-urchin got herself home and dry, and doing quite well by the look of her. Or maybe, and that's the thought that come to me, Mr Stug, *maybe they already do.*"

The same thought, at the same time, amid the whirl of speculation, had already occurred to Stug. "You think she's working for the government?"

"Well, Mr Stug, she was a bright enough spark, she was, but running a business? By herself? Now that's the sort of thing I don't believe would be going on without she had someone setting her up, and *backing* her up. She's only a mort when all's said and done."

"Well," Stug said. "That's very interesting, Simms."

"I thought it was the sorta thing you might want to know, Mr Stug."

"Indeed. Indeed." Stug leant back in his chair. "I am gratified to find you so careful of my interests."

"You're a generous employer, Mr Stug, I'd be a fool not to do my best for you."

Stug took a key from around his neck and opened a drawer in his desk, extracted a tin box, and opened that with another key. He took out a sheaf of notes and passed them to Simms. "I hope this will be acceptable?"

"Most kind, Mr Stug, most kind." Simms tucked the notes away in a pocket inside his jacket.

Stug raised his brows. "You're not going to count it?"

"Now, Mr Stug, I'm sure we know each other well enough that I can rely on you to do the right thing."

"I believe I may have another little job for you, soon."

"Always a pleasure."

"I'll be in touch."

"You know where to find me, Mr Stug."

"Yes, yes I do," Stug said. "Quite often on my doorstep, as it happens."

Stug smiled. Simms smiled back. He closed the door with precise quietness as he left.

Stug leaned back in his chair.

So, the girl was not one of the Folk. Not if Simms knew her – a more earthbound creature than Simms was hard to imagine. She was – or had been – a common thief.

The sense of relief he felt went through him like some weakening dose. Anxiety immediately rushed up in its wake. Was she now working for the government? It seemed absurdly far-fetched, but if Simms was right, what did it mean?

He knew nothing of the girl, except that she did, indeed, appear to be running a business – ridiculous in itself. But why would the government be interested in him? His dealings with his tenants skated up to the very edge of the law, but very, very carefully avoided tipping over the brink. He knew exactly how far he could take things.

And his... other arrangements, were of no-one's business but his own.

The children? Of course, he had made the mistake of allowing himself to show an interest; that should not happen again. But then, if all went well, it wouldn't need to.

The idea that the government might interest itself in the disappearance of a handful of slum-brats was ridiculous, too. And if it did, he had, as Simms pointed out, a respectable reputation. He had been very careful to maintain it – until this latest business. Once this was over, his reputation would remain untarnished – and he would ensure that anything that might tarnish it, or any*one,* would not be getting in the way.

The girl... yes. She had broken in – the nonsense about 'operatives' was just that, nonsense. That in itself suggested Simms was telling at least a part of the truth. And he could, himself, find out a little more. He had a few contacts, a few people that he and Cora had met at the better sort of gathering. Any digging must be done carefully, very carefully. He had hopes, where the government was concerned.

Of course, if Cora... He really could not rely on her for this sort of thing, she was, like all women, an indiscreet chatterbox. What *could* he rely on her for? He felt a dark welling of anger, and pushed it down. He could not afford to be distracted and Cora was, for the moment at least, an insoluble problem.

He would try to find out, at least, whether the government had at any time had an interest in the girl.

As for Simms... Yes, his information about the girl *might* be useful. It would, at least, provide leverage should she become difficult. *If* it were true. Until it was confirmed from another source, he would not rely on it. But he did know, because he had taken advantage of the fact, that Simms was a man of dubious reputation. It helped keep the tenants in line, having someone like that. Stug kept the knowledge in the back of his mind, taking it out only when he needed it. A useful sort to have around, Simms. But Stug was no longer certain he was controllable – he fancied himself a little too much. There was something in his swagger that suggested he might not always be content with his current role. If he was to become pushy, threaten to be indiscreet...

He was useful, but not indispensable.

However with a man like that, a man of no morals, simply telling him his services were no longer required might in itself be a problem. Another solution might have to be found.

Stug found himself drawing back from his desk, as though the thought that had entered his mind had manifested itself there, on the blotter, staring at him with flat, unblinking eyes.

Respectable men don't think of murder.

Very well, respectable men probably do, but they don't actually contemplate arranging it.

It may not come to it.

If it does?

It's not as though Bartholomew Simms is a good man.

He's a bad man, a wicked man. The world, surely, is better off without such a man.

I'm not a wicked man. I create wealth, I provide homes.

And the girl… if the Queen accepts her she'll have a life of unimaginable wealth and luxury.

So long as she continues to please…

But in Limehouse, only one fate awaited her. Anything is better than to end up some degraded, diseased creature, outcast, despised.

And the others… I gave them a chance. They failed to please the Queen, and Simms took them off my hands. What he did with them is not my concern. I know nothing about it. I did nothing wrong. Their parents could give them no life, that boy, that first boy, the Queen herself pointed out that he had bruises, he had been beaten, it was obvious. Wherever he went it would be better than that.

I am a respectable man. I have done nothing wrong.

And the girl? Evvie… Eveline Sparrow, Eveline Duchen. She was probably only some silly girl playing at business. And if not… she would see what happened when some little street-urchin troubled a respectable man of business like Josh Stug.

The Sparrow School

SHE HEARD THE argument through the classroom window before she even got to the house. Ma Pether, and Mama. A crowd of girls jammed by the door, whispering.

"You lot," she said. "Out of it. If you ain't got a class, go practise whatever your next class is. Now."

"But Miss Sparrow…"

"I don't want to hear it. Out."

They scattered like scared hens.

Eveline stood for a moment, gathering herself, and listening. Part of her had known this was coming, that juggling all the sides of her life was not something she could do forever… but she'd thought she'd have a solution before everything came to shouting.

Not that Mama was shouting. Mama never shouted, and the louder Ma Pether got, the quieter Mama got, until she could hardly be heard.

"… isn't suitable," Mama was saying.

"What's not *suitable* is pretending you don't know what goes on and trying to stop the girl from making her way, the best she knows how, what's pretty good being as it was *me* what taught her."

"You kept my daughter alive and I am grateful to you, Mrs Pether,"

"It en't Mrs. Ma'll do, thank you."

"I am grateful, but you also taught her a way of life that is dangerous and, need I actually say this? *Illegal.* I do not want to see my daughter transported or hanged, do you understand? I have lost one child" – now Mama's voice was rising – "I cannot bear to lose another, because I was not there to stop it, do you understand me, *madam*?"

Evvie swallowed, sent up a brief prayer to whoever might be listening, and opened the door.

There they both stood, Mama with her hair falling out of its bun, her hands, stained with oil, clasped in front of the leather apron she wore when working. Ma Pether, all rolled shirt-sleeves and weskit and oddly elegant hands – those long-fingered hands which had made her such an extraordinarily good dipper – fisted on her hips.

"Eveline."

"Evvie."

Eveline suddenly felt very small, and young. It was all wrong. She thought of Bat with his broom, and the whole thing, the school, all of it, felt like Bat's broom: ridiculously unwieldy and only appealing because everyone thought it was funny.

And she was utterly, blisteringly furious with the pair of them.

"What," she said, "do you think you are doing?"

"Eveline!"

"Evvie Sparrer if I..."

"I'd like you both to come with me, please. Over to the House. I'll get them to send tea." She kept her voice calm and small and quiet so they both had to lean in to hear.

The staff house was set away from the school buildings, a small square place of red brick that had a pleasant, homey glow. The window frames were peeling and specked with rot, the floorboards sagged worryingly in the corner of the dining room and a leak had tracked green down the wall in Evvie's bedroom, but it was home.

She led them into the parlour. "Eveline," Mama said.

"Mama, please, after they've brought tea? It won't be a moment." Fortunately the girl Evvie had collared to bring tea had seen something in her face, and was quick.

Once she had gone, Evvie shut the door, made sure the windows were down, poured the tea and then said, "Please, sit down."

They sat, and both drew breath. Before either could let it out, Eveline slammed the teapot down so boiling tea surged out of the spout and drowned the sugar-bowl.

"How *dare* you argue in front of the girls! How am I supposed to be in charge if you undermine me so?"

"Ev…"

"No! I am the *headmistress,* remember? Ma Pether, you should know better, if anyone does. Would you have had this? Well, would you? Someone shouting your personal business in front of us all? And as for you, Mama… it's bad *manners,* never mind anything else!" She could feel herself on the verge of furious tears, but had had enough practice at not crying that she would not let them fall, gripping her hands and throat tight, keeping her head up. "What are you trying to do, bring the place down around my ears? What if it gets back to the parents?"

"I was not shouting, Eveline."

"No but you knew damn well you were saying things that would make *her* shout, Mama."

"Eveline, what are you teaching those girls?"

"How to make a living," Ma Pether said. "At least, that's what I *thought* I was teaching 'em for. And if you'd kept your nose out…"

"I *live* here. This is my home and my daughter, I'll remind you."

"I live here too, and if it weren't for what she learned offa me your daughter wouldn't still be here."

"*Do you think I don't know that*?" Mama said. "There isn't a day goes by I don't think of what could have happened to her when I wasn't there to protect her. Not a *single* day. So do not, madam, lecture me, if you please. She is not a street urchin any more. She has no need for this…"

"Will you both be quiet and *listen*?" Evvie had spent enough years on the street that her best screech could just about shatter granite.

Shocked into silence, the two women looked at her.

"I am trying to keep this place going, legal and all, but I can't do it if you make trouble for me, either of you. I got plans. I didn't want to say before in case it all went wrong, but the whole point of training the girls like we been doing is so we can provide security. Offer protection against thieves and cons. There's plenty of places need it, plenty of businesses. It's good solid work and no-one better suited than you, Ma Pether, to train them in it."

"Security," Ma said.

"Oh, Eveline," Mama said. "Why didn't you *say,* you silly girl? I think it's a very clever idea, so long as it *is* legal. But what about the school, I thought it was doing well?"

"It ain't – isn't – doing well enough, Mama. We're not getting enough paying pupils. I had to do *something.*"

"Well, I think it's an excellent plan. Do you not, Mrs... Ma Pether?"

Ma said nothing.

Madeleine gave her daughter a hug. "You are a clever girl. I was worried you were getting back to your old ways, and I needn't have been. And I'm sorry that I made a scene; I should have trusted you. I hope we haven't disrupted your classes too badly." She glanced at Ma Pether again, but Ma's face was set like one of the Egyptian statues in the British Museum, and she said nothing.

Madeleine looked at Ma Pether, and glanced at Eveline.

"I'd like a word with Evvie, private, if you don't mind," Ma Pether said.

"Eveline?" Madeleine said.

"All right," Evvie said.

"Then I shall take my tea to the workshop," Madeleine said. She poured herself a cup, and closed the door quietly behind her.

"You shoulda told me, Evvie," Ma Pether said.

"I thought you'd tell me I was being stupid," Eveline said, watching Ma warily. It wasn't like her to be so quiet.

Ma took the remains of a cheroot out of her weskit pocket and turned it over in her fingers. "I never peached in me life. Never. Now you're asking me to turn against my own? Well, you ran a con on me all right, Evvie Duchen. Oh, yes. But no-one's making Ma Pether into a chaunter, especially not some mucksnipe I took in hand and saved from the street. I'll be fetching my things now."

"Ma?"

She aimed the cheroot at Evvie. "What did you think, that I'd just go along with it?"

"Ma, we wouldn't be harming no-one! Just stopping them from getting in some places and taking off a few marks, it's not like there's not plenty more!"

"It's taking the side of the law, Evvie, that's what it's doing. It might not be peaching, but it's bad enough. And I ain't doing it."

"You're…"

"I'm leaving. I won't be telling no-one where you are, or nothing, so there's no need to look so green. But you'd better think where you're going, Evvie. You were good. You were nearly as good as me." She paused, head on one side, staring into the distance. "Maybe better, I'll admit it. And you can try as hard as you like to back away, but you got the taste for it and the smell of it on you. You're one of us, Evvie. You always will be. And them respectables, there'll always be those that can smell it. You won't last, you'll slip, and they'll get you in the end. A rough foot in a satin shoe'll always trip, you mark me."

"But Ma…"

"And you watch that Thring. He's crooked as a thorn bush, for all he's giving your Mama the sheep's eyes.

"'Bye, Evvie," Ma Pether said. "And don't think I'm not grateful you gave me a chance. I am. But it ain't gonna work." She lit the cheroot, and walked out. Steam from the pot rose to mingle with the fading smoke.

Eagle Estates

STUG PICKED A box from a shelf, opened it. The herbs inside were losing their scent, he must get some more. He would have to order them. Or would that be worse? Evidence… Perhaps he should go himself, or send Simms. No, not Simms. Jacobs.

But what if Jacobs became suspicious? No, he would go himself. He had relied too much on other people. It would be better if he did it himself.

He put the box back on the shelf, aligned it with the edge. Noticed a smudge on the lid and polished it with his handkerchief. Not that anyone else would ever see it, of course.

That little witch of a female, Sparrow, not that he cared what she thought of his housekeeping. She should never have been here.

He had sounded out his contacts, carefully, very carefully. It had been difficult, and only possible to do at all because the gentlemen he was dealing with had had certain temporary financial embarrassments that he had, in the past, been able to assist them with.

"Duchen, Duchen… oh, there was something," Robert Delaney had said, over brandy in the Conservative Club. "I believe it may have been to do with the Britannia School."

"The Britannia School?"

"Oh, my dear chap, have you not heard? Well, no, I don't suppose you would have. Quite a scandal, if it ever broke, but I can trust *you* not to go to the press. I don't have an interest there, praise be."

"A school hardly sounds like a place for scandal," Stug said, topping up Delaney's glass.

"It is if it's being used as a convenient cupboard in which to store embarrassments," Delaney said. "Cheers. Really the number of gentlemen who are incapable of discretion – by-blows left, right and centre, old boy. Boys one can get into the professions, of course, one way or another – but girls... well. Can't have them ending up on the streets, never know when someone might recognise the family conk, what?" He tapped his own purplish and veiny nose, grinning. "So they got shoved off to the Britannia."

"This girl..."

"I heard her name in connection with a rather unfortunate case – some chap with a touch of the other, you know." Delaney looked around, then leaned forward, and said, "Not just the other. Half-Folk, old boy. *Definitely* the result of an indiscretion. His Papa had connections, got him a government post, he tried to act like a gentleman, but well, blood will out, as they say. Rumour has it he ended up going native in some godforsaken outpost, and disappeared. The girl was involved in some way, whether she was his by-blow or he'd taken her along for entertainment, who knows? Didn't realise she'd surfaced again. If she's popped up now to go after the family's money, I suspect she's out of luck – the chap's father, old Holmforth, laid down his knife and fork soon after the news came through, and it all went to some distant cousin or some such."

"What about government money? She's not someone they'd still have an interest in?"

"I doubt it. Once young Holmforth had disappeared there was a distinct sense of relief in the department, frankly. Still, might be worth keeping an eye on – you never know when someone will prove embarrassing. But after all, she's a female on her own – there's a limit to how much damage she can do."

Stug had put up with Delaney's increasingly garrulous and eventually maudlin company for the rest of the evening, took him to a card game, and ended up with Delaney deeper in his pocket than ever.

It wasn't as though he had intended it, of course, but Delaney was a gambler by nature, and who was Stug to dissuade him from his pleasures, or refuse to lend him money? The fact that he happened to have more than sufficient on him was simply a matter of him having visited his banker earlier that day, in the normal course of business, and getting out a little extra, just in case.

He wasn't a bad man, not a *criminal,* not like the girl, if Simms was to be believed. Not like Simms himself, in fact. He was simply helping out an acquaintance.

And as a respectable man, an upstanding citizen... it was unjust. All these men who produced bastards as easy as winking! Not that a girl more or less would make any difference – Stug would never leave his carefully built-up business in the hands of a woman – but it just went to show how utterly unjust the fates could sometimes be. Here he was with a good reputation and a healthy business to leave, and no son.

Whatever he had to do was only a question of rebalancing the scales, making things the way they should be, after all.

But had the Queen decided? He was up here every dusk, and every dawn. Cora used to complain that he was never at home, but she had, to his relief, stopped that nonsense.

The Queen hadn't turned the girl down straightaway. *Surely* that meant it was going well?

He didn't dare go back before the date she had given him. She was such an impossibly capricious creature, as bad as any human woman, but with power. Terrifying power. So he came here, and waited, in case she should send a messenger, as she had done before.

He didn't use the flute. It made them angry when he did that. He could only wait, and be conciliatory, and crawl on his belly to them because they had all the cards.

The sky outside the window thickened. Yellow-grey fog pressed against the panes, like something trying to get in. Stug fidgeted with the cover of the book on the table – if that stupid girl was half as smart as she thought, she would have taken this, a genuine antique, rare and ancient. He wondered what would happen to her if she attempted to use any of the spells it contained. Even the spell of summoning that used the elder-wood flute required will, and concentration. It might look simple, but then so did a bolting horse.

His thoughts were everywhere this evening. He pulled out his watch. It was hard to tell if it could any longer be considered properly dusk, with the fog – but the Folk took little account of time as it was measured this side of the Stream.

It was very quiet. The last shift-change had been minutes ago; and the ever-present humming roar of a modern city had dulled. The stillness got on Stug's nerves.

He would wait one more minute, then...

The creature appeared absolutely silently, without so much as disturbing the crow feather that lay on the shelf behind it. Stug bit down on a shriek, but could not prevent the jolt backwards which sent him staggering. He would have fallen if the chair had not been right behind him. He sat down with a thump, his teeth jarring together.

The creature watched him with its head on one side. It showed neither amusement nor any other emotion; its huge faceted eyes, like great black glittering mourning brooches carved of jet, held no expression he could read, and its mouth was a rigid downwards curve. Its head and body were approximately human, though the limbs were excessively long and skinny. Gleaming wings were folded against its back.

"Wha..." Stug cleared his throat, and sat up straight in the chair. "Are you from the Queen?"

Its head tilted the other way, but it made no answer, though its wings shivered, making a low humming and sending the crow feather floating to the floor.

"Now, my pet," said a voice. "Discourteous to startle the man in his own place." The young man who appeared beside the creature seemed to step out of the air, as it had done, but more leisurely. Stug caught a glimpse of the landscape behind him, glimmering softly, its light entirely out of place on this grim, dank evening.

The insectlike thing shivered its wings again and rubbed its head against the young man's arm.

He was beautiful, like all the High Folk; his hair danced in shades of copper and gold. His clothes were those of a gentleman – frock-coat, trousers, waistcoat, high-collared shirt – though their colours and materials, their glistening bronze and shimmering topaz, were nothing any respectable man would wear.

He patted the creature on the head and folded his legs up under him, balancing midair, and regarded Stug with blue-green eyes.

"I bring a message from my lady mother," he said.

The son, then, Aiden. Even such a creature as the Queen had a son. A fine boy, if he had been human. *What does she say? Is it yes? Finally, is it yes?* Stug forced the questions back down his throat. "I hope she found my gift pleasing?" he croaked.

"Oh, the girl is well enough. But Mama…" He shrugged. "She has become… troubled, of late. Things please her for such a short time. Even those things that formerly were most amusing, now fade from her pleasure like flowers at summer's end. She is becoming concerned, and plans for the future. Just think, my lady mother planning for the future! It is quite amusing." He tilted his head, like the insect-creature, and his eyes, though human, and amused, glittered just as coldly as did his pet's. "Perhaps it is your influence."

Stug attempted a self-deprecating smile. "So humble a creature as myself could hardly hope for as much," he said, loathing the shake in his voice, loathing the words. *Only until I have what I want,* he told himself. *Only until then.*

"Indeed," the young man said, his voice perfectly expressionless. "Now, where was I? Oh, yes. My lady mother… has been troubled. And there is something particular that troubles her. There is an old woman."

The silence stretched out. Eventually Stug could no longer bear it. "An… old woman?"

"Yes, a terrible, ugly, tyrannous old woman, without grace or beauty, without *finesse*. She thinks herself a rival to my mother."

"How could anyone be so foolish?" Stug quavered.

"Oh, the arrogance of this loathsome creature must be witnessed to be believed. One would laugh, except that it is an insult. You understand?"

"I..." No, he did not – the endless dance of the Folk and their rivalries was of no interest to him at all. He only wanted one thing from them, and never to have to deal with them again. But the gift was not yet in his hands, and he would have to bow and scrape and attempt to follow the steps a little longer. "Yes, of course it is an insult."

"She has got above herself, recently. She crows. She flaunts. It is not to be borne. So my dear mother has decided that she must be put in her place."

What is this to do with me? Stug clenched his hands and held his mouth shut, feeling a muscle along his jaw jump and twitch.

"And you will assist her in this."

"Me?"

"Yes. If you wish to be assured of her continued goodwill, that is."

You were warned. A voice in Stug's memory, the voice of his father, colder than stone. *You were warned about dealings with the Folk, like dealing with a blackmailer. Always more than you thought you would have to pay, and always with a sting in the tail, always a twist on the bargain. You were warned, Joshua. You chose not to listen.*

But his father was dead, and his sententious pratings had no place in this deal.

"What does the Queen desire me to do?"

"The old woman has a subject here. He has a child. She wants it."

"A subject?"

"Yes. Our boundaries, to some degree, reflect your own; and like you, we have ambassadors. The old woman has a human subject, who is an ambassador here, the ambassador has a child, my lady mother wants that child. You are to get it for her. You understand?"

"I... I..."

"Need I say it again?"

"Only, my lord Aiden, the name..."

"Oh, I don't know his *name*," the boy said. "I've seldom troubled to learn the names of humans." Something passed over his face, a shade of... grief? For a moment he looked almost human himself.

"Not his name, lord. The name of the old woman, her country." Stug clenched his hands, feeling the sweat pool in his palms, his nails digging, stinging. *Who... who... let it be some pitiful little colony, some place where the 'embassy' is two rooms on the outskirts of Kensington, with a guard in an extravagant uniform shivering on the pavement.*

"The old woman is Baba Yaga. It is the country of the bear. Russia."

Russia. Dear god she wants the Russian Ambassador's child.

Stug felt his knees weaken, and locked them.

"I hope that is sufficient information," Aiden said, "as I begin to find this conversation tedious, and this place stinks. And roars."

"My lord..."

Aiden raised a hand. "Oh, you will get what you wanted," he said. "Once it is done. You will be given a son, under the conditions you requested. My lady mother keeps her word. I hope you will be wise enough to do the same."

"Jacobs, where are the documents for the Shoreham properties?"

"With the lawyers, sir. I took them over yesterday."

Damn.

"What about the takings?"

"Banked on Monday, sir."

"Hmm. You've been exceptionally efficient lately, Jacobs."

"Thank you, sir." The boy radiated keenness... and was in the damn way.

"Take a half day," Stug said. "You appear to have earned it."

"A half day, sir?"

"A half day, boy, a half day. You have heard of such a thing, I presume?"

"Sir. But there's the documents for the Shoreham properties, sir."

"It will wait. Go... go to a horse-race or whatever it is you young men do."

"Do you want me to come back and finish off these papers, Mr Stug?"

"I told you it will wait!" Stug saw the boy flinch and moderated his tone. "I'm trying to give you some time off, boy. Don't act like a beaten dog who's not sure the chain's off. Stand up. Take life by the throat. Now get out of here."

Jacobs scurried away. Stug shook his head. What a sorry creature the boy was! His son would be different. Sturdy, bold, a man. He would have a clean and untroubled life, with no need to know what his father had gone through, the things he had been forced to.

But certain things had to be got out of the way first.

"Sir?"

"I thought you'd gone. What is it?"

"That woman's due to come back today, sir. Sparrow's Nest Security. At three."

"Yes, yes, I'm quite capable of reading a calendar. Do get on, boy, the day'll be gone."

"Sir."

Jacobs was useful, but Stug hoped he wasn't getting too curious about things that were none of his business. Although he would be easy enough to get rid of with a word in the right ear and an offer of another higher-paying position. It was Stug's experience that most people could be bought off. Even the Queen of the Folk. If you had something they wanted.

The girl turned up on the dot of three, just as Stug's watch pinged the hour.

Stug ushered her in, glancing up and down the street.

Simms. Simms was there, watching from the shadows. He made sure Stug saw him, tipped his hat to an even-more-insolent angle, and strolled away.

He was *definitely* going to have to do something about Simms. And he couldn't trust him with this. He was too sure of himself, too cocky – and far too obvious.

But now, he had an alternative.

* * *

"MR STUG."

"Miss… Sparrow, isn't it? Do sit down." Stug gestured her to the hard, narrow supplicant's chair in front of his desk, and sat himself in the expansive and comfortable leather one behind it. "Sparrow… Sparrow…" He tapped the tips of his fingers together. "Now, that doesn't seem right, you know."

The girl looked up from extracting papers from her bag. "What doesn't seem right, Mr Stug?"

"The name. It doesn't quite *fit*. I'm sure another would suit you better. Something of French origin, perhaps?"

The girl smiled. "I've never thought of myself as particularly French in appearance, Mr Stug, but if you are complimenting me on my style, then thank you."

"So the name Duchen means nothing to you?"

"Duchen?" She looked mildly surprised. "It's not a particularly common one, but I can't recall having heard it before."

"Really? How about Simms?"

She put the papers neatly together on his desk. If her hands were shaking, he couldn't see it.

"Should it? Are they perhaps business rivals, that you fear might be after something? I can investigate further, if you wish."

"Now really, miss. Let us not beat around the bush any further."

"I was not aware of doing any beating around any bushes, Mr Stug."

"You are a wanted criminal, Miss… it isn't really Sparrow, is it? Perhaps it isn't Duchen either, but I shall call you that. A wanted criminal, Miss Duchen."

She folded her hands in her lap.

"Am I? How very exciting. What am I supposed to have done?"

"You and I both know that you are a wanted criminal by the name of Eveline Duchen, a common thief and pickpocket."

"I am not aware of there being any police warrant out for anyone of that name, Mr Stug."

Dammit! He had not checked. He should have checked. But Simms was a criminal, and there was no outstanding warrant for him, either.

"You are also of interest to the government."

"Really?"

"Do you remember a Mr Holmforth?"

"I can't say I do."

"A most unfortunate business. There are those in government who are still wondering what happened to Mr Holmforth – and to his female companion."

"Really."

"These people might… *might*… be prepared to lose interest."

"Might they indeed."

"In return for certain activities which you, Miss… Sparrow, should be more than capable of performing."

"And what might those be?"

"Why, nothing more than the sort of activities you have already performed. Breaking. Entering. Illegal activities."

"Are you suggesting Her Majesty's Government might wish someone to become involved in illegal activities, Mr Stug?"

"Only in the cause of the greater good."

"I see."

"The plain fact of it is that the Russian ambassador has come under suspicion. He may be, in fact, working against the interests of the British Empire. It is necessary to put him under pressure. And for this, your particular talents are required."

"What would you need me for? Hasn't the government got people for that? Seems to me they're a bit desperate if they're dragging innocent women in off the street."

Stug leaned forward, searching her face. She still looked utterly calm, even mildly amused. *Could* Simms have been wrong? Or playing some game of his own? He felt a shudder in his stomach. If that was the case, then he would be in so deep he'd never climb out. She would know his name, his place of business.

But he was committed. He couldn't back off now.

And he could deal with Simms… or have him dealt with. He could do the same with her, a sight more easily.

"On the night of the fifteenth," he said, "there will be a ball at the embassy. That should provide a more than sufficient distraction. It has been decided that you, Miss... Sparrow, will on that night find the ambassador's baby daughter, remove her from the embassy, and bring her to me."

"What?"

"You will take the ambassador's daughter and bring her to me."

"But why?"

"It is not your place to question that. You see, Miss Sparrow, this would be by way of... a conclusion," Stug said.

"A conclusion, Mr Stug?"

"Once it is done it may allow certain past indiscretions of yours to be wiped from the record."

Her face went still. "I see. So, you're a government man, Mr Stug?"

He smiled, and said nothing.

Nor did she.

"Are we agreed?" he said.

"On conditions."

"Oh, I hardly think you're in a situation to make conditions."

"Perhaps you're right. Tell me, did they say anything about Mr Fordyce?" She was looking at him with a peculiar, anxious intensity, suddenly – her hands no longer in her lap but gripped together on the papers on the desk, crumpling the top layer.

Fordyce, Fordyce... Delaney had not mentioned anything, but obviously the name had meaning, a distressing one, for her. It might be the other fellow who had disappeared.

"Oh really, I don't think you want me to go into that, do you?" he said. "Rather unpleasant, don't you think?"

She sat back, and slumped. "If I'm to do this," she said, "I'll need details. Of the embassy."

"I'm sure you can find all that out. Isn't that supposed to be your business?"

"But it's only two days... I'll do my best, but... Oh, Mr Stug," she said. "Please put in a good word for me! With whoever it is you're dealing with, please, I never done nothing bad that I wasn't put up to! I bin led astray, that's what it is."

"Hah." *Women,* Stug thought. Weak-minded, that's what they were. "You will bring the child here, at midnight on the fifteenth. I will meet you."

"Yes, Mr Stug."

"And no mentioning this to anyone else. Government business, you know."

"I shan't, Mr Stug."

"Be sure you don't. You wouldn't wish for anything to happen to... anyone, would you?" This, he told himself, was the only kind of thing a creature like this would understand. It wouldn't be necessary, if the little beast did as she was told.

"And the child – I shall know, if it is some street brat. I want proof. Something that shows she is who I have asked for."

"Yes, Mr Stug."

She looked, finally, cowed, when she left. Stug sat back in his chair, his chest expanding behind his waistcoat. Things were finally back under his control. He would get what he wanted, then he need never deal with the Folk – or such street-scum as Bartholomew Simms or Eveline Duchen – ever again.

EVELINE MADE IT around the corner before her knees gave and she leant against the wall, shaking, every swearword she knew and some she'd made up on the spot running through her head. When she was sure she wasn't going to fall, and that she wasn't still in sight of Stug's windows, she went straight to the nearest sausage-stall. Bags o'mystery they might be – but who cared what was in them. When she was shook up, what she wanted was sausage and bread and a cup of tea, and nothing else would do.

She paid for her portion and went and stood in a doorway, chewing, watching the street without really seeing it, the comforting weight of greasy meat and coarse bread gradually calming her clenched stomach.

Panic was no good. Panic threw you off, made you do stupid things. Panic was one of the things that got you caught.

Stug knew something, that was obvious enough. The fact that her name was still floating around in government circles, however little actual information might be attached to it, that was unpleasant, though hardly surprising. But the name Fordyce meant nothing. She'd made it up on the spot, trying to catch him out... and it had worked. Whatever Stug knew about that business, it wasn't much. He was trying the flimflam artist trick of making it seem like he knew everything about you, and failing.

Someone knew something, though. And the other name he'd mentioned... Simms. Bloody Bartholomew Simms. She'd bet a horse and carriage that Simms was the one who'd peached on her. He'd always been a nasty piece of work and it looked as though he'd decided to throw her to the wolves – though why, she wasn't sure. She'd done her best to stay out of his way, while she was at Ma's... she would have to ask Ma.

The memory of that last argument dropped into her stomach on top of the sausage. Dammit, Ma! After all the years they'd spent together... she'd been too thrown to react properly. She shouldn't have to play-act with Ma. All right, maybe she should have told her – Ma hated not knowing things, information was her guiding light, she loved it like some people loved gin or opium.

And like them, she got real narky if she was deprived of it.

Now what? She could not – *would* not – burden her mother with this, not now she was looking so much better, and besides – Mama knew about as much of the underside of the world as a newborn babe, despite what her brother had put her through. It was all his fault, horrible man, if he hadn't come into their lives...

Never mind. That was of no matter now. What mattered was what she was going to do.

And the first thing was to find out what Stug was really after. He was no more government than she was a dancer at the opera, she was convinced of it. But he *was* involved in something underhand and nasty. Those children... that little battered shoe... *it's children. Always the children,* Juicy Peg had said... *the devil's red right hand...*

Bowler-hat. "Oh, Eveline, you *numbskull.*"

It was Simms. Mr Stug's bowler-hatted companion, the one who laid the heavy on the tenants, that was Bartholomew Simms sure as eggs.

And he must have seen her. Why he'd peached on her to Stug she didn't know. But Simms knew what Stug was up to.

So what could it be, and could she use Simms to find out?

Simms was dangerous. More dangerous than Stug, that she was sure of. Simms didn't have a front to keep up. Stug, with his charity pen-set, his certificates, his carefully arranged office that jarred so with the room upstairs, would only do what he could keep at arm's length. Simms would cheerfully murder and go for a pint of porter with the blood fresh on him, knowing that in the places he drank, it would only act as a warning that Simms was a born thatchgallows, a thoroughgoing villain, and you didn't mess in his business.

Not Simms, then, unless she had to. Stug. She had to find out what Stug was really up to, otherwise she'd have no leverage at all. *Knowledge, and the means to use it.* Ma was right about that, whatever else she might be wrong about.

IT'S GOTTA BE you, Evvie Duchen, Evvie the Sparrow. Lady Sparrow, Liu calls you. Don't think of Liu, it hurts. You gotta do it all, because when it comes down to it, you're the only person... not the only person you got, that's not fair to Mama or to Beth. But the only person you got a right to ask it of.

If only Liu was here.

But Liu wasn't here, and it was down to Eveline. She took a deep breath. There was a bit from a play she'd heard, working pockets at the theatre. She'd liked the plays and almost let herself be distracted. Some fella in shiny armour, saying, "Once more unto the breach," and lots of stuff about it piling up with dead. Of course, him being the king, he wasn't that likely to get dead – kings on the battlefield didn't, so far as she could tell. It was the poor buggers without the fancy armour that got dead.

"Once more unto the breeches, eh, Eveline," she said, tugging on her working trousers, and managing a small, lonely snort of laughter at her own joke.

Hair pulled back, pinned, tucked under the cap. Boots that looked too big but actually fitted well – Evvie, having done without decent footwear for so long, loved her various boots with a fierce passion. These were padded, flexible, and soft-soled, excellent for night-time work but scruffy looking to go with her starveling appearance.

Belgravia

STUG'S HOUSE WAS exactly the sort of place Ma Pether would once have sent her scouting out. All pillars and polish at the front, and even the servants' entrance down the area scrubbed within an inch of its life and decorated with a pair of brutally clipped miniature trees in ugly pink and yellow pots. Eveline assessed the pots as at least Chinese though not as old as they were pretending to be, worth a few bob to the right fence but heavy and clumsy to move.

A maid in black-and-white with a frilly apron and fancy beribboned cap opened the door, looked Eveline over and said, "What is it?"

A masculine voice behind her said, "Is that the chimney-boy? Let him in, Ella, there's a love – Herself's been complaining about the dining-room fire again."

"Rat boy, miss."

"Rat boy? Oh, good." The maid stood back. "The dining-room? I thought it was the windows in the drawing-room had her going."

"Smoke had her Ladyship's guests coughing like a bunch of consumptives, *she* says." The man who was speaking was dressed in tight black trousers and a brocaded waistcoat over a gleaming white shirt, and looked Eveline over with a grin. "Here, Ella, get the boy a slice of that pie, he's half-starved."

"That's very kind, sir, but I'd better get on."

"We'll keep it for you, then. Watch yourself around the place, you get a speck on anything there'll be hell to pay."

"Oh hush," the maid said. "You'll have us both thrown out."

Evvie became aware of a chiming sound, quiet, but exactly the kind of noise that if it went on too long would grate on one's nerves as badly as something much louder. There was a board on the wall of the kitchen with a series of what looked like the lids of fancy pots, delicately painted with flowers, bearing two arrows like the hands of a clock, and surrounded with small labels, saying 'Tea,' 'Cleaning,' 'Consultation,' 'Tobacco,' 'Coffee,' 'Whiskey,' 'Brandy,' 'Drinks, Alcoholic, Assorted,' 'Further Instruction.' Beneath each one was a china label with, in fancy script, *White Drawing Room, Smoking Room, Master Bedroom*... Evvie counted twelve rooms in all. One of the pot-lids was slowly revolving, and from this came the chiming sound. One of its arrows pointed, quivering, to 'Tea.' The label below it said: *Blue Drawing Room.*

"Oh there we go," said the man in the waistcoat. "You're on, Ella."

"I hate that thing," Ella said. "It's not natural."

"Coo," Eveline said. "What is it?"

"It's the latest in 'Service Engineering,' they call it," said Waistcoat. "Saves them all the time of having to tell you what they want, then you go get it, then you bring it to 'em. Ever so fatiguing for 'em, don't you know. I don't s'pose you can read, can you? See that label, third around the dial? That says, 'Consultation.' Means you're in for a ticking off from Her Nibs. Might as well say 'Out on yer Ear,' half the time. You want a job as a boot boy? We just lost one, due to him cheeking Herself, only he was mim as a mouse and that nervous he barely managed a word a day. So I dunno how he got so bold all of a sudden."

"You don't half go on, Ned," Ella said, pouring hot water into a teapot.

"Cor, what's that smell?" Ned said. "It's a bit rank, innit?"

"It's the latest thing she's trying," Ella said, wrinkling her nose at the steam. "It's not as bad as the last one. That was enough to turn you green. And she's still taking enough of that Pinkham's Tonic to float a navy, I don't think it's right."

"Everything she tries, she should have enough nippers to fill St Paul's by now." Waistcoat – Ned – grinned. It wasn't a very nice grin. "I reckon it's him. Too busy making lucre to give her a good…"

"Ned! Little pitchers!" the maid said, waving frantically at Eveline. "I 'spect he's heard worse, eh, boy?"

Eveline rubbed her toe on the very clean kitchen tiles. "Ummm."

"Now stoppit, Ned, and let the poor boy get on." Ella lifted the tray.

THE ROOM WAS so full of fancy stuff that Eveline could barely haul the large bag to the corner without knocking over a potted plant on a stand or a vase or a candlestick. Her sleeve brushed a leaflet onto the floor, whereon was printed a woman apparently asleep in a chair and a smartly-dressed man standing over her with what appeared to be threads or wires extending from his fingers towards her. 'The latest in Mesmeric Techniques' the leaflet declared. 'W. Davey, Practical Mesmerist. The Most Recalcitrant Cases Cured.'

"Oh!"

Eveline jumped up, fixing her face into an expression of cringing politeness. "Sorry, ma'am. Rat boy, ma'am."

The woman standing in the doorway, her hands clasped at her breastbone, put Eveline in mind of a giant doll. Her hair was elaborately piled on her head, her dress in what Eveline had to assume was the very latest fashion. Crinolines might be on their way out but this garment was so laden with ribbon, frills, lace and bows that it was barely any smaller than the vast tented skirts that were now fading from favour.

"Rat boy?"

"Yes, ma'am. Here to deal with the rats, ma'am."

"We have *rats?*" She made a scuttering movement with her feet, picking up first one, and then the other, as though trying not to touch the floor at all, and glancing around with wide, horrified eyes.

"Not for long, ma'am," Evvie said cheerily.

"Do you have to *catch* them? I hope it doesn't make a mess!"

"You'll never even see 'em," Evvie said, with some truth. "S'a new method, using Etherics. Drives 'em right out, it does. Don't you worry, ma'am."

"Etherics? What are those?"

"Science o'noise and vibration, ma'am. Very modern. Practically miraculous, what it can do."

"Etherics. Can it be used for... well, other things?"

"S'coming in for all sorts, ma'am. Health and hygiene, all that. Better than mesmerism or any such."

"Really? For matters of... health?"

"So they say, ma'am. I just turns the machines on, ma'am." Evvie kept her eyes on the mechanism she was unpacking. She was working on the fly, conscious of a rising excitement, that heart-speeding, brain-fizzing sense of dancing, turning need and desire to your advantage, playing the odds, playing the mark.

"I don't suppose you have some sort of visiting card?"

"No, ma'am. Sorry, ma'am."

"Well if I wanted to find out more about Etherics, who should I get in touch with?"

Evvie's brain raced. Mama wanted her machines used for people's health, but if she was right, what this woman wanted was beyond what even Mama could do.

And putting Mrs Stug in touch with her would be far too risky.

"I'll ask them to send you a leaflet, ma'am," she said, feeling deflated.

"Please do."

"Certainly, ma'am."

"I have a card..." She got one from the small beflowered pot on the mantel. Eveline tucked it away, with thanks, forbearing to point out that she already knew the address, being as she was in the place at the time.

"So how does it work?"

"I don't rightly know, ma'am. Like I says, I just turns 'em on." Evvie moved a lever and the machine began to chime, gently, a much more pleasant noise than the one that summoned the staff from the kitchen.

"Now if you was a rat, ma'am, that'd be like chalk squeaking on a slate, that would."

Cora Stug clapped her hands. There was something oddly childlike about her, or perhaps unused, as though this doll had been kept in tissue paper in a box, unwrapped only for display to visitors, and never properly played with.

"How terribly clever! Do, please, get your master to contact me. *As soon as possible.* You won't forget?"

"No, ma'am, I'll speak to him the second I get back to headquarters," Evvie said.

"Please do."

Evvie sat back on her heels, wiping her brow and scowling at the mechanism, which was something she'd had Beth knock together, without Mama's knowledge. It made a pretty enough noise but was no more Etheric than the clock on the mantel.

She felt slightly mean, but after all, she hadn't done the woman any *harm*. What would she do if she ever got an actual baby, in any case, one that cried and stank and couldn't be made all modern and convenient? And that wasn't Evvie's problem.

Her problem was still Stug, and what he was up to. She might have some idea what he *wanted*, but what was the business with the children?

She stared at the mechanism, the grooved brass disc on the top spinning hypnotically. Whoom, *chime,* whoom, *chime...*

A wood. A cold wet wood and Charlotte, tired and hungry and with wet feet, getting colder and colder, close to death. Why was she thinking of Charlotte and her little wet shoes?

She nearly died. You thought she had died, but she'd been taken. Aiden took her away and left a changeling in her place, a sad cold thing that didn't even last the night, that you buried thinking it was Charlotte. The thought still caught her throat, even though she knew Charlotte was alive. She had never been able to forgive Aiden. The Folk didn't think like people, but that didn't make it all right, that he had taken her sister and let Evvie think she was dead.

You gotta give something to get something.

A little battered shoe. Juicy Peg and her tales.

Stug's stealing children for the Folk. He's giving them to the Folk, to get a child in exchange, one of his own.

He's raving.

Mrs Stug might have her own madness, with her teas and her mesmerists, but the things she was trying could only fail.

Mr Stug thought he could get a straight bargain from the Folk. Eveline's dealings with them had been limited since she was a small child, and, apart from Liu (who, whatever she said to him, she hardly thought of as Folk anyway) she was happy to go her way and let them go theirs. But thinking that they'd give a straight exchange? That there wouldn't be such a twist in any bargain that you'd end up wishing like hell you'd never made it?

He must be mad. No-one who wasn't mad, or desperate, or utterly cork-brained, would think such a thing. What sort of a child did he think he'd end up with? Not what the Folk would give him, Evvie was sure of that.

The Sparrow School

"Eveline?"

"Yes, Mama?" Evvie was frowning over the account book, only half-seeing it, working out in her head what she would need for the embassy that night. She was still hoping that something would occur to her. Something – *anything* – that would prevent the need for this insane scheme. Could she get the attention of the ambassador? Tell him what was going on? But... he was government, foreign or no, and Eveline's distrust of all things government was strongly rooted. She needed a trick, a scheme, a con. She *trusted* cons. She understood them. Government, so far as her experience went, was a dangerous mystery, run by people with exactly the same motives as a con artist, but a deal more power.

"Come here, dear. I need to speak with you."

There was something in her mother's tones that pricked Eveline's ears and straightened her back. Something was going on, and she didn't like the feeling.

"Mama, I can't, I need to take a class and then..."

"Yes, then what, Eveline?"

"I don't understand, Mama."

"My dear, I think you do." Mama's look was stern. "I have not completely forgotten my duties as a mother, Eveline. You are planning something, and I should like to know what it is."

"I'm trying to do the accounts, Mama, nothing more."

"Eveline..."

Evvie sighed and shut the book. It wasn't as though staring at them would make the figures change.

"Sorry, Mama. I am planning something, it's to do with this work I told you about. Checking security. I have to go out tonight, in fact."

"Why must you do it at night?"

"Because that's when a lot of robbery happens, Mama." Not the sort she'd done, generally – broad daylight and cheeky with it was more her style – but she couldn't tell Mama that.

"Well I hope you're not going alone."

"I have to, Mama."

"No. I will not have my daughter wandering the streets at night, alone. Eveline…" For a moment Eveline thought she would sit in the chair on the opposite side of the desk – the one intended for staff being interviewed or girls getting a scolding – but she came around to Eveline's side and stroked her daughter's hair. "I know… I know you haven't told me so many things, to spare me. I know I have been away from the world a long time, but I am not a complete fool. I do have some idea of what can happen to young girls, out on their own. I think some of it already happened to you, and that's why you took up with that woman. But I'm here now, and you have the school, and your friends. There's no need for you to risk yourself so."

"Mama, we have no money. And I need this work."

"But why must you go alone?"

"Who would you say I should take, Mama?"

"Oh, I wish there was a man about the place I could send with you… where's young Liu? I haven't seen him for days."

"I don't know. He said he had to do some stuff."

"What about Beth? She's a sensible girl."

"Beth! Mama, she's no more idea how to look after herself on the streets than… a kitten. Less. I'd have to watch her as well as myself."

"But when we were in Shanghai, she was remarkably adept."

"No, Mama."

"Then I'll come."

"Mama! No!"

"Then take one of the other girls, at least."

"All right, I will."

"Promise me."

"Yes, Mama." She'd take Adelita, and send her off on another errand, something safe and out of the way, once they were clear of the school. Bad enough Stug knew what he did – and she'd have to do something about that – but if she was caught she didn't want anything else pointing back here.

OCTAVIOUS THRING HUMMED his way along the corridor, hair on end, nodding and beaming at the girls who passed him. Some of them, once he was past, giggled behind their hands, and though he could certainly hear them it seemed to trouble him not at all.

"Mr Thring?"

"Ah, Eveline. How are you today?"

"I'm well, thank you. May I speak with you a moment?"

"Certainly, my dear, certainly."

Eveline took him to her office. "Would you mind turning the key, Mr Thring?" she said. "I'd rather we weren't interrupted."

He did so, looking a little puzzled. "You look very serious, Miss Sparrow. Is something wrong?"

"I hope not," Evvie said. She stood behind her desk and leaned her hands on the blotter. "Mr Thring, what are your intentions towards my Mama?"

Thring's eyes widened. "My dear child! That's a somewhat... startling question!"

"I don't know how much she's told you, Mr Thring, and it's her story to tell, not mine. But Mama's not had an easy life, and she's had... bad things happen to her. She's maybe a bit too trusting. I've seen what comes of that, and I don't intend she should go through that again. So I'm asking again, what do you intend for my Ma and her mechanisms?"

"I see. May I sit down?" Thring said. "At my age, you know…" Evvie waved him to a chair.

"I admit," Thring said, "I'm carrying more flesh than I should be. I did wonder whether the Etherics might be of use in that respect… in any case, my apologies, I don't mean to ramble on. Your mama is a remarkable woman."

"I know that," Evvie said.

"Indeed, indeed, and who better than you? There's great potential in Etherics, you know, and Madeleine has a most superior understanding of the principles – she leaves me quite behind, I admit it. But I believe – forgive me – I believe the financial situation is not… not quite what it might be. Now, I don't intend to pry, and I'm sure you're doing what you can, but I thought perhaps I might be able to put you in the way of a better financial situation for the school. Then Madeleine would be able to work undisturbed and develop her ideas."

"What sort of better financial situation?" Evvie said.

"If the school became a charity. It's quite simple. I can show you all the paperwork. I get the impression that you're a young woman of sense, and will have no trouble understanding it."

"I don't know about that," Evvie said. "Seems to me there's got to be people willing to give money to something, for it to be a charity. We have enough trouble getting the fees out of parents, never mind trying to persuade people to give us extra, just because… what, anyway? What sort of charity would it be?"

"Are you not already running it as a charity?" Thring said, leaning forward. "Many of your pupils, it seems to me, do not have parents who are paying their fees, willingly or otherwise. I don't mean to sound interfering, Miss Sparrow, but it's not a situation that can go on, really it isn't. Financially speaking, it's simply unsound."

"So how'd you find all this out, Mr Thring?"

"It's not exactly difficult," he said. "Butcher's boys turning up with demands, and whatnot. Oh, dear, I do hope I haven't upset you. I just think many of your immediate difficulties are quite easy of solution."

Eveline bit her lip. "Well, Mr Thring, why don't you show me this paperwork, and we'll see, shall we?"

The idea had an appeal. If the school was a charity – well, if everything went wrong, then maybe it would be protected.

Eagle Estates

"THE POST, SIR."

"Just leave it there, Jacobs."

"Yes, sir."

"Jacobs."

"Sir?"

"I want you to keep an eye out. There have been... incidents."

"Sir? I'm afraid I don't follow, sir."

"Things going missing. Robberies. Look out for anything suspicious."

"Er... like what, sir?"

"Do you expect to be spoon-fed, boy? You'll never make it in business if you can't think for yourself! Now get back to work. I want those papers on my desk by five."

"Yes, sir."

Stug sliced through his post impatiently. Begging letters, some Reform Society nonsense, the usual tedium – straight into the elephant's-foot bin with them.

But here was something different. An envelope of heavy, creamy stationery, with a proper seal in deep red wax – one didn't see those so much any more.

He slid his paper-knife under the flap, the seal snapped away.

The handwriting was smooth and confident. The contents were intriguing. The author described himself as a man of business, and believed they might have met at a recent business dinner. 'Having heard certain discouraging rumours from *friends of influence* regarding invidious new taxation likely soon to be imposed upon men in the property business such as ourselves, I have a proposal I would like to put to you, which I believe may be to our mutual advantage...'

It was signed, *Octavius Thring, Bart.*

"Thring, Thring..." Stug knew the name, he'd heard it somewhere, he was sure. Perhaps they had met at the dinner. It had been a gathering of powerful and influential men, certainly. But there was something else... "Jacobs!"

"Sir?"

"Bring me the cuttings book."

"Sir."

A few moments later Stug was paging through the series of articles and photographs that he had had Jacobs carefully paste into a large, impressive book bound in glossy green leather, handsomely tooled.

Every mention of J. Stug, Esquire, every photograph of every social occasion he had attended, every paragraph had been carefully clipped and filed.

Stug leafed through the pages with his usual sense of mixed gratification and bile. Stug, mixing with men of reputation and achievement! Stug, at this charity ball and that dinner and the other opening! Stug, a pillar of the community! Stug, with no son to build on his father's achievements... he shook his head, and forced his considerable will to focus. *There.* The Metropolitan Association dinner was described in glowing terms. Attended by Mr This, Sir That... and there, 'Sir Octavius Thring, Bt. The genial philanthropist, attired in a waistcoat of the most startling splendour...'

There was nothing else about him, but he had been there, and that was sufficient to establish his bona fides for Stug. He lingered for a few moments over the book before shutting the cover decisively. "Jacobs! Take a letter. I want it delivered by hand, immediately."

"Yes, Mr Stug."

Thring, it appeared, was a man of both leisure and decisiveness. He replied immediately, suggested a meeting the following day.

*　*　*

"MR STUG. A pleasure, a pleasure."

Shaking a plump but callused hand, Stug looked Thring over. He had a round, cosy sort of look about him. *Philanthropist.* Stug braced himself. Taxes and advantage had been mentioned, but was this going to be instead some plea for charity? Stug did, of course, give money to charity. The right sort of charity. It was expected of a man in his position.

"Thank you for your letter, Mr Thring. Do take a seat."

"Thank you. A nice place, Mr Stug. An excellent position for offices. Excellent."

"I find it convenient. Would you care for coffee? Tea?"

"No, no, thank you." The twinkle in Thring's eyes disappeared, he leaned forward, slapping the palms of his hands on the desk. "Straight to business, I think, don't you?"

Stug, who had jumped when Thring's meaty palms met the wood, swallowed. "Yes, indeed. Always the best way."

"Now, Mr Stug, you and I are both men of property, and men of the world. We're in the business of providing homes. A pity that others don't seem to see it that way. They see us rather as milch-cows."

"Milch-cows, Mr Thring?"

"Milch-cows. To be drained dry. Taxes, Mr Stug! Taxes! First regulation, hemming a man in so he can barely make a living, then Taxation, taking what he has worked so hard to earn, with barely a by-your-leave! Do you not find it so, Mr Stug?"

"It is hard," Stug said. "One struggles. But what's a man to do, Mr Thring?"

"Oh, there are things a man can do, Mr Stug, as I'm sure you're aware. Entirely legal things. Entirely *respectable* things. Which allow one to claw back some pitiable fragment from the endlessly hungry jaws of taxation." Thring leaned back in his chair and shook his head sadly. "Alas, regulation too prowls the land, seeking what it might devour. There are things afoot which will make it even harder for an honest man to make an honest living, Mr Stug."

"Indeed? What nature of things?"

"New laws. New regulations. New *taxes*. These things will create great problems for us, Mr Stug, for honest men like you and me. Demands that we provide this that and the other for tenants, that they must be coddled like babies, and all out of our own, endlessly emptied pockets! It's shameful. Shameful."

"I've heard nothing of new regulations," Stug said.

"Oh, believe me, it's all being played very close, Mr Stug. For fear, perhaps, that honest men will rise up and decry it as the blatant robbery it is. Fortunately, I have friends." Thring tapped the side of his nose, beaming. The beam sat much more comfortably on his face than the earlier expression of sorrow. "Friends in Parliament, who warn me of such things."

"I see."

"But you're a cautious man, Mr Stug, I can see that. I can see that from your business – how else is one to make a profit in these troublesome times, other than by being cautious? You desire proof. Of course you do. I would myself, in your position." Thring opened the Gladstone bag he carried, and produced a document.

It was a letter, signed with a name Stug knew well. A certain government minister, a man he had in fact met, though with whom he was not on the same terms that the letter suggested Thring was. It was a bread-and-butter note, thanking Mr Thring for an enjoyable tennis party. He read it, folded it, and returned it. "I see. What is your proposal, Mr Thring?"

"One can avoid some of these measures by putting one's investments… shall we say, out of reach? And at the same time one will be doing what is so beloved of the more radical elements of the government – making a donation to charity."

"Mr Thring, I already give to charity."

"Indeed, indeed, Mr Stug, your generosity has been noted. That was why I thought this might be of interest to you."

"I fail to see how giving money to a charity could possibly ensure I *avoid* losing money."

"Why, it's perfectly simple. Here." More documents appeared from the bag – not letters, this time, but calculations. Thring spread them on the desk. "One simply makes a donation – thus – to a charity, such as a school or hospital, but on certain conditions. This allows one to have a hand in the running of the place – purely for the good of those who need it, of course. And after a while, one discovers that, sadly, the place is not working as it should, not providing the greatest benefit to those in need, is, in fact, too far gone to be saved. Tragic, quite tragic. Then," he beamed, "one transforms it into rentable accommodation, still in the name of the charity, without paying a penny in tax, and avoiding those unpleasant regulations – which don't apply to charities!"

Stug looked over the calculations. They all appeared to work. "Do you have a property in mind?"

"I do, Mr Stug. Several, in fact. I thought that perhaps you might care to make a joint investment. I like the way you do business, Mr Stug. We are men of a kind, you and I, don't you think?"

"You'll forgive me if I show some caution, Mr Thring – but I know nothing whatever of your business."

"Indeed, indeed, and how should you? I like to keep myself out of the public eye, you know. One has more freedom that way, I find. But there, again, you show caution!" He waved a finger, grinning. "I like to see caution in a man. Here." He extracted one more document from the bag. It was a letter from a bank.

The amount shown in Thring's account made even Stug, not himself a poor man, widen his eyes. "I see."

"There's little risk," Thring said. "However, knowing you to be a man of sense, I have signed this undertaking that I will invest exactly the same amount as you. Just to assure you that I believe this to be a thoroughly solid investment. And as you can see, I have it to invest."

"It all looks very promising," Stug said, going over the documents again. "However, the properties…"

"Oh, yes. There are several, but one must be cautious, you know. People sniff about so. I thought just one to start with. The one I think offers the best opportunity is The Hospital for Incurables, in Streatham. There's also a home for fallen women – that sort of cause is very fashionable at the moment, and although the returns might be smaller, the, shall we say, *impact* of such an investment on one's standing could be considerable. And of course, should fashion change, casting it aside can be seen as improving the moral fibre of the nation. Oh, and there's the Sparrow School, that's the smallest investment, but I don't really think…"

"Did you say the *Sparrow* school?" Stug narrowed his eyes.

"You know of it?"

"I have heard of a firm by the name of Sparrow's Nest Security, but not the school. They might not be connected."

"Oh, yes, they are – not a going concern, though, not at all. Run by the same person, a woman, well, hardly more than a child. And quite mad, my dear fellow, full of ridiculous notions."

Stug considered. Could this man know who the Sparrow girl really was? Obviously the school was some ploy, or perhaps a desperate bid for respectability.

"I had no idea it was a charity."

"At the moment, it isn't, though it should be. That's the neatness of it. I persuade them to *become* a charity – believe me, the place is tottering, they can't pay their butcher. They'll be more than willing to grasp at any straw a man can offer them. But I'm not sure it's worth the time – it's a small concern, the investment required is less than the others, of course, but…"

"That one," Stug said. "That's the one I'm interested in."

"Really?" Thring leaned back in his chair. His eyes still twinkled, but their expression was extremely sharp. "Now, Mr Stug. That interests me. You're a shrewd businessman, anyone can see that. Why would you be interested in this particular project?"

Stug tapped the papers with his forefinger, thinking rapidly. It was none of this man's business if he had a personal interest in the school – and in finding out as much as he could about that interfering young woman, thus increasing his hold on her. Stug was conscious of a rising excitement. If he was to free himself of Simms, which he would have to do, and probably sooner rather than later, then someone who not only had dubious morals and experience of criminality but was far more completely under his control, someone like Eveline Sparrow, would be very, very useful. She almost certainly had, or could find, some low bully-boy types she could call upon for the more physical aspects of protecting his interests.

And should things go wrong, the loss would be small, and blame could easily be guided towards the young woman of known criminal background who was running the place.

"As you say, Mr Thring, it's the cheapest of the lot. And as you've noted, I'm a cautious man. I'd prefer to start small." He peered at the papers. "Also, a school – I think, as you say, the business can be discounted – the improvement of young minds, is, after all, the most worthy of causes, and if one should find that those young minds are being guided in ways that are... *unsuitable,* it would be one's public duty to put a stop to it. Don't you think?"

"Neat," Thring said, nodding. "Always better if one can fill out one's reputation at the same time as one's pockets."

"How did you come across the school?"

"Oh, I keep my eyes open. I prefer to investigate such opportunities myself. One can use agents, but they do *miss* things, and are far too easy to spot. If I go myself, why, I can go as Octavius Thring, a private gentleman with a number of interests and a charitable bent. You'd be astonished what people reveal to a would-be reformer, Mr Stug."

"I'm sure I should."

"Well, if you're fixed on this particular one to start with... should it work to our advantage – though as I say, on this particular investment the returns are not as great as with one of the others, do you think you could, later, be persuaded to invest in one of the larger projects?"

"Perhaps. I should prefer to wait until I can be convinced of this project's worth."

"You're a shrewd bargainer, Mr Stug. There's no getting one over on you, I see."

"Well," Stug said, "I like to get my money's worth."

"I can see that you do, Mr Stug. I can see that you do. If you would be so kind as to sign here, here and here, I shall put things in motion. Would you like to visit the place?"

"Oh no," Stug said. "They've already dealt with you, and you've obviously gained their trust, so I think it's better if you do the negotiating. If you're willing."

"Certainly, certainly."

Stug signed, and shook hands, and smiled. Thring was his sort of businessman. One who understood things. His cherubic features and avuncular manner might be deceptive to others; Stug could see the sharp brain behind them, a brain like his own.

When Thring had taken his leave, Stug leaned back in his chair, laced his hands behind his head, and allowed satisfaction to rise in him. Oh, if only that annoying little... even in the privacy of his own head, he hesitated over a word that was, by no definition, respectable... annoying little *bitch,* knew! He'd have her dancing to his tune, and he would get the Queen what she wanted, and all would fall into place, as it must.

The Sparrow School

"YOU LOOK MORE cheerful, Beth," Evvie said. "What's up?"

Beth waved the newspaper. Evvie gave it a scowl. "First time there's been anything in there to make you happy. Thought it was all misery and disaster."

"No, listen! 'The Russian ambassador, M de Staal, will be giving an embassy ball on the fifteenth. All the ladies will no doubt be eager to see Lady Staal displaying the latest in fashions from the glittering Imperial Court.'"

"Didn't think you were interested in all that, Beth, fashions and so forth."

"It's not about the *ball,* Evvie. It's the fact that he's *giving* one, and the way the article's written."

"I don't follow." Something was giving Evvie an uncomfortable feeling in the pit of her stomach, which didn't at all match Beth's cheerful expression.

"The paper's not talking about how Russia's trying to take over territory, it's talking about the 'glittering Imperial Court.' And there's a list of people who are going, and lots of them are government. That means things are calming down, after Panjdeh. There's probably a proper article somewhere, that will explain it, only somebody's taken the main bit of the paper."

"'Things are calming down,'" Evvie said, her voice sounding rather too far from her body. "Oh, good."

A Russian doll. What if you told her you had a Russian doll.

"Evvie, are you all right?"

"Did they say he had a daughter?"

"Yes, a little girl. Evvie?"

Baba Yaga. The Queen has some quarrel with Baba Yaga.

"Beth, you understand this stuff better than I do. Say something happened, to the ambassador's family. Maybe while he was at this ball, with his wife, if something happened... what would that mean?"

"What would it *mean?*"

"Say his little girl got... you know. Hurt, or kidnapped, or something."

"Why on earth should something like that happen?"

"Never mind why, what if it did?"

Beth bit her lip, frowning. "Well... it probably wouldn't be good. Not just now. I mean, actually, it might be pretty bad. Especially if the ambassador thought it had been done on purpose, I don't suppose he'd be that interested in making it all right again."

"D'you think it could mean a war?"

"On its own, normally – no. Maybe not. But just now, with everyone still so riled up about Panjdeh? And from what I read it was the Russian ambassador himself who did a lot of work to stop there *being* a war – he'd think – well, probably *everyone* would think – that it was done on purpose." Beth whitened. "Evvie, what is it? Do you know something?"

"I gotta think," Evvie said. "I... I gotta think."

The Queen wants the Russian Ambassador's baby. Because she's got some stupid quarrel with Baba Yaga.

Maybe Stug really is working for the government – or maybe he's a spy – or maybe it's just about the baby, maybe that's all it is? Does he not know? Not care?

And what do I do now?

She looked at Beth, and thought about Beth's Uncle Berry. And about Old Jeff and Jenny Blake, and Davey, Bobby, William, Frank, Joe and how many more? How many Russians too? Dead and maimed and broken and grieving.

Because one man was mad for a son, and one vain, inhuman creature wanted to score a point over another, they would risk a war. Because neither of *them* would be fighting it.

It's not right. It's not right that they get to mess us about this way; Stug and people like him, and the Queen and Folk like her. They don't care, they don't care nothing for all of us that bleeds and breaks and mourns. Not a bit.

She sat silent for so long that Beth took away her cold tea and put another in front of her without her noticing until she burned her mouth on it. "Ow!"

"Sorry," Beth said. "I told you twice it was a fresh one."

"My fault. Beth… that ladder you were making for me. Is it done?"

"Well…"

"Usable, I mean?"

"Yes."

"Good, show me."

"Evvie, what are you doing?"

"I got an idea. I think. But I need your ladder, and I need to talk to Liu." She pulled the little jade fox out of her hidden pocket, and stared at it. "Hear that? I need to talk to Liu." She saw Beth watching, and flushed. "I dunno," she said. "He says he can tell when I need him, because of this, but… I don't know if it still works. Or if he'll come."

"Tell me what you're doing."

"I can't. I'll be off out tomorrow night. I need your ladder. I should be back by two. If I'm not… you don't know where I went, you don't know me by any other name than Sparrow, and we never met before you came here."

"Evvie…"

"It's safer this way, Beth. You know where the money is, and who has to be paid."

"Evvie, please…"

Eveline gave her a swift hug. "Don't be a worry-wart. I'll be right as rain."

"Oh, Evvie, are you sure?"

"'Course I am."

*　　*　　*

EVELINE FOUND LIU, eventually, seated on the roof of one of the old sheds in the grounds, which caught the sun in the afternoons. He hardly seemed to notice when she clambered up alongside him, but sat with his arms around his knees staring over the field where the shadows of the trees lengthened with the dying day.

"Liu... I'm so glad you're here. Funny how you do that."

"Do what?"

"How you're always here when I really need you to be. Is it the fox? Or just you?" She grinned at him, but he didn't smile back. He hardly seemed to have heard her. "I'm sorry," she said.

"Sorry?"

"I'm sorry I shouted at you. I didn't mean those things I said."

"It is no matter."

"Yes it is. I had a lot on my mind, but that en't no excuse for going for you like I did."

She waited for him to ask her what was on her mind, but he only plucked a bit of broken slate from the roof, and began digging at the moss with it.

"So are we all right?"

"Of course," he said.

"You sure?"

"I would not say so if I were not." He still wasn't looking at her, but at his own fingernails, as though there was some mystery hidden under them. Evvie couldn't see what it could be, since his nails were always so clean it was astonishing.

"Liu, you sick or something?"

"Sick? No. Only, like you, my mind has... things on it."

"You going to tell me?"

"Oh, it is all terribly dull. Tell me what you want instead."

"How do you know I want something?"

"I know."

"Matter of fact, I did want to ask you a favour. But I didn't come up here just for that, you know," she said.

"I know that, too." His smile this time looked more like the one she knew.

She smiled back. "You said I shouldn't get involved with the Folk. Well, I'm taking your advice, but... I need your help. Because I dunno who else to ask."

"Go on."

"Would you be able to get me something, from them?"

"What?" The glance he threw at her was almost desperate.

"Is something up?"

"Not at all. It seems I must travel across the Stream of Blood in any case, it will be no trouble to bring back something."

"You must? Oh, good. I need a baby."

"What?"

Evvie snorted. "Your *face!* I mean a changeling, you daft ha'porth. Not a *real* baby. Can you get one? Well, when I say a baby... nearabouts three or four years. Little girl. Dark headed." She'd managed to find out that much, at least. And it would be night, and the child would be well wrapped. It would have to do.

"That should be possible," he said.

"Only it'd have to be soon. By tomorrow night."

"Ah. That might be more difficult."

"Liu, it's real important. I can't tell you why, because it might get you in trouble. If you don't know, then it's not your fault, right? Only it's probably best no-one knows about it, or as few as possible, anyroad."

"Oh, Lady Sparrow, what have you got yourself mired in?"

"I been asking myself that. But I got to do it, there's no-one else. It's not for me, see. It's... well. Oh, I wish I could tell you but I *daren't*. But it might stop a lot of bad things happening." Liu looked at her, frowning. She sighed. "I'm sorry. But a doll en't going to work. I'd ask Beth but I don't think she could make something in time."

"I will get you your changeling," Liu said. "By tomorrow night. At the foot of the big oak," he pointed to one of the huge old trees that edged the school's grounds.

Evvie grabbed his hand and squeezed it. "Liu, you're a bene cove, you are."

He squeezed back, briefly, and then let go. "If I cannot bring it myself, then I will send it."

"Why wouldn't you be able to bring it yourself?" Evvie said.

"Well…" Liu looked at his fingernails again. "It is possible I might not be coming back."

"What? Why?" Evvie felt a sudden hollow in her stomach.

"I am, as you recently reminded me, half Folk. I think perhaps I have spent too much time here of late. Pleasant though this has been…"

"You're leaving?"

Liu shrugged. "I might. I might not. Life here can be entertaining, but then, so is life among the Folk, you know."

"I see." She kept thinking she knew him, and then, he behaved just like Aiden – fickle, unreliable, not really caring for her or anything but himself.

Don't lose your temper, Evvie. This changeling's the best chance you've got to deal with this business.

And if you're nice there might be a better chance he'll come back.

"Well," she said, "that will be a shame, you know, but I suppose you know your own business best."

The Crepuscular

PRESSING HIS WAY through today's entrance – a curtain of brilliant blue morning glory, that had, somehow, been coaxed open even in the soft light of the Crepuscular – Liu could not help but make comparisons. The Court of Ao Guang was, there was no getting away from it, of a level of magnificence that made the Queen's Court seem... a little countrified. Of course, she favoured living décor – flowers, beasts, birds, her own peculiar pets. Ao Guang was more inclined to the unchanging glories of lacquer and gold.

Yet for all that the Queen's Court had a liveliness of spirit, a *playfulness* that Ao Guang's lacked. It was not only the glory of Ao Guang's Court that was unchanging – the same faces, the same signs of status, the same dancers in the same dances as rank and position shifted up and down and sideways.

In comparison, the Queen's was a constant Festival of Fools – the unexpected, the frivolous, the wild always hovered at the edges, occasionally slamming up through the very centre of things. It reflected the Queen's own temperament, her capacity for impatience and caprice.

That was one of the things that made it so appealing – and so extremely dangerous.

Behind him, the vines shifted, whispering, back into place.

The Queen was draped across her throne. Her colours today were all blues, delphinium and cornflower, harebell and sapphire, her gown stitched with a thousand tiny pieces of gem-bright silk that stirred and shimmered like butterfly wings. She seemed to have acquired a new pet – a small girl. Her curls were as bright as a polished copper kettle, sitting in the hearth reflecting the firelight. Liu felt a jarring pang as the image conjured up the kitchen in the private part of the school – Beth, frowning over some bit of metal; Madeleine, small round glasses perched on her nose, at the other end of the table, reading or stitching, sometimes exclaiming over the latest scientific development; and Evvie, his Lady Sparrow, scowling over accounts, a swear word throttled at birth as she remembered her Mama was in the room, or plotting something. He could always tell when she had some new scheme brewing, there was a particular mischievous tilt to her smile.

He had always put his fox-self, his Folk-self, first. Footloose and without attachments, charming, risk-taking, irresponsible. Apart from his duty to his father, of course. But until now, that duty had hardly been an onerous one – his father had required little of him, neither company, obedience, or affection. And now... now he was at risk of torture, because Liu had not danced quick enough.

Evvie never required obedience either, of course – but company, and affection, yes. And to protect her he must risk her misery and fury, must risk her believing that he, like Aiden before him, had abandoned her...

He supposed he had his father to thank for that revelation. Caring about someone makes you so much, so terribly much more vulnerable, than only caring about yourself.

The Queen terrified him, even as she fascinated him. And he would not risk her knowing that he had become entangled with the humans. It was just the kind of knife she would love to twist.

He could not see – or hear – the Harp anywhere. Perhaps it had fallen out of favour? He felt a brief hope almost immediately followed by anxiety. If she no longer favoured it, then it would be easier to get it away – but if it had fallen out of favour, then it would not be so valuable to Ao Guang... though if he could keep Ao Guang from knowing... perhaps he could tell Ao Guang that she pretended not to care about its loss to save her own face – he would, might, accept that.

Even as his agile brain was shuffling possibilities, Liu was scanning the Court. Here it was harder to tell who was up and who was down; signs of favour shifted with the breeze.

"Why, it's my Little Fox!" the Queen said. Her fingers twined in the human girl's bright curls. The girl looked up at her with an expression of delighted adoration. Liu knew it well – he'd worn it himself. The Queen beckoned him with one pale, jewelled hand. The girl watched with bright interest as he bowed and walked towards the throne. "Have you brought me a gift, Little Fox?"

"I am desolated that I have found nothing that would even approach sufficiency, Lady," Liu said. "I have searched the courts of this world and all others within my reach, but the memory of your beauty reduced everything I saw to dullness and inadequacy."

"Flatterer," she said, but she smiled. "*Empty* flatterer, to come thus empty-handed."

"Oh, not quite, most radiant majesty. I have information that may please you, a little, though it is of course of the least consequence."

"Information?"

"Perhaps I had better call it… gossip?"

Her eyes brightened, tilting up at the corners. For a moment she looked mischievously young, almost as young as the girl seated at her feet.

"Gossip! How delightful. What nature of gossip? Come, sit by me."

He felt the waves of irritation and disapproval break against his back as he took his seat at the other side of her throne from the red-headed girl, and despite the more than slightly desperate nature of the circumstances, he could not help but take pleasure in it. Some of them tried far too hard to win her favour. And here he was, dancing along the edge of disaster, gambling with barely a card to his name…

He felt her fingers in his hair, and shivered. "So different," the Queen marvelled. "Midnight and fire. Here rough curls like a little dog, and here so straight and silken. Perhaps I shall keep you both, to decorate my throne room. What say you, Little Fox?" Her fingers ran down his nape, to feel the tremble of his skin.

"Who could ask a more decorative fate?" Liu said. "But I fear, that without the chance to leave your side and pick up my little fragments of chatter, my petty and unworthy gifts, you would soon find me dull company, and wish you had never seen me. Then my heart would be broken."

"Perhaps," the Queen said. "Tell me your gossip."

So he launched into a set of the kind of trivia best calculated to appeal to the Queen: fragments he had heard from the wild Folk who never came to court, minor bitcheries, small tragedies, the proud brought low and the cunning triumphant. He would not mention Ao Guang, yet; it would not be politic.

She smiled and even laughed once or twice, but soon her fingers tightened on his nape, the threat of her nails pressing chilly crescents into his flesh. "Nothing from the human world? No new gifts that might please us, no news of the clumsy attempts of Our rivals to decrease Our influence there?"

"The human world grows ever more dull," Liu said. "Noisy, and stinking, and tedious. They work and work like ants, and look only at what is in front of them; not what is behind, and around, and below. I beg you, Lady, do not ask me to speak of them, for I fear I cannot find a single entertaining thing to say on the matter."

"Strange," she said, sliding her fingers under his chin and forcing his head up, so he must look into her eyes. "I thought you most captivated by them. You have spent a deal of time there of late."

"Being what I am…" He shrugged. "I felt something – I know not what. Sorrow? Despair? For I will never truly be one of your Court, Lady – never truly be one of your own. I am here only by your great grace and indulgence. I am a half-thing, and I know it. I sought some comfort, perhaps some brief escape from this knowledge, among the humans, but there is nothing there to compare with this. Yes, I am a traveller by nature, but if ever I thought I could be truly one of them, I know now that I cannot. For this, this wonder, this festival of all that is beautiful, and capricious, and terrible, and ever-new, and ever-old, and you, my Queen, at its glimmering heart – how could I not prefer it? I must travel there again, for that is what I am – a traveller. I am doomed to belong nowhere. But always my heart is here."

His heart was, in fact, jittering along at some speed; he wondered if he had laid it on too thick. Her eyes were opaque as she gazed at him, then she blinked, like a lizard, and they were clear as the sky of a perfect June day, even to the tiny fluttering speck of a rising lark, in each.

He managed a smile at this little conceit, and its message. He was, for now, in her good books. She released her grip.

"Then by all means let us talk of more pleasant things. I shall introduce you to my latest pet; stand up, Pearl my jewel, and show my Little Fox how well you curtsey."

The girl did, neatly and calmly, though Liu could see the hem of her dress tremble as she held it out. It seemed she had learned something of what manner of place she now dwelt in. Already her eyes followed the Queen constantly. Or perhaps she was just young, and fascinated to find herself living in a tale.

He hoped it ended better for her than it did for most of the Queen's pets.

"I think her a great deal prettier than Aiden's, though of course, that one is grown now," the Queen said, patting the girl on the head.

Liu, listening with great care, detected a note, like struck metal, when she mentioned her son; something sharp and unpleasant to bite on.

"Soon," the Queen went on, "his pet will become all crumpled, and bent, and I wonder how he will like her then?"

"Surely he will barely notice," Liu said. "After all, when he must compare every human woman to you, Lady, such minor differences between them must seem trivial. What is one star a little duller than another, when they are all overshadowed by the brilliance of the moon?"

"I see that life among the humans has not dulled your tongue, at least. If you visit my son, you may see her, and make the comparison for yourself. *He* will certainly ask you for news of the Lower World." Oh, there was definitely something there. Liu's mind raced. Aiden had offended somehow; the two were on outs. Of course, the Prince would be reaching his majority. Perhaps he was already testing his strength against her.

Yes. He tucked the knowledge away.

"Lady?" The girl said. Her voice struck Liu immediately – it was unusually deep for such a young girl, with a resonance to it like a violin. "May I ask a question?"

The Queen smiled. "What a curious child it is! Go on, then."

"Why do you call him your Little Fox?"

"Oh, he can explain it to you. Run along, the pair of you, I have webs to weave."

THE GIRL LOOKED up at Liu with a kind of clear curiosity. He shrugged. "She calls me her Little Fox because I am a fox-spirit. Not completely. My father is one. My mother was human."

"Sir, what is a fox-spirit?"

"Someone who can be human sometimes, and a fox other times. Part of me is a fox all the time." He lifted his robe a little, to show her the tuft of his tail.

"Oh! How pretty!"

He bowed. "Thank you, that is most kind. I am fond of my tail, but it makes it troublesome to pass for human, sometimes. Though I have some other talents, which help."

"Can you do magic?"

"A little. I can do some things a fox can when I am human and some things a human can when I am a fox. And some other things. I don't always have to look like this." *I can deceive and persuade and steal and lie and hide and sneak and hunt. Better than most humans, better than most foxes.* But he didn't want to say those things to this small, vulnerable girl. "How did you come here?"

"I was brought by a man, sir. Because Papa has no work and they can't pay the rent."

"Oh... and how are you finding it?"

She looked up at him with those clear eyes, and he could see her calculating what would be safe to say, and what would not. "It is very beautiful," she said. "And I have plenty to eat, and no-one is allowed to hurt me, because the Queen would not like it."

Except the Queen herself. That truth hung in the air, unspoken.

"Tell me, have you met Charlotte?"

"Aiden's pet? Yes."

"And do you like her?"

"She has been very kind to me," Pearl said. "But I think..." She glanced away, and pointed. "Look, apples!" She ran towards a grove of trees, where rich red fruit hung gleaming among thick drifts of pink and white blossom.

Liu considered telling her that she was safe saying what she wished to him, but was it true? If he showed too great an interest in her the Queen might question whether he was as bored with humans as he claimed. Sending them off together this way could have been a ploy; in this place there were always a dozen eyes and ears ready to collect titbits for the Queen.

The girl came back with an apple in each hand, and held one up to Liu. "Would you like one?"

"Thank you," he said. "I will save it for later." He knew the Queen's tricks, or some of them, at least. He wouldn't eat the apple, not here. For the girl... but she had already bitten into it, with loud relish. "You must please the Queen very much," he said. "She used to have another pet, but I did not see him. Perhaps she has tired of his music."

"Oh, the Harp?" Pearl said, around a mouthful of apple, and shook her head. She swallowed. "She sent him away, sir."

"Oh?"

"I didn't mean for her to," Pearl said, looking down at the remains of the apple. Its flesh was very white, like frost. "It was just I couldn't help it, he sang so sad, and it made me cry. She didn't like that."

"Well, no, who wants to see little girls cry?"

"She might." Pearl looked up at him with those clear green eyes. "She might if I displeased her."

"Then I hope you will not," Liu said. His tone was light, but he knew his eyes were telling a different story. Oh, he did not need this, to worry about this stray scrap of humanity. She was a bright girl, and already, it seemed, had found her feet as best she could in the ever-shifting dance of the Queen's favour. She must make her own fate. He had enough to worry about keeping Eveline from the Queen's notice. And rescuing his father.

He had never been sure what exactly had set Min on such a vengeful course. Min, it seemed, being very traditional, had never approved of Chen Shun's rise to Ao Guang's favour – but they were hardly rivals. Min's rank and status were so long-established as to be carved in granite.

Perhaps he was just of a vengeful nature. It was not something Liu himself much understood – if one was bested, one was bested. Better, surely, to move on, and find something more amusing to occupy oneself with.

Such as getting Eveline what she wanted, saving his father's skin and, preferably, his own.

He looked at the girl again. "Do you know where he was sent?"

"Somewhere called the Valley of Sighs, sir."

Liu sighed himself. "Of course he was. You need not call me sir, you know. I'm not of so much consequence as all that!"

"Oh. May I ask you something?"

"By all means."

"Will you be going ho..." She corrected herself. "Back to the Lower World?"

"Oh, yes, I fear I must."

The child looked around. From a nearby waterfall came the sound of laughter, chilly and clear. Some small, glimmering creature, about the length of Liu's hand, flew past the girl, circled them both briefly, and paused, its wings a blur of rainbow mist, its small pointed face with glittering faceted eyes atilt as it watched them.

"Nothing," the girl said. "I am glad not to be there any more."

Liu nodded. "I am not surprised," he said. "I expect where you come from is much less charming than this. Where was it, exactly?"

"Limehouse."

"Oh, I know of it, a most unpleasant place. I am sure you were glad to leave."

"Yes," the girl said, watching him carefully. "Yes, it was ugly and smelled bad. I did not know then, that I could be so very lucky."

"I would not be surprised if you had changed your name," he said, with great casualness. "Human names are so ugly and odd!"

"Oh, the Queen was pleased to like my name," Pearl said. "It is Huntridge. The sound makes her laugh."

"I'm sure! It is most amusing," Liu said, "and even in Limehouse, perhaps quite unusual. I am sure there cannot be very many people of that name, should one check. I might even do so. Perhaps I shall become a scholar of human names, and write a treatise, and bore everybody..."

The glittering creature flew off.

"I think if you checked," the girl said, "you might find that the name is mostly found about Hind Street."

"And the man who brought you here, did he have an amusing name?"

"Oh, yes, it was Stug. Is it not ridiculous?"

Stug. Stug. He had heard that name before... *oh*.

"Yes," he said. "A most foolish name."

IN THE VALLEY of Sighs, the wind moans in the bare branches. Here, indeed, the sedge is withered from the lake, and no birds sing. This is the place of exile, where those banished from the Queen's regard drift like ghosts among the empty trees.

Some drift no longer. They stand, or sit, or lie, unmoving. A faint shimmer, a gleam like mica or moonlight, encrusts their skin, flickers in their eyes; but they are gone, lost. These have been too long banished. It pleases the Queen, and those who would avoid the same fate, to assume that, too long out of her notice, they have succumbed to despair. But despair has less to do with it than the air of this place, imbued with a magic older even than the Queen's, that will fold into its everlasting embrace any who stay too long.

The still-moving avoid the stilled, seldom even glance at them, except unwillingly, from averted eyes. Are they alive, trapped in their chilled, glimmering, immobile flesh? The rest try not to think of it, and cover their ears, or sing loudly, whenever they think they might hear lost voices, wailing among the trees.

Oh, yes, the banished sing. They make songs for the Queen, of their loyalty and love. They create, as best they can, entertainments for her averted ears and eyes, hoping that the guards or one of her hundreds of little spies will report back to her, will plead their case for return to the Court; or that she, on one of her rare visits, may be pleased to… be pleased. The faintest rumour of such a visit runs through the place like plague, sending them all into a fever, rattling the trees with songs and dances and demonstrations of wit.

In this grey place, all falls flat, echoless and thin. But sometimes, the Queen will deign to notice their efforts, may, even, take one or another back into her favour. Their desperation feeds her. She requires, lives upon, their longing.

Liu, feeling his mouth stiffen with loathing and nerves, steps lively and bright-eyed among the whimpering trees. He knows dozens of eyes are on him. Visitors are positively encouraged by the Queen – she feels it does no harm for her people to remind themselves of what happens to those who fail in their worship.

The guards glance at him, and turn away, pretending unconcern. His presence will be the source of bitter, anxious gossip and speculation within moments. The guards are members of the court whose exile is temporary – theirs are lesser offenses, their punishment is to see every day the fate that awaits them should they fail again. Or should the Queen's whim change, or some rival whisper successfully in her ear that they have transgressed against perfect adoration.

They make very good guards.

He listens, fox-eared, fine hairs aquiver. *There.*

Faint and melancholy, the low moan of a breeze that is not quite the breeze in the branches, not quite a voice.

The Harp.

He is alone, in a clearing. His base rests in grass that nods with heavy silvery seed-heads, dancing to the music he cannot help but make.

He is not playing. His hands are limp at his sides. His eyes are shut. His gilded skin, still perfect and youthful, glimmers smooth and still. But his strings shiver in the faint constant breeze, a sigh of notes. The breeze plays him, denying him even the stubbornness of silence.

A harp. A harp whose frame is a young man's body, its strings woven of his flowing hair and living nerves.

Liu must be very careful. He has calculated as best he can, but there are still so many things that could go wrong, through spite or sheer bad luck. And as he looks at what was once a man, a young harpist skilled enough, handsome enough, unfortunate enough to catch the Queen's attention, Liu shudders all the way to the bottom of his soul.

He could still run.

But if he fails, his father will suffer for it.

It is so quiet here, apart from the hum of the wind in the Harp's strings. There are no birds to sing, not in these bare and melancholy trees.

Liu looks at the Harp for a long time, trying to work out his best approach.

The Harp's eyes open.

They are dark brown eyes, dreadfully weary, painfully human in that perfect, gilded, unageing face. Liu realises with a terrible, mortal tug, as though he too had strings, that the Harp's eyes are the same colour as Eveline's.

"Am I summoned?" The Harp's voice is beautiful, too; or it should be. Its harmonies are arranged in a way that should be pleasing. But weariness soaks every word.

"No," Liu says.

The Harp's eyes close again, in something that looks a great deal like relief.

"I have… a thought," Liu said.

The Harp does not answer.

"Tell me, what do you wish for?"

The Harp remains silent, though the corners of his mouth tighten the merest fraction.

"I can help you," Liu says.

"No," the Harp says. "No, you can't."

Liu detects a footstep behind him, and a scent he knows. Surprised, he turns.

"Well," Charlotte says. "I hope you're learning as you're supposed to."

"ME OR THE Harp?" Liu says, keeping his tone light. What is Eveline's little sister doing here? She looks much the same; she has grown only as far as is pleasing to her master, and will, if he wills it, be fourteen for long ages – though even he cannot make her as long-lived as himself. Glossy curls cascade to her waist; her skin is palely perfect, her face and figure unmarked by the hardships Eveline has known.

"Both of you," she says.

"Is that why you are here?" Liu says. "To remind yourself what becomes of those who… upset the Queen?"

"Why else would I be here?" Charlotte gives an exaggerated sigh.

"Why else indeed." Liu forces back his exasperation; he is getting nowhere with the Harp, and although Eveline did not ask for news of her sister, he knows she longs for it, as does her mother.

Is Charlotte here on purpose to see him? He hopes she would not be so foolish as to make it obvious, especially here.

Not that the Harp would betray such a thing, or, probably, even notice; his lack of interest in the petty intrigues of the Court is one reason he has been banished to the Valley.

"I suppose she's cross with you, and you're hoping to get back in her favour. Though I can't see why talking to *him* will be the least use." Charlotte avoids looking directly at the Harp.

"Oh, one may learn from others' mistakes, you know. Isn't that the purpose of the Valley?"

"And what do you think you may learn from me?" The Harp says. He turns his gaze to Charlotte. "What but despair? That will not please your Queen."

"Well, I don't know why I should talk to you, if you're only going to be miserable," she says.

"That is now my function, I believe. Easy enough to fulfil."

"I could help you," Liu says.

"Leave me be," the Harp says. "Let me…"

He falls silent, closes his eyes, as though he could make them go away.

"Let you what?" Liu says. "Become like these others? A statue to your own memory?"

"What can you offer me that is better?"

"A chance."

"At what? Home? What do you think they would make of me there?" He laughs, a terrible, wrenching sound. "Can you make me a man again, instead of this thing, this grotesquerie, this wretched, gilded nightmare?" The Harp writhes in his own frame. "You cannot," he says. "Only the Queen has such power, and she will not do it. But even were I a man again, and could escape to the Lower World… what is there for me there? Everything I knew, everyone I loved, is dead a hundred years and more, dust on the wind. My home, if it is standing, houses strangers. The fine folk I played for, they have died, their velvets and satins shat out by moths. Leave me. Let me crumble away. All I have left to share with the world I knew is my own decay. Leave me that much. Go away."

"Are you sure?" Liu says. He knows he is being cruel. But what he offers, surely, is better than this, he tells himself. "Are you sure you will crumble? Some of those who have stilled here, they are very old, they have been here a hundred mortal lifetimes and more, and have not crumbled. And none knows, if what is within them is fled… or not."

"Better that," the Harp whispers. "Better that than she use me as she has before."

"Surely a luxurious captivity is better than such a cold fate."

"Don't!" Charlotte claps her hands to her ears. "Stop talking about it."

"Yes," the Harp says. "Stop." He looks at Charlotte. "Poor child. I at least came willingly to my fate, although I did it in all ignorance. Poor child."

"Don't call me that!"

The Harp closes his eyes.

"So you came to see the Harp," Liu says, "despite the fact that he obviously upsets you."

"Why else?" Charlotte says. "Don't think I wanted to see *you*."

"I would not be so foolish. I expect I remind you of your visit to the Lower World."

"Maybe."

"And it's not as though you want to know anything of it."

"No. Why should I? I suppose they're still alive, if you can call it living."

"Yes, they are."

"Don't be foolish enough to think I can get them anything, jewels aren't the fashion any more," she says, "even if I wanted to."

"They do not want jewels."

"Well they couldn't have them anyway." Charlotte's eyes flicker towards a patch of green, like a leaf, that has appeared on one of the leafless trees. It is not a leaf. It looks a little like the mating of a mouse and a frog, with a mouse's large, quivering ears.

"Although the Lower World is so horrid, I expect jewels could hardly make much difference. I can't imagine anything they'd need that would make things better there. I'm so lucky Aiden took me away."

"He too, of course, is the Queen's subject," Liu says, averting his eyes from the little spy in the tree. "Does he ever come to the Valley?"

"I don't know," Charlotte says. "Why?"

"I am merely curious."

"I can't see why he would."

Liu's frustration increases. How is he to say what he needs to, surrounded, as they are, by eyes and ears? He eyes Charlotte. He believes she is neither as unconcerned or as stupid as she takes care to appear, but if he is too subtle neither she nor the Harp will pick up on what he needs.

"You are his favourite, are you not?" he says.

"Sometimes," she says, and something underlies the carefully casual tone, something that jabs.

She has learned a great deal, in her time here; in her own way, she may be almost as cunning as Eveline. But not quite. And she is still human. She still feels things, needs things, that the Court can barely recognise.

In time either she will become so much like them as to be indistinguishable, or she will fall. Either will hurt Eveline terribly, and he would do much to prevent it, but he cannot see how.

And what of you, Liu? What will you become – or will you fall?

He will be an honourable son, he will save his father, and he will continue to dance, hopping from one world, one Court, to another – because he is Liu, the Little Fox, and it is the only way he knows.

"Favourite is a most enviable position," he says.

"He has redecorated his Court," she says. "Everyone is talking of it. You should come and see."

Good girl.

"If he will permit."

"Oh, I think so. *I* want you to. And as you say, I am his favourite."

"Goodbye, sir Harp," he says, and gives Charlotte his arm.

The Harp does not answer, keeping his eyes shut, hoping only for the endless silence of stone, but the breeze, uncaring, continues to tug at his strings like an importunate child.

"CHARLOTTE TOLD ME my lord had refurbished his court," Liu said, straightening from his bow. "It is most charming."

"I find it pleasing," Aiden said. He was in his full growth, now – bearing the form he would wear as long as he lived, tall and lean and pale. His hair, coppery gold, flowed over his shoulders. He was dressed, almost, like a human – close-fitting trousers, gleaming leather boots, a splendidly embroidered waistcoat – though no shirt. Charlotte sat upon cushions at his feet.

Musical instruments were scattered about – a silver flute, a lyre, a fiddle and, in pride of place, much more recent creations. A concertina, a saxophone.

The Queen relied on the Lower World for gifts, and worship, and entertainment. But this... this suggested a fascination of a different nature. The throne on which Aiden lounged was an extraordinary construction of glass and brass, pistons, cogs, and fat buttoned leather. The throne room, a great gleaming hall, roofed with soaring iron and glass, put Liu forcibly in mind of St Pancras station. *Well, well.*

"Does it move, my Lord? The throne?"

"Oh! No. Why, do you think it should? That might be amusing."

"I believe motion is generally the function of pistons and cogs."

"Oh, must things have a function? Then what is mine?" Aiden's tone was casual.

"Why, my Lord is not a *thing!*"

"But still?"

"Then surely my Lord's function is to be adored? And to provide others with a lesson in aesthetics?" Liu gave his smile just the edge of anxiety he thought would be sufficient.

"Ah, lessons. Yes." Aiden's attention, never easy to hold, drifted. He was regarding another new acquisition – a great box of a thing with levers and pedals and pipes, painted with cherubs and flowers and adorned with small figures that stood stiffly in position, ready, it seemed, to dance or to play the tiny instruments they held.

"My Lord, may I ask? What *is* that?"

"That is the Orchestrion," Aiden said. "An intriguing device, but dull for all of that. It will only play the same tunes, in the same way, over and over again." His eyes, as changeful as his mother's, clouded dark as he looked at it. "They dance, and the music plays, and it shines. But it is all only the same thing again and again." He whisked around. "I hope you have something new to bring me?"

It was a risk. Liu knew it was a risk – anything that drew attention to Eveline was a risk. And yet, Aiden's favour might, perhaps, protect her from the Queen. This part of the game was one he did not enjoy.

"My lord, you may... possibly, remember a human you once knew. Her name was Eveline."

"Oh, my dear Charlotte's sister, of course I do. How could I forget?" Aiden stroked Charlotte's hair, and she rubbed her head against his palm, like a cat.

Liu pushed aside his discomfort. Had he not done exactly the same, when the Queen favoured him with her attention?

"She is still alive, is she?" Aiden said.

"Indeed, my lord, but somewhat... melancholy."

"Oh?"

"She misses her sister."

"Ah." Aiden's gaze sharpened. "I hope you do not intend to try and persuade Charlotte to another visit to the Lower World. I should not permit it. Last time upset her dreadfully, and I do not like my pets upset."

"I am desolated, my Lord. No, I should not dream of such a thing. But I did wonder if perhaps I might persuade my lord to a little gift, a... memorial, as it were. A small thing, for one of my Lord's power, but it would mean a great deal to Eveline."

"What would that be?"

"A manifestation, my Lord. Of Charlotte, as she was, when she was first fortunate enough to take your Lordship's interest."

"A changeling?"

"Well, something like, my Lord, except there would be no human in exchange. A memory of her sister, as a small child."

"I see. You think that would please her?"

"Yes, my Lord." Charlotte was playing with the spider-web lace on her dress, as though she had not heard.

"What do you think, my pet?" Aiden put one finger under Charlotte's chin, and lifted her face towards his. "Would this please your sister, do you think?"

Charlotte shrugged. "Perhaps, my Lord. She was always a strange creature. It might."

"You don't think so?"

Charlotte glanced at Liu, and back to Aiden. "Perhaps it would cheer her. And of course, it would remind her of you, as much as of me…"

"Yes," Aiden said. "I suppose it would." He smiled, and leaned back in his chair, his eyes glittering. "Yes. Very well. But Charlotte as she was, not as she is?"

"If it please my lord," Liu said, sweating. A facsimile of the grown Charlotte would be no use at all, would ruin Eveline's plans, probably upset her, and he would have reminded Aiden of her existence to no good purpose at all. *Think, idiot!* "Although I know it is long ago, and perhaps it is a great deal to ask that my Lord should remember…"

"Long ago? My dear Little Fox, you talk like one of them. Of course," Aiden said, still smiling, "you are, at least partly. One forgets." *Be careful of asking favours, Little Fox,* his eyes said, not smiling at all. *Remember who I am, and what you are.*

"Oh, I am too aware, my Lord," Liu said, "of the gulf that separates us. But, being what I am, I may perhaps claim some little knowledge of humanity. And I think a lasting manifestation is not necessary, and would, perhaps, be unkind. Something that fades, gently, like a flower, leaving only a pleasant memory, like a perfume upon the air… that would give her time to encompass her grief, and yet remember that her sister is not truly lost, but far better off than she would be had she stayed."

"I appreciate your concern, Sir Fox, however, should a more lasting illusion be required, I do not think I would find it *too* fatiguing a task." Ice, ice over deep waters. Charlotte drew into herself, her eyes wide and dark, peering at Liu through her hair.

"I know my Lord could do so, if he wished – merely that it is not necessary, and as I am already asking a great favour I have done nothing to deserve, I did not wish to impose even farther. Indeed, I have already troubled my Lord too much with my foolishness. Perhaps the Queen..."

"No. No, I will make it, and you shall take it to Eveline, with my compliments. Yet, still, I feel a doubt, a nagging discomfort. I suspect, for all your courtesies, you doubt my abilities, Sir Fox. Let me see, what could I do to reassure you?"

"Doubt you, my Lord?" Liu's panic was not, this time, entirely feigned. "How could I be so foolish?"

"Because you are part human, perhaps."

For the first time Liu wondered what it was like for Charlotte, and the other human pets of the court, to hear their people so roundly and frequently disparaged. For himself, he felt he had the best of both worlds, and perhaps he had been known to despise both human and Folk more than a little. But to hear, every day, what fools and weaklings she was born to... still, it was not, could be, none of his concern. He had other fish to fry... or webs to weave. He bowed deeply. "Yes, indeed. And as such, hardly fit for my Lord's notice. The fact that the Queen sees fit to welcome me about her is a continual source of astonishment and gratification. I am more fortunate than some in that."

"Indeed you are. Take care she does not change towards you. I do not think the Valley would suit your constitution."

"Indeed not. To see one formerly such a favourite there..." Liu shuddered.

"Oh, the Harp! He is a most tedious creature."

"Yet, I fear your lady mother misses him."

"She has confided in you?" Aiden laughed, high and clear, the laugh of a child. Liu hid the cold that crawled down his spine at the sound.

"My lord is pleased to jest. Confide in such a lowly member of her court, indeed! Why, I tremble at the mere suggestion!"

"So, sir Fox, what makes you think she mourns him?"

"Oh, little enough, my Lord, only a certain look, sometimes...

her remaining musicians cannot tune themselves to her liking, and the songs that once pleased her she seems to find tedious."

"Indeed she has been... restive, of late, and hard to please." Yes, it was there, that note of metal. A little tap in the right place, and it could be bent to Liu's purpose. "Perhaps she needs some new entertainment. She is not like me. I am more constant in my affections," Aiden said, twining a lock of Charlotte's hair around his forefinger.

"Yet of all her courtiers, the Harp has held her favour the longest."

Aiden's fingers stilled, and he looked directly at Liu. "More so than me?"

"Forgive me, my Lord, surely you are not one of her courtiers, being master of your own Court?"

"That rather depends on one's point of view," Aiden said. His eyes were opaque, like a morning fog.

Liu left a little pause, before saying, "Whatever her feelings, unless the Harp shows proper remorse, her Majesty cannot simply cancel out his punishment – she is the Queen. I do not know what is to be done."

"If the Valley and his eventual fate there is not enough to make him remorseful, then I doubt there is anything," Aiden said. His tone had shifted, he was in danger of becoming bored with the subject. Liu leapt.

"I wonder, my Lord... you have given me an idea."

"Oh?"

"Well, it is probably most foolish, but since your Highness has been pleased to look kindly on making one manifestation... I know of your great fondness and honour for your mother. I wonder if another might perhaps amuse her?"

"Go on," Aiden said, still playing with Charlotte's hair. She sat very still.

"Should the Harp, perhaps, see himself, once more playing before the Queen, apparently at the heart of her affections, I wonder if that might shake him from his folly?"

"A manifestation of the Harp?"

"Yes. Oh, truly, it is a foolish notion. I forgot, it would need to play."

"Yes," Aiden said. "Yes, it would... it would need to play excellently."

"And like a human," Liu said. "It was that sensibility that first drew the Queen's attention, was it not? Oh, I am a fool. Forgive me, my lord, for wasting your time with my chatter." Liu bowed very low, and his eyes were on the glittering marble floor when he heard Charlotte gasp.

"There," Aiden said. "That will do, I think."

Liu looked up.

A small child sat on the floor at Aiden's feet, dressed in layers of clothing, its legs straight out before it. On its feet were a pair of cloth shoes, stained with snowmelt. "I... I remember those shoes," Charlotte said. Her voice was not quite steady.

"Now, you're not going to cry, are you?" Aiden said.

"Of course not," Charlotte said. "Only it is curious to see oneself so. What a solemn little creature I look!" She smiled, and if she could not bear to look at the changeling for more than a moment before her eyes flickered away to something else, only Liu noticed.

"Why, my Lord," Liu said, recovering his breath. "How perfect! Eveline will be quite delighted, I'm sure."

"Yes, yes. Well, you may take it whenever you wish. As to the Harp... I think, perhaps, something can be managed. Yes, indeed. And a surprise would be something new, would it not? She does so adore a surprise."

He leaned back, and cocked his foot over his knee, steepling his fingers in front of his face. "You know that the facsimile will fade, in time. Unless I should decide to keep it from doing so."

"My Lord."

"After all, if it should happen that the real Harp does not make his way back into the Queen's favour, for... whatever reason. She would be most disappointed, I think." Aiden's gaze drifted. "But then, to have a facsimile in her court..."

Liu remained silent. He could only begin the dance, and set the music playing. The steps the dancers took after that were not his to steer.

Aiden laughed. "Very well, I'll play your game, Little Fox. At least, this part of it. What is the rest, I wonder?" He snapped his fingers, and a harp appeared before him. "A tune from the Lower World. What do you say, Sir Fox, something mournful, perhaps?"

"I bow to my Lord's superior taste, in this as in all things."

Aiden began to play a song of lost love and hopeless longing, a song that had not been heard in the Lower World for at least a hundred years. Liu cast one final glance at Charlotte as he picked up the changeling and bowed himself out, and hoped that if Aiden noticed her tears, he would think they were the result of his playing. After all, he did play excellently. Whether he played excellently enough to fool the Queen, that was another matter.

"WHAT ARE YOU *really* doing?"

Liu turned. Charlotte had followed him out of the hall, and stood twining her finger in her hair and glaring at him. She still avoided looking at the changeling.

"I don't know what you mean."

"Evvie wouldn't want that horrible thing. You may think I don't remember anything about her, but I do, and she wouldn't."

"Charlotte..."

"Oh, you needn't worry, Aiden doesn't let any of his Mama's spies in here, and he doesn't have many himself. I know them all, they're not here." Charlotte flung herself on a couch decorated with green and bronze silk cushions, then immediately jumped to her feet again. "What are you doing? Are you going to get Evvie into trouble?"

"She does not need any assistance from me in that endeavour."

"Stop being so clever. Just tell me what's going on, you needn't talk all around something like you do with..."

"With them?" Liu sighed. "You have obviously learned a great deal, in your time here, Charlotte, but you should still take great care who you confide in."

"I *know* that."

"So what makes you think *I* am to be trusted?"

"Who says I trust you? But I do think you care about Evvie, or you'd never have taken me to see her that time. So tell me what's happening."

"The changeling *is* for Eveline. She wants it for a scheme she is playing out. I can't tell you more than that as she has not told me."

"And why should I believe you?"

"You are correct. I care for her."

"Are you lovers?"

"No. We are friends."

"Oh. So what about the Harp?"

"The Harp is nothing to do with Eveline."

"So what are you doing with him? I don't believe you want to get him back in the Queen's favour, and *he* certainly doesn't wish to be."

"Why do you care about the Harp, Charlotte?"

She shrugged, sat down again and began to pick at a corner of one of the cushions. "I don't."

Liu sat down next to her. "I think you do. You weren't in the Valley to see me, were you?"

She hunched her shoulders.

"Charlotte…"

"Can you get him away?"

Liu took a breath. "I mean to try. If anyone knows, though, it will go very badly for me."

He could not quite bring himself to look at her. This strange, half-grown, half-child creature… Eveline's sister. And he was as good as lying to her. He knew what she thought. The idea that he might take the Harp anywhere other than the human world would never cross her mind.

"How do you mean to get him over the Stream? He can't move, you know."

"I hoped I might… persuade someone to help me."

"You want me to help you," Charlotte said, her tone flat.

"No. If I put you in danger Eveline would never forgive me."

"Why would you tell her?"

"She will ask me about you."

"You mean you wouldn't lie?"

"I try not to. Not…" *Not to her.* He shrugged.

Charlotte stood. "When the performance is arranged, come here. To this room. I'll tell them to let you in. I'll get you some help." And without further farewell, she was gone.

"I'LL PAY WELL," Liu said.

The goblin grinned.

"I can get you pearls. And coral," Liu said.

The goblin's eyes sharpened. "Indeed? But I mislike the Lower World now. It bellows and shudders, it grates, it stinks, it offends against the whole person all at once. For such an errand, are pearls enough? Even coral has small healing powers against all that roar and rumpus."

"What, then?" Liu knew he was not being as careful as he should, that this fellow would claw him for all he could get, but he felt time pressing on him like a weight, shortening his breath and his patience.

"Oh, a little thing, a tiny thing. The very smallest, easiest thing. A scale."

"A scale."

"From the owner of that most splendid palace, that my friend is visiting."

"Now why?"

"And why would you need to know that, my sharp-eared one? Hmm? But if my price is too high I am sure you can find another who will run your errand… and remain discreet."

Liu sighed, and shook his head. "It will be difficult. Very difficult."

"Too difficult, then."

"No." Liu gave the goblin a mournful look. "I honour my debts. Deliver this for me, now, and you will have your scale, though it comes drenched in my blood. But it must get there before moonrise in the lower world."

"Oh, no fear for that, bright eyes. No fear for that. And it is to be left… in this place? Are you sure? Such a precious burden should, surely, be delivered in person."

"It is to be as I have said." It was not enough, to keep Evvie safe, but it was the best he could do. There was no time for more.

The Sparrow School

EVVIE, DRESSED IN her servant's gear, neat, respectable, and as close to invisible to the eyes of lords and ladies as it was possible for a normal human girl to be, approached the oak tree.

It was dusk. The wood shivered with the last birdsong; small creatures scuttered and fussed in the under growth. An owl floated silently overhead, like a ghost or a dream.

The bundle lay on the ground. She heard it whimpering.

Liu was nowhere to be seen.

She moved towards it as though in a dream, half-expecting to look down and see her own childish legs and feet, the skirt of a long-gone woollen dress. She knelt on the wet leaf-mould and folded back the blanket.

The ghost of her sister's face looked out at her. She gave a little sobbing cry, and jolted back, as though a spider had run over her hand.

The movement sent a piece of paper sliding to the ground, and she caught it.

I'm sorry, it had to look like this. I hope it does what you need. Be careful.

There was no signature, but a faint paw-print, narrow and light.

The Crepuscular

RUMOURS THAT THE Harp was to perform, to try to regain the Queen's favour, swelled and shivered through the Courts, drawing hundreds of the denizens of Faerie. They gathered in a shimmering, muttering mass, bright-eyed, whispering behind their hands, drawn by the promise of a scandal, the fear of being left out of a notable event, the hope of a clue into the Queen's heart.

In the Valley of Sighs, strange vapours curled among the trees. Distracting sounds and obscuring motions shifted the attention of the guards, whose thoughts were already on the court. Some had been granted permission to attend, and were already there; others were still sending petitions and pleas, bouquets, bibelots, sonnets, sestinas... and anxiously watching for returning messengers.

Only the Harp seemed calm; and was largely ignored. When escorts came for him, those still remaining pretended indifference.

In the Queen's Court, the crowds pressed close. Every balcony and bannister, every lamp and vine and bloom and pedestal shivered with wings and eyes.

The Harp stood in the room's centre, waiting.

The Queen was late, as was her pleasure and privilege.

The Harp stood with eyes closed and hands folded. *He makes such a show of indifference,* the whisper went around. *But if he were truly indifferent, he would not be here...*

Eventually, the Queen arrived, in a fuss of servants and fans and goblets of nectar and singing birds. Her gown was of spider-web and moonlight, her hair dressed with dew. Having declared gems out of fashion, she wore only a single perfect pearl on the finest of chains.

"Well, Sir Harp," she said. "I understand you wish to play for me. Is that so?"

"Yes, Lady."

"And why should I permit it? I may, in a moment of weakness and due to the softness of my heart, have given you permission to leave the Valley, but I am not sure I can allow you to trouble my Court with your wailings."

"Oh, Mother, do let him," Aiden said. "If he succeeds, or fails, he will provide a most amusing spectacle, and an object lesson for those who seek to return to your favour, will he not?"

"WHERE ARE WE going?" the Harp said, with a kind of weary resignation.

"It is the Court of Ao Guang – the Dragon King of the East China Sea," Liu said.

"You are taking me to be a slave to another tyrant."

"If you used that sort of language it is no wonder the Queen banished you," Liu said. He knew he was being snappish, and unfair. Guilt and weariness had worn his nerves too close to his skin.

"It is the nature of tyrants to dislike the truth," the Harp said, closing his eyes again. "It is the nature of true art to speak it, whether the artist will or no. What does it matter now?"

"I had to do this."

"That is what the Queen said. She had to have my voice, my music... and when I first failed to please her, she made me a monster."

"I am not doing this for myself!"

"No?"

"No."

"Tell me, then."

"Ao Guang wanted you, because he hates the Queen. Please,

please don't tell him you were out of favour. Please. Only by bringing him something she valued can I save my father."

"Your father has displeased him?"

"Yes. It is all a foolish misunderstanding but…"

"And what will you bring next time Ao Guang is displeased? The girl, Charlotte? Or her sister? Tyrants cannot be satisfied. They are a dry and bottomless well, and one may drop into them everything one loves and everything one is, and they will never be filled up."

"What would you suggest, then, O most wise Harp, O true artist?" Liu snapped. "That I should let my father be destroyed when I could have helped him?"

"I did not say that it was in my nature to speak truth, only that it is the nature of true art to reveal it. As for wisdom, I gave up all claim to that when I accepted the Queen's invitation."

Liu slumped down by the side of the Harp, and put his head in his hands. "Please. Just… please."

"Why did you not bring *him* the facsimile?"

"Because once it fades, my father would still be here, and still at his mercy."

"And when the one you have left behind fades?"

Liu shrugged. "I think it will not. Not yet." *And when it does, will the Queen remember that I was there? Will Aiden tell her that I was party to deceiving her?*

Well, there was nothing he could do now. Aiden and the Queen had their own games to play, and that particular one might still be on the board long after Liu himself was nothing but dust and bone.

The Russian Embassy

"Oh, isn't it splendid!" Cora breathed.

"Really, my dear, there's no need to gawp. It's not as though you've never attended a function before. Now, let's see who's here…" Stug looked around the room. It was certainly colourful. The sombre clothes of businessmen and government officials set off the splendour of white or scarlet dress uniforms glittering with rows of medals. The ambassador himself was impossible to miss, in his dark green diplomatic uniform, the jacket embroidered with twining leafy branches and small gold stars. Under his arm was a matching bicorn hat, also fringed with gold, and he wore a pale sash with thin bands of colour. He had no beard – Stug would have expected a Russian to have a beard – but an impressive set of sideburns. The woman hovering nearby was, presumably, his wife – Stug normally had no interest in such accoutrements of the powerful, but he checked her over, to see whether she seemed abnormally anxious. He knew that mothers had powerful instincts when it came to the safety of their offspring – though judging by the Huntridge girl's mother perhaps not all of them. Not that the girl was in any danger. And nor would the Russian infant be. None at all. In fact it would probably live longer than it would here, especially if there was another war, and the ambassador was forced to return to Russia, which was, so far as Stug was concerned, little but a palace of barbarian splendour in the midst of a wilderness of snow, bears and brutalised peasants.

The woman seemed calm enough – there was no glancing over

her shoulder, no summoning of servants. She was acting the elegant social hostess, calm and pleasant, and apparently reasonably fluent in English.

Cora was already in amongst a crowd who were exclaiming over the ice-sculpture of a double-headed eagle that towered over their heads. The candle-flames threw their reflections deep into its glassy substance. This flaunting symbol of the power of the Romanovs could hardly be objected to, here in the Russian embassy, but Stug thought it a little vulgar. As he watched twin drops of meltwater dripped from the eagles' beaks, little flecks of fire in the candlelight.

He found himself rubbing his mouth and forced his hand away. He must not seem anxious, or distracted. There were useful people here he should talk with, remind them who he was. The Sparrow girl was completely in his power, and he already knew she was practised at thievery and deception. Why, at first even he had been fooled by her respectable appearance.

Stug hoped the girl wouldn't be foolish enough to come looking for him or send some scruffy street-urchin to track him down. He surreptitiously wiped his hands against his coat. Surely she wouldn't. That would attract notice, something neither of them could afford.

He glanced at the fabulously gilded clock that towered over one end of the room, and blinked. Surely that couldn't be right? He wanted to check his watch, but it would seem so ill-mannered. Nonetheless his hand crept towards his pocket.

"Ah, Mr Stug. An illustrious gathering, isn't it?"

Robert Delaney. Of course, he would be here, damn the man.

Stug snatched his hand from his watch-pocket, and held it out. "Indeed, indeed."

"A great relief, it has to be said," Delaney said, glancing around. "When you consider how things were a bare week ago. De Staal is a neat-footed man, to have got us all through it, though don't let anyone know I gave him so much credit."

"Through…"

"My dear chap…" Delaney lowered his voice. "I know as a

businessman you don't concern yourself overly with politics unless they're of direct interest, but even you must have realised. Came damn close to war, you know. Damn close. Had things been otherwise, this might have been another Duchess of Richmond's ball."

"Duchess of Richmond? Is she here?"

"I'm talking of the night before Waterloo, old chap. Are you feeling quite the thing?"

"Oh, oh, yes, quite. Well, it's all calm now, then."

"Insomuch as things ever are, these days." Delaney sighed. "Sometimes I think that perhaps I should get out of politics. Retire to the estate, you know. Grow potatoes and whatnot. Leave the game to younger chaps. It's no good for the nerves, all this, knowing what rests on the right word at the right time. Or the wrong one."

"Oh, surely you're at the peak," Stug said. "A shame to terminate such a brilliant career." Inwardly, he shook his head. Weakness, and at the very heart of government! It wasn't by giving in, losing one's nerve, that one succeeded. It was by taking the world in both fists and forcing it to do one's bidding. And if a small voice whispered to him of the possibility of war, he crushed it. It wasn't his affair, it was the duty of politicians to trouble themselves about such things. If the man couldn't stomach his job, maybe he should leave it. But then Stug would have to find another useful connection in government, and these things took time, and patience. "I can't imagine," he said, "that they could find someone sufficiently able to replace you."

"You flatter me, old chap – but perhaps you're right. Besides, my wife would never let me hear the last of it. Speaking of wives, how is dear Cora?"

"Blooming, as you see," Stug said, waving in the direction of Cora, who was now chattering like a squirrel with some plump, overdressed female with a pink face.

"Marvellous, marvellous. I must say," Delaney said, "you're a lucky man."

Stug smiled. *I don't believe in luck. I make my own.* And Delaney was part of it. Should suspicion ever fall on Stug, however unlikely that might be, why, he had been right here, with his wife, talking to a government official. He would leave at a perfectly respectable time, meet the girl, make his delivery, and everything would be done. Everything would be completed. Cora would never even know what had happened. And one day soon she would say to him, "My dear, I have news..."

Ao Guang's Palace

LIU HAD CALLED in a great many favours so as not to have to pass through the Lower World to reach Ao Guang's Court; he did not dare. He had no idea how long ago the Harp had first been taken to the Queen's court, but he knew it was at least two centuries, and feared that if the Harp were to even brush the reality he had been born to, the descending years would crush him to shards and powder.

They appeared in the Outer Court, among the columns and white marble and bright, smoothly flickering bodies of the tame carp, directly before the gate. The Harp rode upon a form of rickshaw, which Liu had endeavoured to make look as elegant as possible.

"Look," said the lion.

"I see," said the lioness.

"He has returned. And brought…" The lion extended a curious claw towards the Harp.

"A gift for Ao Guang, and for him alone," Liu said. "I request that my presence be announced in the proper fashion."

"Oh, he does."

"He requests."

"That it is done in the proper fashion."

"How else could it be done?"

"We only know of the proper fashion. Only such creatures as he know of improper fashions. I am not sure such creatures should be announced."

"Indeed not."

"Perhaps, then," Liu said, "it is a pity that the eel who just disappeared through the window up there, has already undoubtedly taken to Ao Guang the news that what he desired is here, but is being unnecessarily delayed."

"What eel?" said the lion.

"Even if one such was there," said the lioness, "and even if he should have carried such dishonourable rumours and folly to Ao Guang, our Lord knows it is our function and honour to guard…"

"To protect his court…"

"However, since you are such a feeble little creature, and that… thing seems harmless, out of our great generosity and wisdom…"

"… we will permit you entrance."

"Now hurry, and do not keep Ao Guang waiting."

Liu bowed, picked up the shafts, and drew the Harp through the gates.

The Sparrow School

BETH OVER-TIGHTENED A nut, muttered, and undid it again, scowling at the scatter of parts, bolts, housing, tubes, rags and bottles. A low green shimmer came from one of the bottles; a purplish glow, slightly discomfiting to the eyes, from another. She was doing nothing useful. She couldn't concentrate. Her eyes kept shifting to the window, as though she might see Evvie, or something, or someone...

It's gone wrong, I know it has. It's all gone dab, like she said.

"Beth?"

Beth jumped like a scared cat, dropping the spanner. "Oh, Mrs Sparrow..."

"Beth, dear, have you seen Eveline?" Madeleine was twisting her hands together, her hair coming loose from its bun.

"No, Mrs Sparrow." Beth didn't like the way Madeleine was glancing around, distractedly, as though she feared something might leap at her from the shadows. She looked too much the way she had when they had first rescued her from the Bethlehem Hospital: anxious and adrift. "Is something wrong?"

"I don't know, but... oh, is that the *Sacagawea*'s engine?"

"Some of it," Beth said. "I know there's a way of improving her speed without her shaking herself to pieces, but..."

"I'm afraid engines aren't really my speciality. Octavius..." Madeleine drifted off. "I think I may have been very foolish."

Beth picked up a polishing cloth and began to clean part of the engine housing. "I'm sure you haven't," she said.

"I've forgotten how to be a mother, or at least… I knew how to be one when Evvie was a little girl, but now… she's a grown woman with troubles of her own and oh, dear. I only meant to… I worry so, and now I can't find her and I'm *certain* she's doing something dangerous and I think it's my fault."

"Tea," Beth declared, as the safest thing she could think of, and scurried for the kettle. As it boiled, she chewed her lip. Evvie would be furious if she told, but if she didn't… and Evvie *was* up to something dangerous.

"Thank you, dear." Madeleine stirred her tea, though there was no sugar in it, she never took any. "You've met Octavius, Beth."

"Yes."

"Did he seem… I mean, do you think Eveline took a dislike to him?"

"I don't think so, Mrs Sparrow. She hasn't spoken of him to me, not really."

Madeleine put the spoon in the saucer with a decisive clink. "No, she'd have no reason to. But… do you know of our situation? Before?"

"Some. Evvie told me about Uncle James, and how he stole your work…" Beth swallowed. "I think he was lucky he died of the gout," she declared. "*I* think he should have been hanged."

"My dear child, how fierce you are!" Madeleine smiled. "I admit, there were times I would have happily *slaughtered* the wretched man myself, brother or no. But I think… well, I know Eveline went through some… some dreadful things, when she was alone, and I *am* grateful to that Pether woman because without her taking Evvie in – I'm sorry, child, I know I'm making little sense. But I thought Eveline excessively suspicious towards Octavius, and I realize that even if she was wrong perhaps she had reason, and now she thinks she can't trust me *either,* and if you know where she's gone, please tell me."

"It's not that," Beth said. "I mean, yes, probably, she's *cautious,* but I don't think he's that sort, although…"

"Although?"

"Well, Ma Pether... Ma Pether thought he was a little too well-dressed, for an inventor, because she didn't know any rich ones. But then Ma Pether mostly knows criminals, really."

"Yes. And so does Eveline, doesn't she? Beth, what *is* she up to?"

Beth chewed her lip again, looking down at her cooling tea. "I *promised,*" she said. "It's not because she doesn't trust you, only she's scared. She wanted to be sure that whatever she did, the rest of us were safe. The school – the girls – you. Liu can probably take care of himself."

"Oh, that boy! He's a nice enough young man but... oh, what is that to the point? Beth, tell me, *please*. I can't... I can't bear the thought that she's in trouble and couldn't come to me."

"She's gone to the Russian embassy, I think. I don't know why. And she says it will all be all right but she wouldn't let me go and now I don't know..."

"Wait, Beth, please, I have no idea what you're talking about."

"That's all I know, that's all she would tell me."

"Right." Madeleine leapt to her feet, slapping her mug of untouched tea down on the bench so hard it sloshed over the side. "Is that machine working?"

"What machine? *Sacagawea?*" Beth put her back protectively against the vehicle. "Well..."

"Is it or isn't it?"

"It will, once I've reconfigured the flow and reattached..."

"How long will that take?"

"About a week."

"That's no good then." Beth slumped with relief, which was short-lived.

"We need something else," Madeleine said.

"For what?"

"To go get my daughter out of whatever unholy mess she's got herself into, that's what."

"But how..."

"Do you know where that woman went?"

"Who?"

"Ma Pether. Do you know where she went?"

Beth frowned. "Wait. I might... she said something... about a place she kept in... Bermondsey? By the river."

"I think we need her. Can you find her?"

"Maybe. I have... other things. I'll go. I'll find her. But I'll need a compass."

"A compass? To get to Bermondsey?"

"No. To find Ma Pether."

IN BETH'S TOOLKIT there was a secret compartment that no-one else knew about. It held a small phial of grey shimmering dust that moved like oil, a pale green stone, worn smooth, a feather so white it seemed to glow, and a few small silver charms.

She bit her lip, took out the phial, and scattered a few grains of the dust into a piece of paper, took them to the workbench and working with neat, concentrated speed, began taking the back off the compass Madeleine had found for her.

Ao Guang's Palace

LIU AND THE Harp were kept waiting, of course. Punctuality might well be the courtesy of kings, but such as Ao Guang – and the Queen – did not think it a necessary part of their dealings.

The Harp did not speak, or show any interest in the splendid carvings that surrounded them. Liu bit at his nails. He had involved himself in a hundred schemes, in a lively and interesting life, but never one that relied so much on the cooperation of others. If the Harp confessed his banishment from the Queen, if he refused to play for Ao Guang... everything could go wrong, and Liu had nothing to offer him.

He looked at the gilded creature beside him, so weary and so desperately alone.

Perhaps one thing.

"Listen," he said. "If you will let Ao Guang think that the Queen most treasured you, and will be furious that you are gone, if you will play for him, even once, if he asks it... I will do my best to get you what you want."

"There is only one thing I can still desire."

"I know," Liu said. "And I will try. Please?"

"You have not the power to do it yourself."

"No. But... I know Ao Guang. And the Queen."

The Harp sighed, and even in sorrow and without a word, his voice was beautiful; it shivered in his strings. "I am weary of promises."

"I know."

"I am weary of… everything."

"I know."

"Will you help me? Truly?"

"Yes."

"Very well."

Liu, listening to the sounds of Ao Guang's musicians, wondered how hard it would be.

Bermondsey

BERMONDSEY WAS HORRIBLE. Beth had come as far as she could on the steam-bus, but once she got off she was almost entirely reliant on the compass, desperately hoping that she'd got it right and that it wasn't playing tricks on her as it led her into increasingly darker, smellier, louder, poorer bits of London.

And this bit of it was the worst yet. Beth huddled in her cloak and clutched the tool kit tightly, praying that no-one would notice her, as she scurried through the crowds. A man fell out of a pub doorway and almost knocked her over, landed on his hands and knees and started to puke loudly into the gutter. Beth held her breath and hurried on. Two women were shrieking at each other in an alleyway, a small child stood naked and howling in the middle of the street, a man with wild hair and wilder eyes stood on a crate and ranted "Judgement" and "End Times" at the mostly-indifferent passers-by.

She could still hear him when the compass needle stopped, quivering, pointing at what was probably a doorway. The house around it was so grimy and slumped it looked like a half-empty sack of coal.

Beth swallowed hard, and knocked.

She heard footsteps, but the door remained shut. She sniffed... *pipe smoke.*

"Ma? Ma Pether? It's Beth."

The door creaked open. "How the 'ell did you find me?" Ma Pether said.

"Does it matter?"

"Bloody right it matters. You could be the law. Or various people of unhealthy intentions who might happen to be wanting to find out where I'm hanging my hat. So you tell me how you tracked me."

Beth slid the compass into her pocket. "Something you said, about Bermondsey. In the corridor that time. Then I… asked."

Ma looked at her with narrowed eyes. "Good thing you en't a peeler, is all I can say. So what're you doing here in such a kerfluffle?"

"Evvie's in trouble. And her Ma thinks you can help. Well, so do I, only I don't know if you will."

"Hah!" Satisfaction exploded out of Ma Pether in a cloud of pipesmoke. "I knew it! I knew she'd overreach herself. Come on then." Ma went inside. Beth hung on the threshold. She spent her days surrounded by oily rags, but the filthy bits of cloth that sagged across the doorway made those rags look like freshly laundered handkerchiefs.

"Come on, what you waiting for?" Ma's voice boomed.

Scrunching up her face and protecting it with her forearms, Beth pushed through, convinced the cloth was leaving stripes of some unspeakable vileness on her clothes and hair.

The floor scrunched and stuck to her boots. The corridor was so dim she could not, thankfully, see what she was walking in. She heard a click and a creak, and the soft glow of a lantern outlined a doorway. She scuttled towards it. "Wipe yer bloody feet, was you born in a barn?" Ma said, pointing down to something on the floor that might have been a square of hessian.

Beth wondered what earthly point there could be to wiping her feet in such a disgusting place, but obediently did so. Ma stepped back, and Beth stepped into a room that was so colourful and crowded that at first all she could do was blink, trying to define what she was looking at.

Dresses, cogs, segments of brass housing, hats, bags (beaded) and bags (Gladstone). Copper wire twining amongst perfume bottles and photographs. Shoes, boots, tankards, flasks, and waistcoats both fancy and plan. The brass head of a mannequin apparently in conversation with a bronze bust of a distinctly disgruntled-looking gentleman Beth thought might be Socrates.

It was like finding a dragon's hoard around the back of a junk shop.

In amongst the shimmering piles were two chairs; one large, squashy version speckled with the small burns of spilled pipe-tobacco, in which Ma settled herself, and one fragile looking item with a blue-velvet seat that Beth lowered herself onto with great caution. It creaked and puffed dust, but held.

Ma repacked her pipe with callused, brown-stained fingers and stared at a point somewhere above Beth's head. "What..." Beth said, but Ma raised a hushing hand, and Beth subsided. Ma's eyes narrowed, widened, narrowed; her thick greying brows shifting up and down, the smoke of her pipe rising to the ceiling where it gathered like a storm. Beth stayed silent and tried not to cough.

"So. What's she gone and got herself into?"

Beth took a deep breath and went through it again.

Ma listened, and nodded, and puffed smoke, and asked a couple of brisk questions.

"Hmm," she said, when Beth came to a halt, and took her pipe out of her mouth and contemplated the chewed end. "Never had a stab at that end of the market, bit too rich for my blood. Nice takings, but risky. Peelers all over it like a case of the itch, and I heard nasty things about them Cossack guards, too. So. Evvie's gone to snatch this bantling, then. That don't sound like Evvie, that don't."

"She said it would be all right but she wouldn't say why."

Ma nodded. "Smart. Don't spill every bean to every bleeder and there won't be beans all over the floor to slip on."

Beth considered this phrase for a moment in silence, then said, "So will you help?"

"What d'you want me to do?"

"Help us get Evvie out."

"Hmm. And what makes you and her Ma so convinced she's in need of getting out?"

"I don't know," Beth said. "It doesn't make sense, I mean, she's clever, isn't she, Evvie, she's always got out of everything before, but this time…"

"You got a tickle?"

"I don't know what that means."

"A tickle, an itch, a tightness in your belly, a feeling you missed something what's important. That."

"Yes… Both of us, I think. I mean Mrs Sparrow had more reasons, but…"

Ma made another satisfied puff of smoke. "Hah. Reasons, words, them comes later. You seen or heard or felt something, and didn't know what it was at the time, that's what. Something she or someone else done, or said, or had about 'em. If you ignore that tickle it'll snap a chain around your ankles, sure as eggs."

"It's not *my* ankles I'm worried about," Beth said.

"Well," Ma said. "We need some o' the girls, and we need a vehicle. Because yours is out, en't it?"

"The *Sacagawea*? Yes. I was trying to improve it, but I took it apart and added bits and I'd never get it back together in time, not safely."

"And we need a driver. That'll be you."

"Yes ma'am."

"Don't go ma'am-ing me, I ain't the Queen. I can get a vehicle but… ah, you'll do, 'cording to Evvie there ain't a machine made you can't get to walk and talk." Ma gave her a sharp look, catching the smile on Beth's face. "Yes, it's nice to know she thinks well of you, but is she right? Don't you say you can do it if you can't."

"I don't know until I see the vehicle," Beth said. "But… yes."

"Honest, at least. Well, we'll see. If we can get it off the old fool."

"What are you going to do?"

"I'm going to round up the best of the girls, and get them to meet us. We're going to get us a vehicle. And then, we're going to drag that silly chit out of the mire."

The Russian Embassy

BARTHOLOMEW SIMMS SAW the girl silhouetted in the window, with a bundle in her arms. He'd been right.

Stug had been planning to do him over, replace him with this chit. What use did he think she'd be? Sharp enough, yes, but who was going to be afraid of a little thing like her? The man was a fool. Not the first Simms had dealt with and wouldn't be the last – and like the others, he'd have to pay for his folly. Not right away, no. This time, Simms would do what should have been his job in the first place: get Stug what he wanted – payment would come later. Once you turned your back on Bartholomew Simms you'd better grow eyes in your spine – and you still wouldn't see him coming.

If you didn't know better, Duchen looked just like any respectable maid; in a place like this, you could pass as a lower servant easily enough. The building was crawling with them. The ones in livery were hard to mimic, but at the lower end – skivvies, boot-boys, nursemaids – easy. The gentry didn't look at such lowly faces much, or if they did assumed someone new had been taken on. That was how he'd got his information from Stug's offices – no-one noticed chimney-boys, and the starveling scraps were always eager to earn a few extra pence.

Getting in was shamefully easy; he shook his head at it. And this the ambassador's residence! But with everyone arriving for the ball, all this coming and going, sliding in was simple enough. Dress like a respectable servant, hold your head up, look confident, and find the right person...

The maid was harried, skinny, and young, her arms full of towels. She was also Russian, and looked at him blankly when he said, "Where's the nursery?"

"*Ya ne ponimaju.*"

"Nursery!" Dammit, the chit would be out of here with the baby before he could stop her. Simms crushed down the impulse to put his hand around the stupid girl's skinny white throat, but something must have shown in his eyes. She backed away, shaking her head, and casting frightened glances about her – looking for some help. She'd yelp out if he didn't calm her. He took a breath, and smiled. "Don't take on, love. I just need to find where the baby is. Baby, baba." He made a rocking motion with his arms. "I have medicine, for the baba." He took a bottle from his pocket, made coughing sounds. "Medicine. Doctor. Baba."

"*Rebjonok bolen?*"

"Baba." Rocking motions, hand to brow, checking for a fever, serious look, shaking head. Giving medicine. Smiling. All better. What a raree-show, he felt a proper fool, grinning and capering like some penny gaff mummer. Maybe he'd come back for this girl, pay her out for forcing him to make such a show of himself.

"Oh!" Finally, she seemed to get it. Pointing up a set of servant's stairs, gesturing, turn left.

"Thank *you.*" He gave her a grin which made her glance nervously behind her again, and headed up the stairs.

He'd have to be quick. The maid might be foreign and beef-witted, but he'd pushed a trifle too hard and maybe she'd have second thoughts about the stranger she'd let upstairs, tip the office to whichever footman she was mooning over.

Ao Guang's Palace

EVENTUALLY, THEY WERE summoned. Unlike the Queen's court, it was below the dignity of most of Ao Guang's followers to show too much interest in such a lowly visitor as Liu; the formal dance of the Court, the movement of each to and from their appointed place continued much as it always had, with only a sidelong glance here and there, from behind a sleeve, or a fan.

Liu looked about for his father. There he was, looking entirely comfortable and playing at Go. Liu felt a surge of resentment. Everything he had gone through, everything he had risked – and his father was not even in prison.

Not that he wished for that, he told himself fiercely. Not at all, not for one moment.

Ao Guang sat upon his throne, dressed in scarlet and gold. His form was human; usually a sign that he was in a good mood, and did not feel the need to impress his followers with terror. He was manifesting as an elderly man with a long white beard. Dignity and wisdom, then.

Liu prostrated himself.

One of the dozens of little lion dogs that infested the place scuttled up as the Harp was set down, to sniff at it. Liu showed his teeth at it, and the dog, its dignity affronted, growled, before being swept up by a dignitary and carried, yipping, away.

"So, it seems you have succeeded," Ao Guang said. "Rise."

"Thank you, Great Lord." Liu got to his feet.

Ao Guang rose from his throne. His manifestation did not

extend to tottering like an ancient; the cane he carried was purely ornamental, his walk as sleek and powerful as that of a warrior at the height of his strength.

"So, Harp," he said. "What do you make of my Court?" He spoke in English, to the annoyance of those of his court who could not.

Liu held his breath.

The Harp's gaze scanned the walls, the lacquered columns and silk robes, the enamelled boxes and painted scrolls. "It is most magnificent," he said. At the sound of his voice, a stillness passed through the court, quieting the soft shuffle of feet, the whisper of garments.

"More so than the place from which you have been freed?" Ao Guang said.

"There are riches here the Queen dare not dream of."

Ao Guang smiled. "And now you are here."

"I am."

"Play for me, Harp. Show me what it was that made the *gweilo* Queen so eager for your skills."

"My Lord, I will do my best."

And he began to play, reaching back with his hands in a way impossible to one still human, to strum his own strings. It looked, and almost certainly was, painful.

He began to play, and to sing.

Liu had spent a great deal of time in Great Britain, one way and another, and in its shadow world. He had learned some of their ways and heard a great deal of their music. But the voice of the Harp was unique. It made his ears quiver and his brush puff out. Tragedy wound through every phrase. The most lilting tones took their shape from sorrow carved pure as crystal. Had he once, Liu wondered, been a merry singer? Had he sung of shining spring days unmarked by frost, of happy lovers hand in hand? What would a merry song become, if he were to sing it now?

His sorrow was beautiful, even as it tore at the heart, even as it wrenched Liu with every regret and loss he had ever encountered, as it brought Liu's mother's face before him, drawn with the ravages of her last sickness. And something else began to tug at him. A sense of some other, terrible loss; of some awful tearing sorrow. Something that began to send steely threads of fear winding along his veins.

But even as he listened, and shivered, Liu was still what he was. And he was aware that things were not... *right*. He tore his gaze from the Harp.

The Court was still; listening. Waiting on Ao Guang's verdict. But their faces...

The Harp came to the end of the song. The last note hung in the air. He folded his hands on his breast, and lowered his head.

And then Ao Guang yawned.

"This?" he said. "This is the taste of the great, the mighty Queen of the Isles? With this she charms her court? I am surprised their ears do not fall from their heads and crawl away."

The Harp's head rose, the merest fraction. Liu wondered what might be in his eyes. Some vagrant flicker of pride? Some sense of insult? *Don't...* he thought. *Don't be a fool.*

But the Harp's head sank down again.

Liu was already thinking, as fast as he could. The music of the English, of course, was not the music of the Chinese. He might have become used to it, even learned to love it – but here, the harmonies that charmed an English ear fell heavy and strange.

Ao Guang was disappointed. This had to be turned around, and fast.

But that sense of terror and loss was twisting up in him, making it hard to think.

"Indeed, O great Lord," he said. "But how could I have convinced you, without the work of bringing him before you?"

"Hah." Thin threads of smoke curled from Ao Guang's human nostrils, and the long white moustaches he wore wavered as if in a slow current. "If nothing else you have convinced me the Queen has even worse taste than I suspected."

Then, of course, because it was inevitable, Min leaned forward and bowed, not looking at Liu. "Great Lord," he said, "how can we be sure this is the Harp she loves so much? Surely this could be some scheme or trick, designed to free Chen Sun from your most righteous justice?"

"Hah," Ao Guang said. "Indeed." He pointed one long, gilded nail at Liu. "Speak," he said.

Sometimes Liu wondered if life would be easier if Ao Guang ever thought for himself, instead of relying on his advisors even for this. But probably not. "Great Lord, he is the very one – I was forced to create schemes and tricks indeed, in order to obtain him, but they were to fool the Queen, not your noble self. That would be far too hard a task."

Normally Ao Guang was susceptible to such easy flattery. But this time, with Min at his ear, he shrugged, and turned away.

Think, Liu. It was getting harder. His heart shivered in his chest. *Evvie.*

Evvie was heading into trouble. The jade fox he had given her was trembling with the racing beat of her heart.

But his honour demanded he save his father; that was the pact of fathers and sons – and there was the Harp, who he had dragged all this way with half-promises, only for him to be humiliated and dismissed. Broken though he was, it was surely a bitter thing.

Think! Are you not the Fox, the tricksy thief with a foot in both worlds? Talk, use that tongue of yours!

But his heart was beating *Evvie Evvie Evvie* and suddenly there was a terrible pain in his side, and as a strange chilly grey, the grey of a London smog, began to creep across his vision, he heard the voice of Ao Guang saying, "Take him away. Put him in the Room of Reflection, and there let him contemplate his failure, while we decide on his fate. And let *that* go with him."

He was aware of the faces that turned towards him as the Shi lioness padded across the floor towards him. The raised fans, the whispers. Min, his heavy face pulled even further down by a look of bitter satisfaction. And his father, who turned from his game, shocked, his mouth opening, his eyes darting from Liu to Ao Guang. *If you'd been paying attention, you could have run,* Liu had time to think before the teeth of the lioness closed on his robes, and he was carried away, dangling like prey, like a toy. Servants lifted the Harp and carried it after him.

He could not stop himself from glancing at it. Its eyes were closed. He could not bear to think what expression might be in them.

And the pain in his side worsened, and worsened, and his heart was shivering as though it had been plunged into a winter river.

Evvie...

The Russian Embassy

SIMMS DIDN'T ATTEMPT to creep up the stairs. It was the best way to attract attention. Stride everywhere as though you owned the place, and doors would open.

He glanced into rooms as he passed, noting some very fine things, things that would be worth a second look, but he wasn't here for such frivols.

There, a door opening, and there she was, looking down at the bundle in her arms. Simms slipped himself into another doorway. As she came past, he noticed that she held the bundle slightly away from her. At least the bantling was quiet. Let's keep it that way, nip out, hand over her mouth, pull her back into the room, smooth, not jerking, no need to wake the cub. She writhed and tried to bite, that was Evvie Duchen, but he was bull-strong. She went limp, but he knew that trick, and didn't loosen his grip. He put his mouth to her ear, feeling her writhe away from the tickle of his whiskers. "Now, now, Evvie, where are you going to run to, eh? Be a good girl. Just hand me the nipper, and we'll keep it all quiet."

"*Bartholomew Simms?*"

"Large as life and twice as handsome. Now you just be still. Don't want 'em all pounding up the stairs to see what's wrong with the precious little kinchin, do we? Let's just keep her sleeping. I'll take her now."

"What? What are you doing here? You can't!" Evvie said.

"Oh, yes, I can, and I am." He slid the knife out of his sleeve, and pressed it against her side. "What you feel there," he said, "is my chiv. And I expect you might've heard, it's an experienced blade, it is. Knows its job." He heard her breathing catch and quicken. "Don't make a fuss, and it won't be getting no more experience, not tonight."

"But... I'm supposed to..."

"I know exactly what you're supposed to, young missy. Only Stug sent a girl to do a man's job and I'm going to prove to him the error of his ways, bring him what he asked for all nice and neat and no questions asked." Though he did have questions, oh, most definitely. He had a whole barrel of questions, not that he'd ask them of Stug, he'd find answers his own way, as to just what business his employer was getting his soft, pale, clean gentleman's fingers into now. This was high-class business. Maybe some might consider it a little rich for the blood of such as Bartholomew Simms, but he'd never been one to turn down an opportunity before giving it a good looking-over. He moved around so he could get an arm under the baby without taking his blade from Evvie's side. "Give her over."

"You won't hurt her?"

Bartholomew mentally shook his head. A typical female, it wasn't as though she even knew this cub. "And why would I harm a hair of her precious little head? She's why I'm here."

Reluctantly, she eased the child into his arms. It barely stirred – Bartholomew wondered if it was doped, or sick, but that wasn't his problem, so long as he delivered it whole and breathing.

"Now, as for you, missy," he said, the little girl safely tucked inside his jacket, the flat of his blade still against Evvie's side, "what shall we do with you?"

"You've got what you wanted," she said. Her hands hung limp at her sides, as though she'd given up. "Just go, I'll try and get out after you've gone."

"How'd you get in?"

"I climbed."

"And there's me thinking you'd jawed your way in. And climbed how? I had a look and it didn't seem any too easy to me."

She jerked her head towards something in the corner. "Steps. They fold up. My... someone made them for me."

He could just make it out. "Clever. How'd they work?"

"I can show you..."

"No," he said. "No, I don't think so. You're a sly-boots, Evvie Duchen. Slippery as waterweed. What if you should decide to call the servants up here, tell 'em some bad man went off with the little girl, eh?"

"Why would I do that? I'm no more s'posed to be here than you are!"

"Why? For vengeance? For spite? To take their minds off you or get in with Stug? Who knows, not me, and nor'd I care, not a whit. I just ain't inclined for taking a risk. I'm a careful man, Evvie."

She had guessed, and started to twist away. He drove his hand forward. She let out a breathless grunt, dropped limp over his arm.

He lowered her to the ground, grabbed the folding steps, saw in a moment how they opened. Neat, very neat. He swung up the sash, ah, this was like his old housebreaking days, before he'd found his real calling. He had his legs over the sill and his feet on the ledge below in a wink. The steps shook out, silently unfolding down into the dark below like Jacob's ladder in reverse – they were even painted splotchy to hide their silhouette against the brickwork and disguise any shine. When he reached the bottom he rested his hand on them for a moment – seemed a shame to leave such a neat device – but then... he glanced up at the window. No. It would make it obvious she'd broken in, and if by any chance she was still alive – he should have checked, but his back hairs were telling him to get moving – anything she might have to say would be given the lie by this same device, so clever, so obviously burglarious in intent.

Simms shook his head and resettled his bowler. A waste. She was a clever girl, but now, alive or dead, she would be shut away in prison to rot. If she was so foolish as to mention Stug's name, who was going to listen to her? All the same, he should warn Stug to come up with some tale, maybe even provide him with one. Which would put Stug further in his debt, whether he liked to acknowledge it or not.

Supporting the child's slight breathing weight with one hand, Bartholomew Simms strolled into the night, a man well pleased with a job well done.

Bermondsey

BETH HUDDLED CLOSE behind Ma as they walked. The area only seemed to get worse. The tiny narrow streets, the dense increasing stench, the grimy shuffling figures that sometimes scurried out of the way like vermin disturbed by light. Men lounged in doorways with their caps tipped over their eyes, but she could feel those eyes following her and Ma.

Eventually Ma gave a huff of exasperation and pulled Beth after her into a doorway.

"Wh... what is it?"

"Listen, you daft ha'porth," Ma hissed. "You wondering why I keep the place I live in the way I do? Think I like that stinking mess out front? It's all deception, innit. Anyone sees that, they en't looking for something to prig, nor even somewhere to lay down less'n they're proper desperate, and proper desperate I can deal with even caught sleeping. Now you see me? See how I walk? Place like this, you walk like a mouse, there's going to be a dozen cats after you. You got to walk like the biggest savagest bastard dog that ever ripped a bullock's throat out and ate tigers for afters."

"Me?" Beth squeaked.

Ma looked her up and down. "Din't you learn nothing from that actress at yer old school?"

"I'm no good at that stuff," Beth said. "I'm not like Evvie."

"No, you en't. But you gotta have some armour, you gotta... here. You're good at mechanisms, engines, right? Best in the school. Best outside it too, probably, better'n me, better'n this old fool we're going to see, I en't got no doubt at all. You're an engineer like no-one else, the tip top at engines, you."

"Well…"

"So you get that in your head. You get that in your eyes and your chin and your shoulders and your stride. Anyone or anything makes you nervous, you just think – *I can build an engine that'd run right over you, if I'd a mind. I can hear the heart of metal and make it beat to my drum, I can, and you en't nothing to me.* Right?"

Beth stood for a moment blinking, as though in sudden light. "The heart of metal," she said. "Oh, yes."

"Good. Keep that in yer head and come on." Ma let go of her arm and stalked off, the biggest savagest bastard dog in the street.

Beth started to scurry after her and thought, *I'm an Engineer, I know the heart of metal.* And she set her feet to a beat of brass, and strode on after Ma.

THE 'OLD FOOL' turned out to be a skinny, grimy, whip of a man with a few strands of grey hair crawling across an age-spotted skull, hugely-knuckled hands so ingrained with oil and random dirt that every crease and line stood out like a contour map, and a high pitched whinny of a laugh.

He peered at them around one side of a great heavy iron double door, set in a high brick wall beyond which Beth could hear enticing clangs and smell the scent of machine oil.

"Oh, so you wants a favour, eh?" he said. "Well well, what's brought Ma Pether so low?"

"I don't want a favour," Ma said. "I don't ask for favours, Augustus Drape. I come for a payment."

"What payment?" Augustus Drape scowled. "I don't owe you no payment." He pulled the door closer, so only one eye, a long nose, a strip of scalp and a few fingers were visible. He put Beth in mind of the grumpy, wattled cockerels she'd seen glaring out of their cages at the market.

Ma looked at her fingernails. "Little matter of a job down Southwark way, last June, and a piece of equipment what was supposed to turn up, and didn't, and me getting away by the skin of my grandmother's last remaining tooth. You owe me, Augustus. You owe me 'cos I didn't come and drag you out of your hole and chuck you in the Thames with one of your engines tied to your scrawny neck."

"Ah. Southwark, was it? Don't know as I remember that…"

"Oh, I think you do. Having a bad memory, in your business, that'd be unfortunate, that would. Do your reputation no end of harm, that would. And since I'm being generous enough *not* to take it out of your hide, Mr Drape, I'd thank you to let us in like a proper gent before… well, let's say before I remember how long I had to hide in the sewers that night. In June. When it was hotter'n hell and twice as stinksome."

Ma Pether seemed to have got taller as she was talking. She was taller than Drape to start with, but somehow during this conversation she had stretched, and he had shrunk. She loomed and he scriggled up like a dried pea, and then with obvious reluctance edged open the door just enough to let the two of them pass.

The door led to a half-roofed yard, lit pale and hissing with gas-lamps, full of carts and steam-cars and even what looked to Beth very much like a steam-tricycle; every sort of vehicle, some half-built, most in poor repair, including at least one that was so neglected it was hard to tell what it had been before it became little but rust and holes.

"So what can I do you for?" said Mr Drape, who, having given up on keeping them out, seemed to have recovered a kind of pessimistic cheer.

"I need something as is fast, carries at least five, and won't get noticed," Ma said.

"Well," he said, rubbing his grey-bristled chin, "to be fair, you can have one, or you can have t'other, but likely not both. I does machines, not magic. Who's this then?" He said, looking Beth up and down.

"She's an engineer," Ma said. "And she knows a rivet from a watchspring, so don't think you can pass off any old rubbish, Augustus. You try, and... well."

"All right, all right, there's no need for unpleasantness, now is there?"

"Not if you get us what we want, there isn't."

"Fast, and unnoticeable. Depends which's most important. What sort of place you taking it into?"

"High-class."

"Hmm. Buildings close together?"

"Probably."

"Peelers?"

"Likely."

"People? Crowds?"

"Maybe."

"What sort? Fancy?"

"Most like. Maybe mixed, but mostly toffs."

"Now, see," Drape said, "what you want there, I reckon, ain't inconspicuous. You turn up in something looks like a butcher's cart, it's going to stick out like a spare prick at a wedding, that is." He saw Beth's blush, and snickered. "Engineer, is it?"

"She's been brought up proper, unlike you," Ma said. "Don't pay him no mind, Beth, he's a dirty old codger. He's right, though. So, what you got that's fancy?"

"Oh, I got a few things. But it depends on the price."

"What price?"

"Look, I understand, but you got to give me some room here, Ma. I lend out one of my best pieces, I got no guarantee it's coming back whole, have I?"

Beth, looking around the yard, could see little that could be described as whole, never mind fancy. And this was taking far too long.

"Ma."

"In a minute, Beth."

"Ma, there's nothing here. It's all rubbish. We need another way."

"Now, don't you be so quick to judge, young madam," Drape said.

"I can see your stock. This lot? Most of it would take even me a week to get into running order, and we've not got time. Ma, let's go, please? Find someone else?"

"There ain't no-one else got what I've got," Drape said. "You come along of me."

"Come on," Ma said. "We'll give the old fool five minutes, then, we're off." She fixed Drape with her steely eye. "And you'll *still* owe me."

Reluctantly, Beth followed them along an oily track between the half-dismembered machines. Normally she'd have been longing for a chance to rummage, polish, tighten – to find usable parts, to take apart what couldn't be rescued and rescue what could, make it better, make it gleam and speed. But now, all she could think of was Evvie, and what might be happening to her. Her gut kept tightening with every minute that passed.

Drape shoved aside a rusted sheet of corrugated iron, and ducked through the resulting gap. His hand came out and beckoned.

Ma frowned. "I don't *think* he's stupid enough to try and pull something," she said, aloud, obviously not caring if Drape or any of the oily shadow figures among the machines heard, "but you stay behind me, girl. I got me popper." She pulled something out from inside her coat. Beth saw the thing in her hand and stifled a groan. Ma was fond of a bit of tinkering herself, and the 'popper,' a kind of pistol, was one of her latest toys. Beth had no idea where she'd found it, but though it was fancy-looking as all getout, judging by recent events she wouldn't trust it not to fire up, down or backwards.

"You're a suspicious old bat, Ma Pether," came Drape's voice, echoing back from a large space.

"Not suspicious enough, or I'd never have got mixed up with you," she growled. "Come on, Beth."

Ma wrenched the opening wider, but her bulk blocked any chance of Beth seeing what was ahead as she wriggled after her.

Into a treasure chamber.

The lamps in here were no more nor brighter than those outside, but every surface their light fell on threw it back tenfold. Shining glass and gleaming brass, bronze glowing like a flame. Glossy paintwork: burgundy, ebony, forest green. There was a superlative Serpollet fit for a duke – and probably formerly belonging to one (so sleekly black and plumply cared for she almost expected it to purr) and a chunky De Dion steam tricycle.

And in the corner, on a stand, by itself... "Oh," Beth said.

"What's that when it's at home?" Ma said.

"S'an aerial steamer," Drape said. "Ain't working, though." He patted the Serpollet. "Now *this* beauty'll chew up the road and spit it out behind her, she will."

"Beth? Beth!"

But Beth hardly heard Ma Pether's voice as she wandered towards the beautiful, extraordinary machine that crouched in the corner like a hawk ready to leap for the air. "Oh," she crooned. "*Look* at you."

Carved into the cherrywood of the prow was a name. *Aerymouse.*

Beth ran her hands over the chassis, her clever fingers feeling out seams and rivets, her eyes roving over levers and dials, cogs and handles. No, she wasn't working... but she *could.*

Beth slid the padded straps from her shoulders and swung her toolbox to the ground.

"'Ere, what's she doing?"

"Beth, you stop that!" Ma snapped. "You're telling me this thing *flies*?"

"Should do, yes," Drape said. "Up in the air. Seen it meself, but something inside went awry and now she won't move for no-one."

"She will for me," Beth said, emerging from the flyer's innards. "Can you pass me..."

"Now get off there!" Drape scurried towards the machine. "What do you think..." He reached for her, but Ma grabbed his shoulder.

"I don't *think*, I *know*," Beth said, grabbing a spanner from her toolbox, and a phial of liquid that shimmered iridescent blue-green. "She'll fly for me, she will."

"Well you can stop," Ma said, jamming her hands on her hips, her frown formidable. "Stop right there. If you think you're getting me into that thing…"

"Ma, it's a *flyer*. I can make it *work*."

"It's an abomination against nature is what it is!"

"Can she?" Drape said.

"What?" Ma said.

"Can she make it work?"

"Oh, I don't doubt it… but I'm not…"

"Here, girl."

"What?" said Beth, not looking up from the rivet she was tightening.

"Want a job?"

"No. I just want this."

"I'll make you a bargain," Drape said.

"Not with that thing!" Ma barked. "Beth, you listen to me! I am not getting in no flyer for no-one!"

"Oh you're worse than Evvie," Beth said. "Ma, it's safer than a horse. I can make it *work*."

"Can you fly it?"

"Yes!"

"Where'd you learn that then?"

Beth paused. *From a book* would not reassure Ma. "Just trust me. I don't think we've time to waste."

"You got a tickle?" Ma said.

"Yes. Only… it's more like a toothache," Beth said. "Ma…"

"Right," Ma said. "Augustus, we're taking your flying machine." She raised her eyes to the roof. "And if it goes wrong, my girl… I'll crawl out of the wreckage just to tan your hide."

"Yes, Ma."

Somewhere outside a dog was barking. Voices were raised, and one of them cut high and clear above the rest: "Hello? Hello? Beth, are you in there?"

"Oh, now, what *is* this?" said Drape.

"Mrs *Sparrow?*" Beth squeaked.

Ma rolled her eyes again. "Oh, just what we needed," she muttered.

MADELEINE SPARROW WAS accompanied by Adelita, Doris, and a slight, scarred, fierce girl everyone called Tinder, from her habit of flaring up. Madeleine stood with her hands on her hips, looking up at Ma Pether, who overtopped her by at least a foot. "Did you really think you could take these girls out of the school on a mission to rescue my daughter without so much as consulting me? What have you got her involved in?"

"I en't got her involved in nothing," Ma Pether said. "If she'd paid attention to her business, 'stead of trying to go respectable for *your* sake, she wouldn't be in this mess."

"You think being involved with criminals and who knows what is *safer* than teaching school?"

"She never got into this mess *teaching,* I never said there was nothing wrong with teaching! She's got some fancy idea about working against her own, that's what it is. *Security,* she calls it. *Treachery,* I calls it. It's no better than being a snitch. I didn't bring her up to..."

Madeleine winced. Ma broke off, and said, "Well, this en't the time to stand around jawing. You girls brung what I told you?"

"Yes, Ma," Adelita said.

"Right. Augustus, find us somewhere outta sight of your crew. We need to change."

Madeleine drew in a breath, and said, "If you think I am going to stand by while you... Is that a *flyer?*"

Beth appeared over the edge of the cockpit. "Isn't she *beautiful?*"

Ma muttered something under her breath. "You can fawn over that infernal thing later. We gotta get ourselves up like toffs." She looked down at Madeleine. "You're right, she's your daughter, but she was one of my girls a long time, and right now I'm minded to haul her out the fire. Anything else can wait."

"Yes," Madeleine said. "Yes, it can." She turned to Drape. "Mr...

I'm sorry, I don't believe we were introduced. Would you be so kind as to find us somewhere out of the way for a few minutes, and then we will no longer impose on you."

Drape gaped for a moment, and then made a strange bobbing gesture that might almost, in a kind light, have been a bow. "Come this way, ladies."

When they emerged a few frantic and pin-jabbed minutes later, Adelita, Doris, and Tinder were satin-slippered, lace-gloved, beribboned and reticuled. A swift application of theatrical putty had covered the worst of the scar on Tinder's neck. Madeleine was elegant in a gown of lavender satin, that only the closest inspection would reveal had been made for someone of more generous dimensions and was now padded out about the bosom with whatever material they had been able to find. She also wore a very splendid and glittering necklace that would, at least by candlelight, pass for diamonds. Drape, torn between a sudden access of courtesy and the sheer incongruity of all this primped femininity in the middle of his yard, made odd little half-bows and inarticulate noises in the back of his throat.

When Beth and Ma Pether emerged he simply stared.

Beth, her hair tucked away under a peaked cap, her hands in leather gloves, her neat little figure wrapped in an excellently cut blue and grey jacket and matching jodhpurs, made for an astonishingly smart chauffeuse. Ma Pether, on the other hand, was dressed in an apron over a brown stuff dress, with a vast mob cap. "Servants get in anywhere," she said. "And dress me as you like, no-one'll any more believe I'm a toff than fly through the..." She glanced at the *Aerymouse,* shuddered, and failed to finish her sentence.

THE *AERYMOUSE* ROLLED out into the yard. Ma Pether crouched in the rear, white-knuckled hands gripping the sides of the seat, her eyes firmly shut. Beth had warned her of all the many dangerous and above all *vertical* things that could happen should she light her pipe while aboard, so it was clenched unlit in the corner of her mouth, jutting up at a defiant angle. Only close inspection would reveal that it was, faintly but constantly, jittering.

Beth, a leather helmet jammed over her curls and a pair of goggles over her eyes, steered the flyer towards the widest path she could see between the lace of rust and dying machines.

Adelita, Doris, and Tinder were in the rear.

Madeleine Sparrow was looking longingly at the engine, unable to get too close for fear of the effect of oil on lavender satin. Blue-green light flickered over it. "Beth?"

"Yes, Mrs Sparrow?"

"What *is* this fluid?"

"It's… well, lots of things. Try not to get it on your hands."

"Does it burn?"

"Not exactly." Beth, in a whirl of excitement and panic, didn't feel this was the time to mention the fluid's occasional odd side-effects, like growing tiny brightly-coloured mushrooms under one's nails.

"One of these days, Beth, I think you and I should have a *talk* about that fluid."

"Yes, Mrs Sparrow. But I think everyone should hold on now."

The Russian Embassy

EVVIE LAY ON the floor, breathing dust, and cursed. It *hurt*. She'd been caught off guard. Blood seeped warm and sticky over her fingers.

She was frightened. She couldn't let herself be frightened.

She'd been caught off guard. She thought she'd planned for everything, but she hadn't planned for Simms. What was she going to do? What now?

Get up. Whatever you decide you can't do it lying on the floor.

It's dusty. You'd think the Embassy would be better kept'n this.

Never mind the dust, you stupid girl! What are you, the housekeeper? Get up!

She eased herself as far as her knees, which hurt ridiculously, as though the knife were still in the wound, twisting. It also set the blood flowing faster. Her heart was pounding, her ears ringing, her hands felt numb and cold as though she'd plunged them in icy water except where her blood, warm and sticky, ran over her fingers. Perhaps if she could calm down her blood wouldn't flow so fast.

The Bartitsu lessons she'd taken hadn't got as far as knives. That had been meant for the next term. If only she'd found a Bartitsu teacher, maybe she wouldn't be in this mess.

Never mind that! Too late! If you don't get out of here, you're going to get caught, in the Russian Embassy! And who will they talk to? Why, the British Government! Who might just remember you after all, and wonder what happened to a certain Mr Holmforth,

last seen in your company, not to mention a Mr Forbes-Cresswell...
last seen being dead.

Or you might provoke a war... all this glitter and music, that was part of it, wasn't it, part of saying we're all friends now so let's have a grand party to prove it...

Her head swam so. She could hear the music from the ball, could imagine the gentlemen in their gleaming shirtfronts and the ladies in their fine dresses, every colour like a flower garden, spinning and spinning to the music... *I'm sorry, everyone. Mama, Beth... I meant to make it better... I meant to sort it all out...*

Evvie Duchen are you giving up? Don't you dare! After everything you've lived through... are you going to let Bartholomew Simms *finish you off? Him? Going to let him ruin everything...*

Devil if I am.

On hands and knees, her side howling and scraping with every move, she began to crawl towards the window, but it seemed, somehow, much too far away, and something like black curtains shifted and flickered around its edges, around the edges of everything... *Yer fainting, Evvie. Don't faint, or you won't wake up.* She bit her tongue, hard, but the sting was dull, like a dream of pain. All the pain was dimming.

Ao Guang's Palace

THE ROOM OF Reflection. Liu had never been in it before, though he knew of it. Mirrors lined the walls, framed with frenetic writhing figures in blood-red lacquer. Even the door was mirrored, except for a small opening crossed with bars, at the base of which two identical carved figures prostrated themselves to each other.

Liu tried not to look at the walls, but though he stared at his feet, or hands, or simply shut his eyes, sooner or later he found himself contemplating his reflection.

He had never been particularly vain about his looks; his face was a canvas to be painted over, when need arose, but he had been aware that he was well-enough looking. Now a ghost looked back at him; a lost thing that he did not want to see.

The pain in his side was still there, though it had subsided to a dull, hot ache. The magic of the jade fox was not his; he had received the thing in exchange for a favour, long ago, and had given it to Evvie almost without thought, as a gesture of friendship. Once before it had called to him when she was in need of help. Then, he had been able to reach her. Now... from this room he could not slip between worlds, even unencumbered by the Harp. And he had called in every favour he could just to bring the Harp here. Even if he should he reach the lower world, he would be half a globe away from Evvie.

He cupped his hand to his side, holding on to the pain. It hurt, and clouded his thoughts, but he welcomed its presence. He was terrified of what it would mean if the pain should stop.

Evvie.

He wondered where his father was. In another of the cells of the White Jade Palace, no doubt. He had talked his way back into attendance at the court, but his son's failure would fling him once more into disgrace – which was, after all, what Min desired.

For the first time Liu wondered why Min hated his father so very much. He knew there had been a woman, yes... there was often a woman, where his father was concerned. And this was a Court of the Folk, yes. Long-held grudges and point-scoring, slights real and imagined, the ever-shifting, obsessive dance of position and favour ran through them all like fat through bacon. But Min, so often castigated by Liu's father as "a dull stick, a creature of muddy mind, with only enough imagination to hold a single grudge for a thousand years..." Min was in all other respects a stickler for proper protocol, for what passed among the Folk as honour and respect; a true servant of his Lord.

He must realise, surely, that the Harp was genuine. Yet he was prepared to deprive his Lord of the very thing that would score him most points in his battle against the Queen.

Yet what did it matter? Liu could not think of a single thing that would work to get Min on his side, or destroy him in Ao Guang's favour. All his manipulations, his deceptions, his cleverness had left him nothing but whatever loathsome end Ao Guang (or rather, Min) could devise for him, and the knowledge that he had betrayed his Father, and Evvie, and even the Harp. "I'm sorry," he burst out. "I really thought I could persuade him, but now Min's convinced him you're not even *you*... I don't know what will happen. I'm sorry."

The Harp opened those beautiful, sorrow-drowned eyes and stared at him.

"I am not me. I was someone called Thomas once, but I have not been Thomas for a long time." He sighed, and the sigh echoed back from his strings, filling the chamber with harmonious whispers. "He is much like her, but perhaps not so clever. I see little difference, except in the music."

Liu winced. Ao Guang was not so interested in playing off his courtiers against each other as the Queen, and so did not have nearly as many informants infesting every corner of his palace, but that did not mean that it was safe to say such things.

"I am sorry." Liu looked up, surprised. The Harp raised his hands, palms out. "I may wish to die, but you do not. I will try to guard my tongue."

"It hardly matters now," Liu said, slumping back against the wall.

"Why does it not matter?"

"I'm... I failed. You just got caught up in it, and I'm sorry. I meant to help my father and all I've done is make it worse... and Evvie... Evvie is hurt and I'm not there. I knew she was getting into something but then, Father... I never meant any of this. I thought I could... I've always been clever. But I wasn't clever enough."

"No. Sometimes I wonder if you're my son at all."

Chen Shun stood outside the door, looking in. His handsome face wore an expression of mild exasperation. "Father!" Liu jumped to his feet. "I thought... what happened? Are you well? What..."

"I am as well as can be expected, under the circumstances. I am disappointed in you. That my son should fail at such a task..."

"I didn't fail! Father, this is the Harp! The very one, the Queen's most prized..."

Chen Shun shrugged, barely glancing at the Harp. "Your task was not to steal the Harp, your task was to please Ao Guang, at which you have, noticeably, failed. And now I must suffer."

"Father, I'm sorry, I thought..."

"What does it matter what you thought?" Chen Shun huffed. "The damage is done. Min drops poison in Ao Guang's ear and I am likely to lose everything."

"But he let you visit me..."

"Well, *I* still have some powers of persuasion. Now, what are you going to do about it?"

"I don't know. I can't... what can I do?"

"As my son it is *your* duty to protect my interests, and help me overcome the influence of such as Min. It is not mine to think of ways in which you can do so. Did I not instruct you? Did you not learn at my feet? And now when I am oppressed on all sides, you will not help me!"

"Father, please, I only…"

"Oh, enough. You whine as much as your mother did. I suppose, then, that I must try and do it all myself."

Liu struggled to find words, but those that emerged were not the ones he expected. "Why does he hate you so? Min?"

"What?" Chen Shun had already begun to turn away, but here he paused, and looked over his shoulder. "Because he is a rigid old fool, with no imagination and less humour. Why else?"

"Was it a woman?"

"A woman! I have better taste than to share a woman with Min! I hope at least you have managed to find yourself a few women and are not a eunuch. What has that to do with anything?"

His side gave a sudden wrenching twinge. *Evvie*. She was a woman, yes, but not as his father meant it. He fought against the pain, and the fear that went with it. "Father, if I knew more about Min, and what happened, perhaps I might think of something."

"Oh, you will never change Min's mind, he made it up a hundred years ago, and now it is set, like a clay pot. Also, hah, cracked like one. Well, now I must clear up your mess. In the meantime, try not to make things worse." He walked away.

Liu slumped down again, feeling, as he often did after dealing with his father, as though he had been trying to get hold of something that constantly evaded his grasp while punching him in the stomach.

His only hope was that Chen Shun would somehow work around Ao Guang; he was very good at persuasion. He always had been.

"Tell me," the Harp said. "Why do you wish to help him?"

"What? He's my *father*," Liu said. "It's honour. And respect. Of course I have to help him!"

"Has he shown you either of those things?"

Liu hunched his shoulders. "Leave me alone. You've been with the Folk too long."

"I do not understand. You are Folk, so is your father."

"I'm half-Folk. I'm not... I have to... no, you don't understand." Liu drew his knees up, folded his arms on them, and put his head down. He didn't want to look at himself, or the Harp, any more.

He heard the Harp sigh.

"The creature has a point," said a voice.

Liu opened his eyes and saw, beyond the bars, Min.

"Well, young man? What do you have to say for yourself?"

"Lord Min..." Liu got to his feet, and stood as straight as he could, hiding the pain in his side. He bowed.

"You have better manners than your father," Min said. "You had some difficulty answering the creature's question."

"I believe I did, my Lord: I honour and respect my father as is only right and proper for a son."

"Strange, that your father should have so carefully instilled in you that quite proper belief, while he himself has neither honour or respect for any being."

Liu remained silent.

"You asked him a question which he, too, found difficult to answer. I shall answer it. It is a simple story. Has he spoken to you of my daughter?"

"No, Lord Min."

"Half-Folk, like you."

Liu was conscious of shock. He had always thought Min despised humans, and such mixed-blood creatures as himself.

"A respectful, dutiful girl," Min said, "most skilled at embroidery." The words were those of a traditional father, to whom girls were an ornament at best, a burden ever. But the crackle in his voice told another tale.

"She made me a gift of a fine robe, and when she was searching for thread to embroider it, your father, meeting her in the guise of a merchant, persuaded her to buy a certain golden thread that he said would bring fortune and longevity to the wearer of the robe, and with it she stitched gold pomegranates, with great skill. But when I put the robe on..." Min paused. "You must have been still with your mother then. There was something in the thread... it acted upon me like strong wine, or opium. I became a clown, for all to see. Dancing, leaping... your father found it most amusing, as did others of the Court."

Heavy Min, cavorting like an acrobat. It might have been a funny image, if Liu had not heard the darkness in his voice. As obsessed with his dignity as Min was, there was more here than mortification.

"I am sorry, Lord Min. That was a foolish and unpleasant trick."

"Yes, it was." Min glared through the bars. "My daughter blamed herself for my humiliation. She threw herself down a well, and died."

Something cold and bitter welled up in Liu. *Was there a woman?* His father had skirted the question – or perhaps had just forgotten that Min's daughter even existed. She had not mattered to him.

He bowed deeply. "That grieves me greatly, my Lord Min. I did not know."

"Yes, I did not think he had told you, or I would not have done so. I get no pleasure from recounting it." Min tapped the bars with one long gilded fingernail. "I think that your father did not train you as well as he supposes. I heard you earlier. It seems you have, somehow, learned compassion. Perhaps it was from your mother. It is said, after all, that a patient woman can roast an ox with a lantern."

"My Lord is kinder than I deserve."

"He is right." The Harp's voice shivered through the chamber. "You are not cruel, Little Fox; reckless, perhaps, foolish, certainly. But I believe you meant to be kind to me."

"As for you," Min said, "you are what the boy claims."

"I have been the Queen's toy for more years than I can bear to count. Long enough to know that all I once knew was dust on the wind before this boy was ever born. I was her favourite, yes. and would be again, perhaps, if I was prepared to pretend I adore her despite all she has done to me. But I grew weary of pretence, and since I would not, she could not. So she cast me into exile."

Min stood for a moment, in frowning silence. "Ao Guang does not know this," he said, "that you were exiled. Better that he does not."

Liu stared at Min. "My Lord?"

"It is also said that a son pays his father's debt. I do not think, on this occasion, that this would be just."

"Do you mean you will help me?"

"I will speak to Ao Guang for you."

"My Lord, may I make a suggestion?"

"If you ask compassion for your father..."

"I ask only this, my Lord. Will you speak to Ao Guang on my behalf, using words I will suggest to you?"

"I have learned not to trust the words of foxes, boy. What is your plan?"

"I would see the Harp freed from his bondage, and I think it can be done in a way that will please Ao Guang."

"And your father?"

"My father," Liu said, "was eloquent enough to be walking about and blaming me for his troubles. I think perhaps he must rely on his own tongue now, not mine. My lord, I can never compensate for the wrong my father did you, or the grief he caused you. He did not mean such a tragedy to happen, I am sure, but that does not mean it did not. If I can ever do you some service, though it will never be enough, I hope you will call on me."

"For that, you would need to be free, and in your right mind," Min said.

"This is true." Liu attempted his most engaging grin.

"You look sickly," Min said.

"I am in some discomfort, my Lord."

"A spell?"

"One that tells me someone I care for is..." Liu's vision misted, and he struggled for the next word. "Hurt."

"Then tell me quickly before you faint."

"Tell Ao Guang..." Liu scrabbled for consciousness, for the words that normally came so easily. "Tell Ao Guang that this Harp is indeed the Queen's favourite, and that he has suffered dreadfully at her hands, because she is a barbarian. Tell him that as he is the most wise and compassionate of rulers, he can prove himself her better..."

"I HAVE DONE my best," Min said, "always to fulfil my duty. This court," he gestured to the assembled notables, "is the heart of all that is most wise and most benevolent." Ao Guang drew his head back, looking very smug. "Is not all that happens here," Min went on, "reflected in the Lower World, and does not all that happens in the Lower World reflect back upon us? And if those of the Higher do not act in accordance with the traditions, how may the creatures of the Lower do so?"

Liu, in pain, exhausted, and frantic with worry, nonetheless reflected briefly that Min would be horrified if he had any knowledge of how rapidly things were changing in Eveline's world. What would he make of Aiden's latest style of decoration?

And if Min, or any here, had the slightest knowledge of the Etheric science that could be turned against the Folk of the Higher worlds... but that thought was so dangerous he crushed it down, in case some hint of it should show on his face.

"My Lord Dragon, I have examined the case, and I believe that the Harp is indeed what Chen Shun's son claims it to be. For it has undergone foul tortures at the hands of the barbarian Queen: centuries of terrible pain, humiliation, and loss. No wonder his music sounded imperfect to your ears – it is the cry of a soul tormented. He has begged the Queen to end his life, and she will not. My Lord Dragon, oh most mighty and most compassionate, I can tell you only that the boy has done what was asked of him."

"I see," Ao Guang examined one claw. He was today a dragon in form as well as name; which could be either good or bad, depending. Liu clenched his hands. He had coached Min as best he could, but... *please, let this work.* "And I am supposed to be content?"

"Why, no, my Lord," Min said. "How could you be? Yet being

of the sharp and noble mind that you are, I am sure you have seen how this unfortunate situation may be turned to good."

"Of course, but after all this trouble I am too weary to explain it all," Ao Guang said. "You do it."

Min bowed. "As it please your Majesty. Why, to show how far you are above the depraved and ugly practices of the barbarian court, you need only free this poor creature from his bonds, and let him die, as he desires. Then your wisdom and compassion – in contrast to the loathsome cruelty of the barbarian Queen – will be as the sound of trumpets falling upon the ear of the worlds. For is it not said that the fragrance of flowers clings to the hand that bestows them?"

"Indeed," Ao Guang said. "Yes, have the Harp brought to me. Was there something else?"

"Yes, your Majesty." Min glanced towards where Liu was standing. "Since his son has striven mightily to honour him, and has fulfilled the request you made to its last detail, I believe you will not, in your great wisdom, hold the boy responsible for its failure to please you.

"Yet his father is still, rightly, in your disfavour. And lest he fail to understand that your compassion is that of strength, I think you would yourself suggest that the boy be returned at once back to the barbarian lands, so that Chen Shun may forfeit the honour and pleasure of having a good and dutiful son at his side."

Liu could not help himself from glancing up at Min in shock. Those were not his words.

Then he looked at his father.

Chen Shun's face was stubborn, closed. He looked away.

"I WILL GIVE you one piece of advice," the Harp said. "I desired the Queen's admiration. I paid with everything I ever loved. Consider always whether what you desire will cost you what you love."

"I wish there had been another way," Liu said.

"Do not wish for things. Make them be. That is two pieces of advice, and it is enough. Goodbye, Little Fox." The Harp looked up at Ao Guang.

Ao Guang, with a gesture so casual it seemed almost careless, waved a claw.

There was a sound like a thousand snowflakes disintegrating, and a shimmer of strings.

A scatter of gilded dust lay on the floor. As the court murmured, like the sound of a breeze in the strings of a harp, a servant with a broom hurried up, soft-footed, to sweep it away.

Aloft

"THERE!" ADELITA POINTED.

"Are you sure?" Beth said.

"Yes, it's the Russian embassy, and look, you can see there's a party! Ma? Ma Pether!"

"I en't looking at nothing." Ma's unlit pipe shuddered between her teeth, and her hands clenched white-knuckled on a strut. The *Aerymouse* tilted and swooped.

Eagle Estates

When the figure stepped from the shadows, Stug's hands came up, clutching his cane across his chest. A thug, a murderer. Not now! Not now, when he was so close! His face clenched in a grimace, and he gripped the cane hard.

"Why sir, you look quite fearsome. Not scared of old Bartholomew, are we?"

"Simms! What are you doing here?" The man looked more like a burglar than ever, with a great sack over his shoulder.

"Looking to your interests, sir, merely looking to your interests."

"I can't deal with you now. I've business." If the girl saw Simms, she'd flee. He could not help glancing down the street.

"If you're looking for that wench Eveline, sir, you're out of luck." Simms shook his head. "Wish you'd taken my advice, that I do, sir, but don't you worry, I've dealt with it."

"What do you mean, you've dealt with it? Where is she?" Stug stepped forward, his cane coming up, baring his teeth. "*What have you done?*"

Stug stepped back, raised his free hand. "I've ensured she won't blab, that's what I've done. Sending a girl to do a man's job, I dunno, sir, really I don't."

"You've ruined it all!"

"Now, that's unkind, sir, when all I've done is ensure there won't be any unpleasantness. Oh, I expect you'll be wanting the prize, sir, won't you?"

He slid the sack from his back with unwonted gentleness, and opened the mouth.

There, fast asleep, her thumb in her mouth, was a tiny girl, wrapped in blankets. Asleep or... her mouth moved around her thumb, and Stug breathed out.

"Is that..."

"The Russian ambassador's daughter, sir, yes it is."

Even as elation surged in him, Stug realised just how much Bartholomew must have known, just how dangerous he was.

But he was a wild animal, and would sniff out Stug's intentions in a moment. Stug must be careful.

"Bring her inside," he said, and unlocked the door to his offices with trembling hands.

Once upstairs, he lit the lamps. The shutters were tightly drawn – he had gone through the place before he left, darkening every window, ensuring no light would escape to spark the interest of that patrolling officer, or any other passer-by. *We shall hunt the badger by owl-light, it is a deed of darkness.* What nonsense the brain threw up. Was it Webster? Or Shakespeare? Now Shakespeare was a man who knew something of ambition. He'd had a son, who had died, had he not? Stug shook his head. Enough. It was the excitement, the nearness of his hopes, that filled his brain with these whispering fragments. "Put her down. Wait. How can I be sure?" he said. "If this is some by-blow of yours..."

"Now, sir, would a child of mine be dressed so fine? Look at that lace. Besides, you'll know tomorrow, the hue-and-cry will be all over London. And further, I should say. All the way to Mother Russia, they'll be wailing."

"Then you'll get paid tomorrow," Stug said. "Late. Midnight." By tomorrow he could have made arrangements to get Simms dealt with. Maybe even with the Folk. That would have a certain symmetry to it. And after that, this foul business would be done, and all would be as it was meant to be. He could wash his hands of it. Make a donation, perhaps, to some charitable organisation.

"Very well, sir, as it suits you, as it suits," Bartholomew Simms said. "Perhaps a little on account, for my trouble?"

"Very well." Stug unlocked the safe, constantly glancing over his shoulder at the child. She was still sleeping, perhaps he had drugged her... would that change things? What if she was damaged? He shoved the money bag at Simms without looking, and took hold of the baby, propping her upright. She opened her eyes, and blinked at him, then her mouth turned down and she began to cry, a thin wail. "Hush!" he told her.

She cried louder. Someone might hear.

"Give her your watch," Simms said. "Let her listen to it. That often calms 'em."

"How do you..." Never mind, it was no matter. He had to quiet her. He whipped the watch from its pocket and held it to the child's ear.

She quieted. "Good. Now, Simms..." But when Stug looked up, Simms, for all his heavy boots and bullish breadth, had disappeared as silently as one of the Folk.

The Russian Embassy

BETH LOOKED FOR somewhere to put down. The space in front of the embassy milled with carriages, horses – already people were looking up and pointing. "Go around," Ma said. She had opened one eye, and was peering at the building. "Dammitall, this ain't natural, this ain't. Go *around,* girl."

"But there's a space…"

"I'm looking."

"For what?"

"There. See?" Ma pointed a less than steady hand. "Under that glim."

"What…"

"Wake up. What'd a ladder be doing there? Think they got some cove in to swab the glazes while all the nobs are about?"

"You think that's where… but I can't land on the lawn!"

"Land, never was there a more beautiful word. Ho, yes, land right by the ladder and draw even more eyes. No, you daft hap'orth, take us down where the rest of the nobs are."

"Yes, Ma."

"And let me know when it's safe," Ma said, clenching her eyes firmly shut again.

"It will be," Madeleine said. "Beth's a natural, aren't you, dear?"

But Beth was no longer listening, calculating the distance, the wind, the amount of space… there… if that carriage stayed where it was… she dropped the speed as much as she dared, the

Aerymouse yawed gently towards the spot she'd chosen, a nice open patch of drive with plenty of room to land. Easy, easy…

A small boy holding one of the carriage-horses looked up, saw the *Aerymouse* twenty feet above him and yelled with surprise.

The horse he was holding laid back its ears and bolted, dragging its carriage, and the boy, right into the path of the *Aerymouse*.

Beth hauled back on the joystick, the engine stuttered, and a blurt of smoke shot past Madeleine and caught Ma square in the face. They'd lost too much speed, they couldn't go around again, they *had* to land.

Building, landscape and milling, pointing crowd faded from the edges of Beth's consciousness. She knew only angles, and speed, and distance. The boy, the carriage, the horse, the ground became shapes to negotiate.

One wing dipped, the undercarriage skimmed a foot from the carriage roof, and the *Aerymouse* touched down, spewing gravel into the crowd.

"What was that?" Ma squeaked.

"We're down," Beth said, blinking. "We're down, Ma." She unlocked her fingers from the joystick, her arms gone suddenly weak with strain.

"Well praise be." Ma cautiously opened first one eye, then the other.

Beth looked up, startled, at a patter of applause. The partygoers, having overcome their fright, were moving towards the *Aerymouse*.

"Beautifully done, Beth dear," Madeleine said. "Ma Pether…"

"What is it?"

Wordlessly, Madeleine took a mirror from her reticule.

"Oh now look," Ma said. "Smutted like a sweep. This thing's worse'n the trains. I'll be going home by hansom if it's all the same to you." She scrubbed at her face with her handkerchief, eyeing the approaching figures.

"We need to move," Ma said. "Beth, you and me gotta go in the servants' entrance. Rest of you, once yer in, you know where to go – find that room where the ladder is. Second floor, north west side, we'll meet you there."

Madeleine, Adelita, Doris, and Tinder headed for the main door.

"Coo," Doris said, "Reckon there's enough sparks between here and the door to keep us in meat for a year, eh?" She regarded a passing matron with particular interest. "Look at them luggers, how's she hold her head up with that lot hanging off her ears?"

"You en't in class now," Ma Pether growled. "Act like a young lady, 'less you want us all hung."

"Yes, Ma."

"What exactly have you been teaching them in your classes?" Madeleine said. "No, this isn't the time. Oh, dear. Come along, girls." Her voice was tight. Beth saw how hard her fingers clutched at her shawl. "She'll be all right, Mrs Sparrow," she said.

"Evvie?" Ma said. "Ah, she'll do. Tough as a boot, she is. You lot, obey Mrs Sparrow, you hear me? *She* knows how to act like a lady, being as she is one. Come on, Beth." She hustled Beth towards the crowd.

"Splendid flying," said a young blood in a crimson waistcoat. "I say, it's a gel! Well done, that gel. Any chance of a spin?"

Beth felt herself blushing, pulled her hat further down and hurried after Ma.

A POLICEMAN STOOD rigid-spined and shiny-buttoned at the servant's entrance. Beth's heart dropped to her boots. But Ma strode up to him, bolder than a brass knuckle. "Hofficer? I got sent over from the agency to help in the kitchen, only I come out the side door for a breath of air and I can't find my way back in nohow, and here's this one sent to wait for her people to come out and she can't find her way neither, and could you tell us where we need to go as if I don't sit down soon my knees'll go on me, terrible, they are, my mother was just the same, her knees were a torment to her, well, it was the scrubbing, see, years of it, should have seen her hands, mine were going the same way, I tried goose-grease on 'em but not a particle of difference did it make…"

Beth glanced at the policeman's face as he slowly backed into a corner of the portico, and rapidly looked away before the bubble of hysterical laughter rising in her chest could burst out.

"Through there!" he said. "Go down to the left, you'll find the kitchens, and if not someone will tell you the way, good evening!"

"There, now, that's very helpful, you're a very helpful young man, you put me in mind of my youngest, gone to sea, he has, oh, he's a very smart boy, not that you look alike, but he has just that way…" Ma continued, steaming down the corridor. Beth, ducking in her wake, risked a final glance at the policeman. He grinned, suddenly looking no older than herself, rolled his eyes and fanned himself with one hand. Beth shot him a smile which felt guilt-ridden and scuttled after Ma.

The back rooms of the embassy were aheave with cooks and maids and footmen, in a dozen different liveries. Ma strode through them without a care, until a large man with a huge beard spilling over his dirty white shirt, who had cornered a maid with an armload of laundry, caught sight of Beth. His eyes widened and he pointed at her, and said something which she couldn't understand, but sounded like a question.

Ma ignored him, and Beth tried to follow her example, but the bearded man strode towards them, put himself in her path, and said it again, bending down to yell into her face. He had great bushy eyebrows to match his beard, and dreadful teeth. Beth stared up at him, her mind racing. He must be Russian. What did he want? Did he suspect something?

Ma stopped and looked over her shoulder. She gave Beth a single hard stare, and then headed away through the kitchen, disappearing into the steam.

Beth swallowed. Several people had stopped and were looking at her, staring.

"He has never seen woman in trousers," said another man, this one in livery, his Russian accent giving the words a heavy, metallic edge. "He want to know if you are boy or girl."

Beth took a deep breath and squared her shoulders. "I'm an *engineer*," she said, and pushed past the bearded man, doing her best to stride. *Heart of metal, I know the heart of metal.*

Her hands were sweating, her heart beating so hard her eyes blurred. Where the hell was Ma?

Never mind Ma, find Evvie.

Behind her, she heard a babble of Russian, and then a wave of laughter.

A maid with an armload of towels hurried through a door and Beth followed her.

Back stairs, a thin strip of worn carpet down the middle, bare, black-stained boards. A single hissing gas lamp sending dim greenish light down and up.

Beth let the maid get ahead, hoping no-one would come the other way and ask what a chauffeur was doing creeping about on the servants' stairs. She would say she was looking for the privy. Or something.

The maid exited at the top, a door opened and shut. Beth emerged into a silent corridor, far better lit, too well lit, she felt like a moth on a lampshade. And she had no idea which direction she was facing.

She made for a window and pushed the heavy damask curtain aside, heaved up the sash, and leaned out.

There, over to her left, she could just make out the line of the ladder. *Why would Evvie leave it there? She wouldn't. Not unless she had no choice.*

Part of Beth's brain was already working on a way to improve the design of the ladder as she hurried down the corridor towards the room, praying that Evvie would be there, that she was all right.

WHEN SHE OPENED the door she saw Madeleine, crouched on the floor in the moonlight, a dark stain seeping up the lavender satin gown, and then she saw Evvie.

"Oh no. Evvie…"

"She's alive," Madeleine said. "But she's unconscious. So much blood… I'll never… I should never…"

"Bust it!" Ma stared for a moment, then pulled the door shut behind her. "Come on, we gotta get her out of here."

"Wait!" Madeleine snapped. "She's still bleeding. We mustn't move her, it could make it worse."

"We don't move her we're going to have forty Peelers on our necks and there ain't much nursing to be had in Holloway neither," Ma said. "Where are the girls?"

"Here," said Tinder. "I got some linens. Get out the way, I can do this, but you gotta get me some light."

"Tinder?"

"I was in hospital," Tinder said. "When I got burnt. I watched 'em. You gotta press on it, bind it up. It'll hold the blood in. Later it'll have to be stitched but we en't got the stuff. Light."

Beth reached into her bag, and pulled out her torch.

Hard white light flooded the room. "Turn it off!" Ma said. "They'll think the place is afire!"

But Beth was looking at Evvie. Her clothes were drenched with blood, her face grey, her breathing a dreadful low rasp.

Hands trembling, she adjusted the little wheel on the side of her torch, and the blazing light diminished.

Tinder made a thick pad of cloth and pressed it over the wound. "Lift her. Careful."

Madeleine, tears pouring down her face, slid her arms under Evvie. Ma moved forward. "*Stay away from my daughter*," Madeleine hissed.

Working quickly, neat-handed, Tinder wrapped linen strips around and around Evvie's torso, under her clothes, binding her like a mummy.

Eveline stirred, her eyelids fluttering. She coughed, and moaned.

"It's all right, my darling, I'm here," Madeleine said. "Hush."

Tinder knotted off the linen, and said, "Water. She'll want water."

Beth, glad to do something useful, grabbed a jug and a mug from a nearby nightstand, and Madeleine trickled water into Eveline's mouth. She coughed again, and opened her eyes. "Baby," she said.

"Shhh, don't try and speak," Madeleine said.

"Baby. Did he…" She coughed again, her eyes closed and she went limp.

"Best move her while she's out," Tinder said.

"How?" Madeleine said.

Beth ran to the window. They might be able to get Eveline down the ladder as firemen did, but… dammit, there were people down there, moving towards the back of the house, a couple, seeking somewhere private. If they hadn't noticed the ladder yet they would, in minutes. She snatched the top bar, hit a small lever, and the ladder snapped together, ratcheting up on itself, good thing she'd designed it to be quiet. It folded down to something that could be carried on the back, so she slipped it over her shoulders.

"Why did you do that?" Adelita said. "We could have…"

"No, we couldn't," Beth said. "People." If only there was a way to make the *Aerymouse* fly in place, hovering as a bee did… but she would have to fly it and land it again, and even if there were enough fuel to do it twice, there was no room in the tiny garden behind the embassy.

She looked at the others. Madeleine and Tinder were both bloodstained; how could they go back through the house? But she suspected if anyone tried to separate Madeleine from her daughter they'd have a fight on their hands.

"Ma?" Adelita said.

But Ma was staring at Eveline, her hands clenched at her sides, as though someone had switched her off. "I never…"

"Ma, we got to get out of here!" Adelita said.

"I know. I just gotta think. I…" With a visible effort, Ma clenched her jaw. "Right. Tinder, get out of them fancy togs. Can you get them bloody clothes off Evvie and your dress on without hurting her worse?"

"Yes, if we're careful."

"Good. Make sure that pad's covered over. What you got under that dress?"

"Only me shift."

"Adelita, I reckon there's servants rooms a spit away. I need a dress, apron and cap fit for a kitchen skivvy. And at least two fancy shawls – or cloaks, if you can find 'em. We need to cover that blood. Don't you get caught."

"Yes, Ma. I won't, Ma." Adelita dashed away.

"What do you plan?" Madeleine said, not taking her eyes from Eveline.

"Tinder goes out through the kitchen, en't no-one going to notice a skivvy. They're worried about people coming in, not out. I'll find me own way, better we're not together. Beth, can you take that bloody machine up again?"

"Yes."

"Good. Ah, Adelita, you got it. Tinder, put it on. Doris, you and Adelita and Missus Sparrow, you're going to have to take her out. Beth, you're the strongest, you got to carry her."

"Me?" Beth knew she was strong, from working with machines, but she'd never picked up someone else.

"I do it they'll notice. You look enough like a manservant it'll seem normal. Keep that cap on and your head ducked. The rest of you can help. Anyone asks, she got overcome by the heat and fainted. Girls, anyone pays too much mind, you distract 'em, you know what to do. Doris, don't you go lifting anything, last thing we need's attention. You lot can't go through the kitchens, they already noticed Beth. I'll let you know when the stairs are safe. Get to that machine and get off, don't wait for me'n Tinder."

Beth stood trembling as they put Eveline in her arms. She wasn't as heavy as Beth had expected, but she was so limp and quiet. Eveline was always sharp and quick, it hardly seemed like her at all. *She's still breathing.*

Ma Pether went ahead of them to the end of the corridor. Music and chatter drifted up the stairs. She held her hand up, *stay.* A man's voice, a gabble of Russian, laughter, a taint of cigar smoke. A door, closing. Ma beckoned.

They crept towards her. Adelita and Madeleine helped support Evvie's shoulders and legs, Doris went ahead. Madeleine had a shawl tied across one shoulder and draping down the front of her gown, hiding the worst of the blood – but the hem was thick with it and patches had smeared past what the shawl covered. Tinder had Evvie's blood-soaked jacket and skirt bundled under her arm. There were already dark red-brown smudges on her dull skivvy's dress.

Beth couldn't stop seeing the blood, blood everywhere for all their care. It seemed to shriek its presence. Surely someone would notice? She almost hoped they would – they would look after Evvie, Evvie who was lying so quiet, getting heavier and heavier in her arms.

But Evvie had broken in, and they would take her to prison, and who would care for her then?

It hardly occurred to Beth that she, too, would probably go to prison.

Ma waved them on and she and Tinder disappeared. Beth felt bereft as soon as she was gone. They started down the stairs; wide, sweeping stairs with fine curved bannisters. The gas-lights hissed, unforgivingly bright. Below, two women passed by, chattering, not looking up at the group creeping down towards them. The hallway seemed huge, the tiled floor stretching for miles to the front doors, and the backs of the pair of Cossack guards standing looking so tall and forbidding. *It's only their hats make them seem so tall,* Beth told herself.

"Hold up," Adelita muttered. "It ain't far."

A burst of music, and a group of men came out of the ballroom, laughing together. "Must go look upon the hedge, old man," one of them said, and started up the stairs. He was young, with a thick mop of blonde hair. "I say, everything all right?" he said.

"My daughter, she fainted," Madeleine said. "The heat."

"Oh, dear, what fragile flowers you ladies are! Need any help?"

"No, no…"

Madeleine's voice sounded thin as mist. *If* she *faints we're done for,* Beth thought.

"Why, sir, that's *terribly* generous of you, but our chauffeur can manage." Adelita rolled her eyes and flirted her fan. "My sister's fainted a dozen times at least, it's terribly vexatious of her." She gave the rest of them a meaningful look. "*Do* take her out, Mama, so at least the *rest* of us don't have to have a wasted evening."

Beth felt Madeleine straighten. "Now don't think I'm leaving you here alone," she said, "... miss. Come along."

"Yes, Mama. Now tell me, are you with the embassy?" Adelita smiled up at the young man. "*Such* an important job."

Madeleine was trembling. Doris moved up to take Eveline's shoulders, glanced down, and muttered, "Hurry."

Beth realised that her arm felt warm. And damp.

The blood was coming through.

"Excuse us," Madeleine said, as they approached the guards. "I have to take my daughter home."

The guards barely glanced at them, but looked back as Adelita approached, all flurry and laughter, "Oh, I dropped my reticule." She bent to pick it up, sweeping a corner of her skirt across the floor. "There, I have it. Mama, wait for me!"

They crunched across gravel. Oh, such a long way, and so many people looking. Beth's arms were starting to shake, and a low, ugly pain was blooming in the small of her back like a dark red cloud.

The *Aerymouse* was surrounded by curious onlookers. Someone had even climbed in the cockpit. "Excuse us," Madeleine said.

"Astonishing thing, what is it?"

"Where does the horse go?" some wag said.

"Have to be Pegasus, old boy."

"My daughter is ill," Madeleine said, her tone icily calm. "We need to take her home."

"Oh, sorry." The man who had climbed in the cockpit looked up, blushed, and scrambled over the side. "'pologies. Never seen – here, let me help. Give her to me."

"We can manage, thank you," Madeleine said.

"Let me at least..." He held his arms out.

"No!" Beth said, clutching Eveline closer, though her arms were shuddering with strain and her back moaned. If he held her he'd get blood on him. *Just get out of my bloody machine, you stupid man!*

Madeleine stood, waiting, until the young man climbed down, looking nonplussed. "Well I must say..."

Madeleine pushed past him and climbed in. "Give her to me."

Carefully, so carefully, aware that their every move was being watched, they manoeuvred Eveline into the craft. Beth laid her in Madeleine's lap, stood straight and gave a croak of pain as something in her back seized.

"Beth?"

"It's all right," she said, clenching her teeth against the pain, fumbled her way to the front, and lowered herself into the seat. She extracted the small glass bottle from her pocket.

About an inch of fluid glowed inside.

Enough. Probably.

Fed, the *Aerymouse* sputtered and shuddered. A few people moved back, others pressed closer. *Aren't you all supposed to be at a party? Get out of the way!*

There was a large black rubber bulb in front of Beth. She squeezed it, and a gout of noise blatted from the *Aerymouse*. "Out of the way, please," she shouted, and hauled the nose around. The *Aerymouse* faced across the lawn. Wheeltracks. The Ambassador wouldn't be pleased. Beth bit her lip, and pulled the bar towards her.

The *Aerymouse* began to move. Two men in conversation walked across her path, and Beth blatted the horn again, making them jump and scurry.

There was barely enough room, less than in Drape's yard. The trees and wall at the end of the lawn rushed towards her. She hauled back. The nose lifted. *Not enough, not enough...* she hauled back some more.

The *Aerymouse* scraped the top of the trees with a horrible sound like claws gouging its belly. "I'm sorry, I'm sorry, please fly," Beth muttered, and the little craft struggled up into the smoke-thick London air.

The Sparrow School

LIU CAME RUNNING out of the school as they landed, his face ghost-white in the darkness. "Eveline?"

"Help us with her," Madeleine said.

"I tried... I couldn't find her... the fox... what..."

"Oh shut up and help," Doris said.

Liu did, taking Evvie in his arms and carrying her into the school, without another word.

Beth eased herself out of the cockpit and climbed down, trying not to cry out. Her back was a red band of pain. She leaned her head against the *Aerymouse's* warm, glossy side, looked up at the moon, a misty smudge beyond the clouds, and cried.

"LIU, I NEED you to listen," Madeleine said, once Evvie was settled in bed. "She's very badly hurt. We need a doctor, a good one."

"One who won't ask questions," Adelita said.

"I..." Liu looked down at Eveline. "Yes. Wait."

And he was gone.

"HOW DID I get here?" Eveline said.

"Eveline, dear, don't try to talk." Madeleine said. "I'll get you some tea."

"Yes, please, Mama. But how?"

"We found you and brought you home. You're safe now. But you're to stay in bed."

"*How*... Beth?"

"Sorry, Evvie," Beth said, hovering by the door.

"You told 'em."

"Evvie, I *had* to. When you didn't come back I knew something had gone wrong. And... there was no-one else. What happened?"

"It was Simms. He took the baby." She looked at Beth.

"What baby?" Madeleine said. "Eveline? What baby? What have you done?"

The Crepuscular

STUG FELT HIS innards writing with impatience as he waited for the Queen's permission to approach. Her gown teased his eyes with constant, flickering movement.

Finally, she beckoned him. Her court shifted and whispered; beast-headed, tree-limbed, beautiful and grotesque and both together, all of them watched him as he walked towards the throne with the child in his arms.

Seated at her right hand was the Huntridge child. It seemed she was still pleased with that gift, too. *Soon, soon...* he imagined what it would be like to carry his son. Not this foreign brat, nor some stinking whining creature from the stews and slums. *His son.* No more of this. This one would buy him what he desired, and that would be the end of it. Once he had dealt with Simms.

He reached the foot of the dais, and bowed low. He realised her gown was made all of butterflies – whole, live insects, fragile legs woven together beneath their tiny furred bodies, wings fluttering helplessly, folding and unfolding, allowing glimpses of the Queen's pearly skin.

"Your Majesty," he said.

"You have brought me what I desire?"

"I have."

"Bring it to me."

He stepped closer, even as the hairs on his neck crept and crawled. The Queen leaned forward, and held out her arms.

Stug put the little girl into them. A few wings, crumpled and broken, floated away.

The Queen looked down. Her delicately drawn brows, curved and fine as a butterfly's feelers, bent.

She leaned closer.

Stug's heart sped up. What was she looking for? The child was the one, it even had the double-headed eagle embroidered on its blanket.

The Queen's head came up, and she looked at Stug. Her eyes had gone the yellow-grey of the sky before a snowstorm.

"Surely," she said, "you did not think to fool *me*, with *this*?"

"I... what? But it is the child, I know, it was..."

"It is not the child. It is not even *a* child." She dropped the baby to the floor, where it began to wail, thin and high and chilly as a night wind.

The Queen stood, and her gown shivered and flickered and hummed with desperate beating wings. "Little man," she said, "what *did* you imagine you were doing?"

"I don't understand."

"You brought me a changeling. A mommet. Something that will fade, and die." She moved towards him, sleek as water, and he stood helpless, trapped by her eyes. "Did the old woman, did Baba Yaga put you up to this? To humiliate me?"

"I... what... no..." He managed to wrench his gaze away long enough to seek out the Queen's son, Aiden, who stood beside her throne. "Your son told me what you wanted, and I had her brought... I risked everything, everything..."

Aiden looked slightly puzzled. Then something... understanding, even amusement, began to dawn on his face. Seeing him smile, Stug felt a jag of hope. He must have done it, he would explain...

"My Lord!"

But Aiden was staring into the distance, thinking of something else, and seemed not to hear him at all.

"You think to plead with my son?" The Queen put her hand to Stug's face, forcing him to look at her. Her fingers fed a terrible, crippling cold through his skin, and his knees began to weaken. "This is between you and me, little man. We made a bargain, and you failed to keep it. Stand *still*."

His knees failed, but he remained upright, held by the light, dreadful touch of her fingers on his skin. His limbs felt like hollow glass filled with water from the Arctic depths.

"They call you Viper, don't they?" the Queen said. "Josh 'Viper' Stug. A name that helps give you power – but not enough. I know it, and that is one of the secrets of *my* power. Shall I make you a snake, to crawl at my feet until you have earned forgiveness?" She leaned back, pressing the forefinger of her free hand to her lip. "No, too dull. Perhaps I should pay you back in kind. Oh, I could. I could give you a son, as you so desire... but one of my design. A son to burden you with lost hopes and broken dreams, to riddle your life with sorrow and loss." She laughed. "Of course, I might have done that in any case. You dared to *summon* one of *my* subjects with the elder flute, and yet you thought this bargain might go in your favour? Yet, I might have been minded to be generous, and give you the child of your heart. But now... oh, what shall I do with you? You are far too ugly and commonplace to be kept about my court as you are. Oh, I know! How perfect!" She turned, and looked at the red-haired girl who sat beside her throne. "My little love, he is the one who brought you here. What do *you* think I should do with him?" She shook her forefinger. "And do, please, make it amusing."

The child turned her green eyes on him. Stug could see nothing there but calculation.

"May I ask him something, my Lady?"

"Of course."

"What did you do with them?" Pearl said. "The ones who were not so fortunate as me."

Even through his fear Stug felt fury rise like nausea in his throat. That this brat should dare..."I... Bartholomew Simms. He took them. Please..."

Pearl turned to the Queen. "This one is very ugly," she said. "Far too ugly to be here, where everything is beautiful. He looks..." She smiled, a charming, innocent smile. "He looks like a pig! Oh, lady, turn him into a pig!"

"Why," the Queen said. "The very thing. But I do not like pigs. He cannot stay here, rooting and snorting and stinking."

"I know someone who would be *very* pleased to have a pig," said Pearl. "They will be so pleased, they will make him into sausages, and eat him all up, from his nose to his tail!"

"Now that is a truly delightful thought," the Queen said.

Stug whimpered.

"And who is it you wish should have a fine fat pig?" said the Queen.

"Why, my own old family in Limehouse!" Pearl laughed. "Of course it is a terrible thing to eat a person, even if they are a pig, so it is a fine trick to play on them, too!"

Stug remembered the room: the single table, the piled clothing. The children, and their ravenous eyes. Would the Huntridge family question the sudden appearance of a pig? Or would they simply fall on him? The children, hollow-cheeked, their mouths open, empty... "No," he whispered.

"My dear," the Queen said fondly. "How sharp you are grown!" And she stroked Pearl's hair. "Are you *sure* they will eat every single bit of him?"

"Oh yes, your Majesty. They are always hungry," said Pearl, looking directly at Stug, her eyes as cold as coins.

"No," Stug said. The Queen took her hand from him, and he fell to his knees, next to the changeling, which stopped crying and looked at him with empty eyes.

"No," he said, and "No," and "No," until he could no longer say "No," or anything at all.

"AIDEN."

"Mama."

"I think you have been playing tricks upon your mother," the Queen said, and pouted. "That is unkind, and improper."

"I had no such intention, Mama."

"Oh?"

"Someone played a trick on me, in fact."

"Indeed?" The Queen tapped her chin. "In that case you shall be doubly punished. For tricking me, and for allowing yourself to be tricked."

Aiden bowed. "Your judgement is, as always, lamentably precise."

"This was supposed to be the human ambassador's child. Here is a thought I find piquant. You shall be *our* ambassador, to the court of Baba Yaga. She has failed to provide much amusement as an enemy, but as a place to exile one's foolish son... yes, thinking of you among *her* court may serve to lighten my tedium, at least until I can find a better use for you."

"I see. I hope you will allow me to take a few of my court? Otherwise, I will make a very poor showing."

"Oh, take who you wish," the Queen said. "Except – no humans. I think perhaps you have been too much influenced by them of late."

"As my Lady commands," Aiden said, and bowed, and returned to his own court.

HE SAT UPON his throne of brass and pistons and cogs and fat buttoned leather, and stormclouds gathered beneath the soaring roof of iron and glass, and lightning flared about the metal and his servants hid themselves. "I become a little weary," Aiden said. A hawk spread wings of gold and steel, stooped from the highest beam and landed upon his raised wrist, tilting its head to gaze at him with a scarlet, enamelled eye. "I am, after all, the prince," he told the hawk. "Yet still I am treated like a child. One day, Mama, you will realise I have grown. Children do that. Yes, even among us they do that." He stared thoughtfully at the hawk, and the thunder and lightning died away. "Charlotte!" he called. "Come to me."

The Sparrow School

"YOU SHOULD HAVE *told* me," Madeleine said.

Evvie, still wrapped in bandages, hunched her shoulders and stared into her mug of tea. She had taken the jade fox out of its secret pocket, and it sat on the dresser, looking forlorn.

"She..." Ma Pether stopped and shook her head.

"If you have something to say," Madeleine said, "please do so."

"All right." Ma straightened her shoulders. "She wasn't going to tell you, was she? You don't approve of her using what she knows, so why'd she tell you? But she should have told *me*." She glared at Evvie. "I coulda *helped*."

"It's your influence..." Madeleine started.

"Oh, stop it, both of you!" Beth said. They both looked at her as though a chair had jumped up and bitten them. "Leave her alone, she's hurt and she's tired. She did what she thought was best, and if you two hadn't been forever arguing maybe she wouldn't have..." Beth stopped, and ducked her head. "I'm sorry."

"Well, well," Ma Pether said. "You've finally found yourself a bit of gumption, haven't you, missy?"

"Yes," Madeleine said, "and since she told *you* and you didn't see fit to inform anyone..."

"I can speak, you know," Evvie said. Her voice was still weak, but her look wasn't. "I told Beth where I was going, that was all. Not why. And don't you go blaming her. I didn't tell you, Mama, because you'd fret yourself to nothing or try and stop me, or both, and Ma Pether, you weren't here, so how could I tell you? 'Sides, you'd have interfered. So I'll thank the pair of you to," she drew a hard painful breath, "to stop it. I looked after meself a long time. And it worked out, din't it? Apart from me getting stuck like a pig, anyways."

"But Evvie, dear," Madeleine said, sitting on the bed and taking her daughter's hand, "you don't *have* to do it all yourself, any more. And besides, if I understand rightly what was going on, do you *really* think I'd have objected to you dealing with that awful man the way he deserved? Yes, I might have advised you to involve the police, but..."

"And get them interested in the school? Mama, we *can't*. We have to stay out of their way, best we can."

"Well what if he turns up again?"

Ma Pether snorted. "He tried to palm off a changeling on the Queen of the Folk. If he turns up, it won't be in the shape he started out. It'll be in a bunch of 'em, all screaming."

"Please," Madeleine said, her hand going to her throat.

"Serves him right, you ask me," said Ma. "Anyways. Seems to me like you need me around, Evvie Sparrow, keep you and my girls out of trouble."

"*Your* girls?"

Ma rolled her eyes. "*The* girls, then. But it's up to your Mama, I suppose."

"No," Evvie said. "No, it isn't. I'm sorry, Mama, but we *do* need her. Only you two better be polite."

"She saved your life, Eveline," Madeleine said. "I was very angry with you, Ma," she said, standing up. "But you did save her life." She offered her hand to Ma.

Ma took it. "You were worried about your girl. I don't take it wrong, f'I hadn't been wrongheaded and taken meself off in a spelter, maybe she wouldn't have got in such a mess." She let go. "Right, I got some business to see to."

"What business?" Evvie said.

"Best you don't know," Ma said. "Not till after."

"Ma! What did you just say not a breath ago? You said I should have told you what I was doing!"

Ma grinned. "I will tell you. Later. Now you be good and listen to your Mama." She left.

Eveline sighed with exasperation.

"Now I think you should rest," Madeleine said.

"You do understand, Mama? Why we need her?"

"She is terribly useful," Madeleine said. "But one day, Eveline, I do hope we can manage without getting entangled in quite such dangerous messes."

"I admit I don't fancy getting knifed again," Eveline said.

"No." Madeleine's face was hidden as she picked up the tea-tray, but her voice was very tight.

"Ma, I'm sorry you were frightened."

"I was, yes. But I'm proud of you," Madeleine said, straightening up. "You did the right thing, my love." She kissed her daughter on the forehead and left.

Evvie stared out of the window.

"You're angry with me," Beth said.

"No, I… well, all right. Some."

"I never meant your Mama to find out."

"I know."

"I don't think you can keep things from her, Evvie. Not any more. Not everything, at any rate."

"Doesn't look like it, does it?"

"Does it still hurt?"

"Yes."

"Do you want some medicine?"

"No. It's got laudanum in it."

"Evvie, what's wrong? You did it. You did everything. You saved the baby, you got rid of Stug… well, probably… and there won't be a war, now."

Eveline shrugged. "I s'pose."

"So what's up?"

"You seen Liu?"

"He's about," Beth said, carefully. "Shall I ask him to come see you?"

"If he wants to I suppose he can bring himself."

"Evvie," Beth said. "Don't."

Evvie hunched a shoulder. "Why not? Running off and not telling me nothing."

"You do *know* he probably saved your life?" Beth said. "As well as Tinder, I mean. Rousted a doctor out of bed in the middle of the night, and sat up with you, wouldn't go to bed. And he looked *awful*."

"He tell *you* what it was all about?"

"Don't be silly, Evvie, why would he tell me? But you should have seen him when we brought you home. He looked... he was crying."

"He was?"

"Don't tell him I told, he'd never forgive me. As for not telling you... why do you think he didn't, Evvie?"

"I dunno, do I? Family business, he said."

"Evvie, for someone so clever, you can be really stupid," Beth said. "Family business? His mother's dead, and she was the human one. Family means *Folk*. They're *dangerous*. Ma Pether's right about Stug, and what the Queen probably did to him. Maybe Liu was afraid for you, like you were for your Mama. Maybe he didn't want to draw their attention any more than you wanted the police getting interested in us. And you asked him to bring you that changeling. He did it, didn't he? What do you think he had to do to get it?"

Eveline folded her arms and scowled.

"You know I'm right," Beth said.

Eveline glared at her. "What happened to you when you were with Ma?" she said.

Beth shrugged. "I found the heart of metal."

"What?"

"Never mind. Anyway. Shall I tell him you want to talk to him?"

Eveline glanced at the jade fox. "No," she said. "Go on, get to class. Someone's got to keep 'em in hand, and now you've gone all gumption and metal, it'll be easy as anything, won't it?"

*　　*　　*

"So there you are," Evvie said.

"How are you?" Liu said.

"Sore."

"Eveline... Lady Sparrow... I should have been here."

"Well, you had something on, didn't you?" Evvie said.

"Yes. It was... a family matter."

She looked back at him. "You going to tell me?"

"It is a long and not very happy story."

"Well, you tell me what you feel like. If you feel like. Only... I didn't tell you stuff, before you left, and I probably shoulda. I'm not in the habit, see." She sighed. "I dunno, I keep thinking I've worked stuff out, and then I realise I'm not near as sharp as I think."

"Now that is a terrible confession you should never make to anyone. Besides, I don't think it is true."

"Flatterer. Liu..."

"Yes?"

"I'm serious. I trust Beth like I trust the ground under my feet, but I didn't tell her what I was doing, and if she hadn't been so damn sharp, well, I wouldn't be here. I nearly wasn't."

Liu swallowed. "I know. I... am very glad she was so sharp."

"Well, so'm I. So I think, maybe, it wouldn't be such a bad idea if we told each other what we're up to, maybe. Next time."

"You are planning a next time?"

"I never plan nothing, well, 'cepting a con, it's just, stuff just *happens*. So, you know, just so you know, 'spite of what I said, I trust you, too, and if I get up in it again, I'll tell you, right? And I'd really appreciate the same from you, because, whatever you were up to, and I get it if you don't want to tell me, but you look like you din't exactly have a holiday by the sea, and you still worried about me, too, so..."

"Lady Sparrow."

"Yeah."

"Yes. I will tell you. This time. And next time, although I hope there will be no next time for a while. I think I would like some peace and quiet."

"Me too."

So he sat in the chair by the bed and told her, as much as he thought she would care to hear. And then she asked questions, and he told her more, until he had told her far more than he ever meant to.

She put her hand over his, where it was clenched on his thigh. "Liu?"

"Yes." He rubbed his eyes.

"You did right."

"I should have been here, Evvie. You could have... I should have been here."

"Well you couldn't know, could you? And..." She picked at the bedspread, with her free hand, the fingers of the other tightening on his. "If I'da known you were going to get yourself in even more trouble, for me... I'd never have asked."

"I know."

"I thought it would be easy, getting the changeling."

"I never told you otherwise."

"I'm sorry."

"So am I."

"You got nothing to be sorry for."

"I wish... I wish I could have brought your sister home. And the red-headed girl... I looked at her, and wondered if she had a sister, like you, at home, who missed her."

"You can't rescue everyone, Liu. You wanted to, because you're decent. Not like..." She broke off, but not before Liu heard the words 'your father,' hanging in the air.

He sighed. "The Harp said to me, 'Consider always whether what you desire will cost you what you love.' I thought I honoured my father, but in fact, I desired his love."

"'Course you did. S'natural, a father's supposed to love his children – but it don't always work that way, does it? If it did there wouldn't be so many children knocked about, or on the streets.

Anyway," she said, "why should you honour him when he ain't done nothing to earn it? I'm s'posed to honour the Queen – our Queen, I mean – just cos she's the Queen, but she ain't never done a thing for me."

"You have done something for her, by preventing a war."

"Maybe I should write and tell her, that'd go down a treat, wouldn't it? 'Dear ma'am, I just saved your empire from a big row, how's about a bit of the cash what you won't have to spend on gunpowder, yours truly, Evvie Sparrow.'"

"Perhaps not."

"I still need money, or this place is going to fall apart."

Liu patted her hand. "Between the cunning Fox and the sneaky Sparrow, we should be able to come up with something."

"Better do it quick, then." Evvie sighed, and slumped back on the pillow. "Give us a minute, eh?"

"Yes, you should rest." Liu stood up.

"Liu? Can you do us one more favour? There's still that hellhound Simms. He knows more'n is healthy. I don't know *what* I'm going to do about him, but while I'm laid up, I'd like to think someone's keeping an eye on him."

"I suspect he need not trouble you for long."

"Oh? What d'you mean?"

"Ma Pether has gone looking for him. If I were him, I would be finding a very deep, dark hole to hide in."

"She has?" Evvie sat up, her eyes wide, and winced. "Gah, that hurts."

"Lie down, please!"

"But Liu... Ma's done a lot of stuff but she's never been a killer, she's never held with it! I don't want her hanged 'cause of me!"

"Eveline... please. I do not know what she was planning, but she had a smile and a large bag and I did not scent murder on her. Mischief, yes. I think Mr Simms may have a long time to regret his actions. Perhaps he will become a reformed character."

"Well, I hope you're right. But I wish she wouldn't..."

"Help you? When you cannot, for the moment, help yourself?"

"Well… all right."

"Sometimes one must accept help."

"Look who's talking."

"You are obviously better, since you are feeling argumentative. But now I think you should sleep."

"Liu?"

"Yes?"

"I'm glad you came back."

"Thank you." He smiled. "I am glad, too. Go to sleep, Lady Sparrow."

"Eveline, come to the parlour."

"What is it, Mama?"

"We've a visitor. Oh, dear…" Madeleine was twisting her hands together, her hair coming adrift from its bun.

"Mama? It's not the carpenter, is it? I told you to let me deal with him."

"No, it's Mr Thring."

"What's going on?"

"You'd better come. He'll tell you."

The parlour was small, and all the furniture, though lovingly chosen, was second-hand. The fire in the grate struggled, chewing on the cheapest coal. Octavius Thring, standing on the threadbare carpet, looked distinctly out of place: altogether too plump, and shiny, and prosperous. Today's waistcoat was embroidered with fleurs-de-lis, in green and silver, and his rambunctious silver curls were already escaping from an inadequate application of pomade. He was looking out of the window to the old stables, from which issued interesting clankings and occasional puffs of oddly-coloured smoke.

"Ah, Miss Sparrow," he said. "How are you today?"

"I'm well, thank you, Mr Thring. My Mama said you wished to speak to me?"

"Yes, well, I'm afraid I have a confession to make. I do hope you won't be too terribly upset with me."

"What sort of a confession?" Eveline was instantly aprickle.

"I haven't been entirely honest with you."

I knew it. Eveline's stomach fell to her boots, but she folded her arms, pointed her chin and waited.

Octavius Thring fidgeted with the scarf he was wearing. "Oh, well," he said, "perhaps it would be easier if I just gave you these." He thrust a sheaf of papers at her.

Eveline looked at the top layer. It was the language of lawyers – impenetrable as a pea-souper. She flicked through, looking for something she could understand.

And there, glaring up at her, was a name she knew, and a signature she had seen before.

Josh Stug, Esq.

A dozen fragmented thoughts jammed into her mind, crashing into each other. He knew Stug. They had worked together. Perhaps Stug had been government after all… was Thring government too? How would she protect her mother, Beth, the girls?

"It's not as complicated as it looks," Thring said. "Fortunately everything was already in place. Did you know Stug seems to have disappeared? I suspect some of his less legitimate dealings may have caught up with him."

Well that's true enough, Eveline thought.

Thring shook his head. "Long spoons, you know. Long spoons. But his secretary is a smart young man, and I made sure everything was in order."

"What do you mean spoons?" Eveline said, grabbing at the thing that made the least sense.

"Oh, well, you know, one needs a long spoon to sup with the devil, and I suspect Mr Stug's spoon lacked sufficient length."

"Mr Thring, I don't know who you really are or what you've done, but I'll thank you to make yourself plain."

"Who I really am? Oh, dear, I quite thought we'd been properly introduced, when I first came to visit your Mama, I'm dreadfully sorry."

"Are you government?"

"What? Good heavens, no. Whatever gave you that idea? No, no, entirely a private individual. I dabble, you know, I dabble – but not in government. Heaven forfend. Merely in mechanics. Your Mama is a far better creator. But she has too much to worry her. It interferes with the concentration. I know you do your best…"

"What business did you have with 'Viper' Stug, Mr Thring?"

"Ah, well, perhaps I'd better start at the beginning."

"Perhaps you had."

"Your mama told me what you were planning – the security business. A most intriguing idea, I must say – I had some thoughts on a device or two that might be of use, I'm sure I had the notes somewhere… in any case, well, I have a little property here and there, and I'd come across Stug's name… there was never any suggestion of anything actually *illegal,* just a sense that perhaps he wasn't entirely *savoury.* So I thought perhaps I should look into it."

"You did, did you?"

"Yes. Oh, dear, you're offended, aren't you? Your mama tells me you're a very independent young lady. Admirable, you know, entirely admirable, but… well, it's too late now."

"What's too late?"

"I'm afraid I did something rather unsavoury myself."

"What?"

"I've dealt with men like Stug before, you know. Desperate for the appearance of respectability."

"Mr Thring!"

"Oh, dear, yes, well. I'm afraid I rather, well, actually, turned the tables on him."

"Mr Thring, if you don't tell me what you're talking about in the plainest language, right this minute, I shall hit you with the poker."

"Oh, please don't. Very well. I gave Stug the impression that he could buy you out, but in fact, I was setting up a charity to support the school. Those papers you signed? It's all entirely in order. But there will be money, from Stug's estate. A nice regular sum. And it's been announced. So even if he does reappear – I did mention he seems to have disappeared? – he can't stop it without looking like a bad sort to the very people to whom he would most wish to appear respectable."

Eveline sat down, hard, on the nearest chair.

"So we've paid the butcher, and the cook, and the grocer..." Beth said.

Evvie nodded. "I think that's the lot."

They were in the kitchen. Liu sat on the table, swinging his legs. "Well, Lady Sparrow, now you have nothing to worry about."

"Apart from Thring mooning over Mama."

"Is he?" Beth said.

"Follows her about like a spaniel, he does."

"Oh. Well, he's nice, I don't see anything wrong with it."

Evvie hunched her shoulders. "Well, it's not exactly *wrong*, I s'pose, but I don't have to like it."

"Why not? He's perfectly nice, and look at what he did," Beth said.

"He only did it to get on Mama's good side."

"That's silly," Beth said. "We *need* that money, Evvie. It's not even his, it's Stug's. Don't tell me you aren't happy to take Stug's money."

Evvie shrugged again.

"Perhaps," Liu said, "you would rather have solved everything yourself. Stopped a war, got rid of Stug, kept the school afloat..."

"It's too easy," Evvie said. "I don't trust what comes easy, not any more. I'm still going to do the security business."

"And?" Liu said.

"And what?"

"Apart from the undoubtedly desirable but perhaps not terribly exciting security business, what will you do?"

"I don't want any more excitement, for the moment, thank you," Evvie said, scratching her ribs, where a thick scar was now forming.

Liu suddenly turned, his lip lifting. Evvie felt the hairs on her arms prickle. "What..." she said.

"The way is opening," Liu said. "Something is coming, from the Crepuscular. I think you two should leave."

"I'm not leaving you on your own! Besides, this is *my* kitchen, I want to see who thinks they can walk in here without asking!"

The air shuddered and split, and the kitchen filled with the scent of cold flowers, and an iron tang of blood. A figure stepped through the breach, slight and finely dressed and looking about with curiosity.

"It's me, Evvie," said Charlotte. "I have to live here now. What an ugly room. Oh, and Fox, you're in *ever* so much trouble."

Acknowledgements

To THE COOL froods of Solaris, my splendid agent, John Jarrold, my constantly-indulgent friends and family, and my ever-beloved Dave. I literally couldn't do it without you all.

About the Author

GAIE SEBOLD LIVES in London, works for a charity, reads obsessively, gardens amateurishly, and sometimes runs around in woods hitting people with latex weapons. She has won awards for her poetry. Born in the US, she has lived in the UK most of her life. Her *Babylon Steel* and *Dangerous Gifts* books for Solaris have won her critical and popular acclaim.

A HEROINE WHO
REALLY GETS UP CLOSE
AND PERSONAL!

Babylon Steel, ex-sword-for-hire, ex... other things, runs The Red Lantern, the best brothel in the city. She's got elves using sex magic upstairs, S&M in the basement and a large green troll cooking breakfast in the kitchen, and she'd love you to visit, except...

She's not having a good week. The Vessels of Purity are protesting against brothels, girls are disappearing, and if she can't pay her taxes, Babylon's going to lose the Lantern. She'd given up the mercenary life, but when the mysterious Darask Fain pays her to find a missing heiress, she has to take the job. And then her past starts to catch up with her in other, more dangerous ways.

Witty and fresh, Sebold delivers the most exciting fantasy debut in years.

**'Ingenious, gripping, and full of pleasures
on every level. Exceptional.'**
Mike Carey, NYT Bestselling author of The Unwritten

US ISBN: 978-1-907992-38-4
UK ISBN: 978-1-907992-37-7

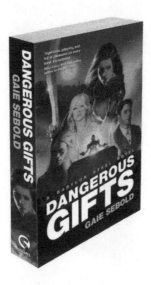

THE VIOLENCE SHE CAN HANDLE.
THE DIPLOMACY IS MURDER...

Babylon Steel, owner of the Red Lantern brothel – and former avatar of the goddess of sex and war – has been offered a job. Two jobs, really: bodyguard to Enthemmerlee, a girl transformed into a figure of legend... and spy for the barely-acknowledged government of Scalentine. The very young Enthemmerlee embodies the hopes and fears of many on her home world of Incandress, and is a prime target for assassination.

Babylon must somehow turn Enthemmerlee's useless household guard into a disciplined fighting force, dodge Incandress's bizarre and oppressive Moral Statutes, and unruffle the feathers of a very annoyed Scalentine diplomat. All of which would be hard enough, were she not already distracted by threats to both her livelihood and those dearest to her...

'Reading Babylon Steel is like having a refreshing chat with that hot, tall, slightly intimidating girl that always looks like she has a lot of fun in her life.'
Pornokitsch on Babylon Steel

US ISBN: 978-1-78108-080-1
UK ISBN: 978-1-78108-079-5

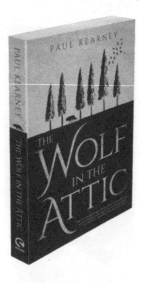

THE WOLF
IN THE ATTIC

Anna Francis lives in a tall old house with her father and her doll Penelope. She is a refugee, a piece of flotsam washed up in England by the tides of the Great War and the chaos that trailed in its wake. Once upon a time, she had a mother and a brother, and they all lived together in the most beautiful city in the world, by the shores of Homer's wine-dark sea.

But that is all gone now, and only to her doll does she ever speak of it, because her father cannot bear to hear. She sits in the shadows of the tall house and watches the rain on the windows, creating worlds for herself to fill out the loneliness. The house becomes her own little kingdom, an island full of dreams and half-forgotten memories. And then one winter day, she finds an interloper in the topmost, dustiest attic of the house. A boy named Luca with yellow eyes, who is as alone in the world as she is.

That day, she'll lose everything in her life, and find the only real friend she may ever know.

'Beautifully written, wryly observed.'
Tony Ballantyne, author of Dream London

US ISBN: 978-1-78108-362-8
UK ISBN: 978-1-78108-361-1

ONE NIGHT
IN SIXES

Appaloosa Elim is a man who knows his place. On a good day, he's content with it. Today is not a good day. Today, his so-called "partner" – that lily-white lordling Sil Halfwick – has ridden off west for the border, hell-bent on making a name for himself in native territory. And Elim, whose place is written in the bastard browns and whites of his cow-spotted face, doesn't dare show up home again without him.

The border town called Sixes is quiet in the heat of the day, but Elim's heard the stories about what wakes at sunset: gunslingers and shapeshifters and ancient animal gods whose human faces never outlast the daylight.

If he ever wants to go home again, he'd better find his missing partner fast. But if he's caught out after dark, Elim risks succumbing to the old and sinister truth in his own flesh - and discovering just how far he'll go to survive the night.

'If you loved Stephen King's Dark Tower series you will find this book right inside your wheelhouse. I loved it.'
Paul Kearney

US ISBN: 978-1-78108-238-6
UK ISBN: 978-1-78108-237-9

**BOOK ONE OF
THE CURSED KINGDOMS TRILOGY**

THE SENTINEL MAGE

In a distant corner of the Seven Kingdoms, an ancient curse festers and grows, consuming everything in its path. Only one man can break it: Harkeld of Osgaard, a prince with mage's blood in his veins. But Prince Harkeld has a bounty on his head - and assassins at his heels.

Innis is a gifted shapeshifter. Now she must do the forbidden: become a man. She must stand at Prince Harkeld's side as his armsman, protecting and deceiving him. But the deserts of Masse are more dangerous than the assassins hunting the prince. The curse has woken deadly creatures, and the magic Prince Harkeld loathes may be the only thing standing between him and death.

**'Her haunting prose reads like Hans Christian Andersen
for twenty-first century adults.'**
Mindy Klasky, author of the Glasswright series

US ISBN: 978-1-907519-50-5
UK ISBN: 978-1-907519-49-9

BOOK TWO OF
THE CURSED KINGDOMS TRILOGY

THE FIRE PRINCE

The Seven Kingdoms are in the grip of an ancient and terrible blood curse. Thousands have died; thousands more yet will. Only one man can end the curse: the fugitive Osgaardan prince and reluctant mage, Harkeld.

The road to salvation is long and arduous. Harkeld has outrun his father's soldiers, but he can't hope to outrun the assassins – the notorious, deadly Fithians – clamouring for the bounty on his head. Even the Sentinel mages who guide and guard him are no match for Fithian steel. Faced with the ever-present threat of death, Harkeld must learn to use his fire magic, or die.

Meanwhile, in Osgaard's gold-tiled palace, Harkeld's sister Princess Brigitta is living on borrowed time, hostage to their brother's ambition. And far to the east, young orphan Jaumé journeys with a band of mysterious, dangerous fighters, heading north for a purpose he does not yet understand.

'Ms. Gee has set up characters and conflicts that have extraordinary potential, and created the opportunity to explore identity issues in a way that conventional literature never could.'
Pornokitsch on The Sentinel Mage

US ISBN: 978-1-78108-240-9
UK ISBN: 978-1-78108-239-3

BOOK THREE OF
THE CURSED KINGDOMS TRILOGY

THE BLOOD CURSE

Those who drink the water shall thirst for blood. They shall be as wild beasts.

A curse is ravaging the Seven Kingdoms. Fugitive Osgaardan prince, Harkeld, is the one person who can destroy it. Guarded by Sentinel mages, pursued by Fithian assassins, he begins the final—and most dangerous—stage of his quest: entering the cursed kingdom of Sault, where drinking even one drop of water means madness and death.

But the mages aren't the only travelers heading east. Princess Brigitta, abducted by the Fithians, is also bound for Sault—unless she can escape. And in close pursuit is her loyal armsman, Karel.

Young orphan, Jaumé, is also headed for Sault—where he will be forced to make decisions that will change the fate of the Seven Kingdoms forever.

A good read. Death and magic, zombies and assassins, fighting and fleeing. What more could you ask for?
Fantasy Book Review on The Sentinel Mage

US ISBN: 978-1-78108-387-1
UK ISBN: 978-1-78108-368-4